Mrs Calc ... ight

Vernon Coleman

ISBN: 9781898146223

Dedication

To Antoinette: Yours for as long as God spares me, and for an eternity thereafter.

Note from Vernon Coleman:
This is the fourth novel about Mrs Caldicot. The first three are *Mrs Caldicot's Cabbage War*, *Mrs Caldicot's Knickerbocker Glory* and *Mrs Caldicot's Oyster Parade*. For a full list of the books by Vernon Coleman which are currently available please see his author page on Amazon or visit www.vernoncoleman.com.

Chapter One

It is often said that things tend to happen in threes.

And thus it was for Mrs Caldicot and the residents who had, with her as their guide and leader, escaped the dull tyranny of the Twilight Years Rest Home.

All three things happened at more or less the same time; enlivening what would have otherwise been a rather dull, spring morning.

The first thing that happened was that Mrs Caldicot received a formal letter informing her that the home they all shared, the former Twilight Years Rest Home, was to be compulsorily purchased by a Government quango.

The Government wanted the house because it was planning to use the best part of a £100 billion worth of taxpayers' money to build a multi-billion pound high-speed railway line connecting London and Tidbury Halt.

'Why are they building a superfast line to a station I've never heard of?' a curious Mrs Caldicot asked Jenkins, her much loved husband. 'Do you know anything about it?'

Mrs Caldicot's surprise was entirely justified. It did seem odd that a previously little used railway station and, moreover, one settled in an infrequently visited part of the country, should have been chosen, almost at random so it seemed to outside observers, to be the recipient of so much unexpected largesse. The surprise was enhanced by the fact that it was reliably estimated, by people who make a study of such things, that the new railway line, suitable for high-speed trains, would cut no more than 15 minutes off the journey time between London and Tidbury Halt.

'Tidbury Halt is a very old station,' explained Jenkins. 'Back in 1963, it narrowly escaped the axe when an indefatigable but sadly unromantic Government employee named Dr Beeching decided to tear up any stretch of line that didn't make a profit and to sell off any railway station that didn't earn its keep.'

Although he was now retired, Jenkins had been a Fleet Street editor and he understood how things worked in Britain.

'A lot of people have wondered why such a small and apparently insignificant railway station has been selected for such special treatment, and why a country which is in so much debt is spending such a huge amount of money on such a curious gesture,' continued Jenkins. 'Cutting 15 minutes off a railway journey isn't a huge improvement – especially now that trains on the existing line are equipped with Wi-Fi. Businessmen who feel the need to travel to Tidbury Halt can continue their money making endeavours while sitting on the train.'

Mrs Caldicot cocked her head to one side and looked at her husband without saying anything for a moment. 'But you know something don't you?'

'Well, I've heard the rumour,' admitted Jenkins. 'It concerns the Government and it may be scurrilous.'

'That's all the more reason to share it with me,' insisted Mrs Caldicot. 'Generally speaking, I'm not one who believes in sharing gossip or rumour. But politicians are fair game.'

'Well, it's been repeatedly denied that this apparently quixotic endeavour has anything whatsoever to do with the fact that two senior ministers and a Permanent Under-Secretary of State have country homes very close to Tidbury Halt,' said Jenkins. 'In addition, I have heard it denied, often and loudly, that they have for some time been exasperated by the more or less permanent Friday night queues on the motorway. The word from Whitehall is that it was deemed politically more acceptable, though probably rather more expensive, to do something to improve the railway line rather than to try to widen the motorway connecting London with the village of Tidbury.'

'So the Government is going to buy our house so that they can knock it down, and they want to knock it down so that they can lay down some very expensive railway lines upon which they can run some very fast and extremely expensive trains. And they want to do all that so that two ministers and a civil servant can save fifteen minutes when they scurry off to their country cottages for the weekend?'

'I'm afraid so,' admitted Jenkins. 'Though, I must admit that given the length of time the new line is expected to take to build, the chances are that the three of them will all be retired long before the work is finished.'

Despite the unfairness of the decision to buy her perfectly serviceable house simply in order to knock it down, Mrs Caldicot was surprisingly unconcerned by this apparently disturbing communication from the Government.

She liked the old house, which had that certain style associated with almost all older buildings, and she had long ago got over the unhappy memories it had once held when it had been known as The Twilight Years Rest Home, and managed by the ruthlessly efficient and penny-pinching Mr Muller-Hawksmoor. She was well aware that the house had been built with much better materials, and far more thought, than most modern homes which seemed to have been designed by bureaucrats obsessed more with the need to satisfy unhelpful and largely pointless regulations than to build habitable homes. Indeed, the newly built homes which she had seen had been so shoddy that she thought it would be a miracle if they lasted 20 years before they fell down.

But Mrs Caldicot had long ago accepted that she, like the rest of us who are without power and authority, must live in a world which is, sadly but unavoidably, far more corrupt, oppressive and tyrannical than we might like to think it ought to be. She was old enough to have diluted her idealism with a good dollop of pragmatism.

More importantly perhaps, and certainly more personally, she was not as upset at being forced out of her home as one might have expected since she was rather well aware that the building, an old one, was now in desperate need of a considerable amount of restoration. The central heating boiler had acquired the temperamental idiosyncrasies common among all boilers of a certain age, and the cast iron radiators and pipes, which had been installed in the year when King Edward VII had been thrilled to find his face on every one of the nation's postage stamps, were vast, prone to leak and predisposed to a good deal of disturbing gurgling, most of which seemed to take place in the early hours of the morning. The electrical wiring, last checked in the 1950s, was now also beginning to show its age. It should have been replaced when the house had been made into an officially approved nursing home but the ultimate owners, a large and powerful property company, had not found it difficult to sidestep that particular onerous financial responsibility. The requirements of the local Fire Officer had been quietly shelved at approximately the same time that the Fire Officer's pleasant suburban home had acquired a rather fine new conservatory at a surprisingly reasonable price. The plumbing, like the central heating system, had been installed in Edwardian times, and although the lead pipes were sound in themselves, the junctions and tanks which helped to manage the flow of water around the house were of an age that always resulted in much shaking of heads and sucking in of air when plumbers were called.

And then there was the roof.

Mrs Caldicot preferred not to think about the roof or the dry rot which Jenkins had found growing in the loft. She did not mind the bats, for they generally kept themselves to themselves and were by no means uncongenial tenants, but it is never easy to know that one is sharing one's loft space with dry rot spores, hyphae, mycelia and fruiting bodies.

All of this meant that Mrs Caldicot was not quite as horrified as one might have expected her to be when she received the official letter, sent by registered post so that its receipt could not be denied, informing her that the Government intended to purchase her house.

The coldly written letter, which was addressed to Mrs Caldicot solely, because only her name was on the ownership papers, made it abundantly clear that she had just one month to vacate the property, that she was entitled to appeal (though it was made pretty clear that this would be a waste of time since she would be appealing to the Government against a decision made by the Government) and that she would receive the allocated sum of compensation in six months' time.

There was no indication in the letter of just how Mrs Caldicot and her companions were expected to find accommodation in the interim period, the five months between having her home knocked down and the arrival of the compensation cheque. This was clearly not a problem which the Government felt it needed to address.

Mrs Caldicot's one relief was that the sum offered in compensation, though naturally on the mean side of parsimonious, was enough to pay off the mortgage and satisfy the bank, which was the ultimate owner of nine tenths of the central heating system, the electrical wiring, the roof, the dry rot and the bats.

The second of the three things which had happened that morning, not in itself by any stretch of the imagination a bad thing but certainly one worthy of inclusion in our list of three significant events, was that Jenkins, Mrs Caldicot's husband, had received an invitation to travel to the United States and to spend three weeks giving a series of lectures to media students at Yale University.

Although now retired from his career as an editor of *The Sunday Globe* newspaper, Jenkins had acquired something of a reputation as a lecturer and writer on the principles and practices of journalism. His two books, *The Role of the Editor in Defending the Truth Against Manipulation by Lobbyists and Politicians* and *The Slow and Silent Death of Free Speech and Democracy* were hardly bestsellers but they were considered required reading for media students on both sides of the Atlantic.

Jenkins had spent several years working on a novel but he was beginning to feel that the book he was writing was not the book he really wanted to write or, indeed, one that many people would want to read. It was, he feared, the sort of book that might win laudatory reviews in *The Guardian*, and maybe collect a literary prize or two, but would never win the hearts of any readers. Despite the fact that he thought that a few weeks away from his novel might prove beneficial, Jenkins's first reaction had been to say 'Thank You but No' to the invitation. He really didn't want to travel to foreign parts without Mrs Caldicot by his side, and he knew that she would not want to go anywhere without her residents. Even if they could afford it, he could hardly drag Miss Nightingale, Mrs Peterborough, Mr Livingstone, Mr Hewitt et al to Yale University for three weeks!

But Mrs Caldicot's reaction was quite different.

'What will you do?' asked Jenkins, when Mrs Caldicot had insisted that he should accept the invitation.

'I'll start looking for somewhere for us to live!' replied Mrs Caldicot. 'The Government has given very little notice so we will have to get a move on.'

'They should pay far more in compensation!'

'I agree! But the Government's valuer doesn't seem to think the house is worth very much. And since he hasn't been inside the house he doesn't know about the problems we've been having with the heating, the plumbing, the electrics, the roof or the dry rot. I'm worried that if he'd looked harder he might have thought his compensation offer a little on the high side. And maybe he thinks it isn't worth much because he knows it's about to have a new railway line built through the middle of it!'

Mrs Caldicot was not averse to fighting when it mattered, but in this instance she felt that fighting would take a great deal of effort and eventually prove to be disappointingly unproductive. The Government makes a difficult opponent since it has most of the money and, in the final event, the right to send in armed men and tanks if it feels peeved, or suspects that it is being thwarted or provoked.

And then there was the third thing.

When there have been two big things, there is nearly always a third big thing.

Mrs Caldicot was well aware that there is no good, scientific reason for this. But she also knew that it was an inescapable fact of life.

And in this case the third thing was, like the first two things, brought by the postman.

The third thing came in a large brown envelope and had been posted by 'special delivery'. As a result of this designation it had to be signed for by Mr Livingstone, who was the addressee.

Mr Livingstone did not receive very much mail and he had never before received a letter that had to be signed for, although he had once received a postcard from a friend in New Zealand who had mistakenly put on the wrong sort of stamp. On that occasion, the postman had rung the doorbell and demanded that Mr Livingstone hand over £1 in excess postage. Mr Livingstone had read the card (not difficult since there were only seven words: 'Arrived safely, having great time, best, Dick') and had decided that ownership of the card was not worth £1. He had, therefore, said 'no thank you' to the postman and the card had duly been taken back to the Post Office to start its long and rather pointless journey back to New Zealand.

That, however, had been some years earlier.

Mr Livingstone was not a man who was greatly troubled by the mails. Occasional letters about his pension were pretty much the extent of his correspondence.

So once the big, brown envelope had been duly signed for and handed over, Mr Livingstone put it on the table and looked at it for a while. He did not expect it to contain good news. His had not, to date, been a life blessed by exceptional good fortune. He did not regard himself as one of those people for whom life always runs smoothly. In shops, the assistants he approached always suddenly found that they had something more important to do than attend to him. In banks and at the Post Office, the 'Position Closed' sign would go up the moment he approached. And if, when walking on a pavement, he came face to face with another pedestrian, he was always the one who had to step off into the gutter.

Everyone else in the room gathered round and looked at the packet too.

Even Mrs Peterborough came to have a look.

She had been watching a television programme of which she was extremely fond and the fact that she had dragged herself away to stare at Mr Livingstone's package was quite a tribute. She liked 'The Shopping Channel' because it was there whenever you turned on the television; there was a reliable permanence about it which she found strangely comforting. Even in the middle of the night it was there, just the same as it was in the middle of the day. It was, she suspected, even there on Christmas Day. Most of all, however, Mrs Peterborough liked 'The Shopping Channel' because the programmes were never interrupted with advertisements or public service announcements.

'What do you think it is?' asked Mr Hewitt, nodding towards the mystery package.

They all knew that Mrs Caldicot had received a letter telling her that the Government was going to buy their home. They really didn't want any more bad news.

'I've no idea,' replied Mr Livingstone who had decided that he really wished the packet would disappear.

'Aren't you going to open it?' asked Mrs Peterborough, whose fingers were itching to tear through the packaging. Mrs Peterborough had always found parcels, packets and envelopes irresistible.

'Later, perhaps,' said Mr Livingstone, whose natural levels of curiosity had long since abated and had, indeed, shrunk at approximately the same rate that his natural aversion to surprises of any kind had grown. 'Let's have a cup of tea, first.'

Even Mrs Peterborough could find nothing to object to about this.

And so the kettle was boiled, the teapot prepared and eventually, some ten minutes later, they all sat down in the living room, added milk and sugar to their cups, as required, and stared again at Mr Livingstone's packet.

'I think it's time to open it now,' said Mr Livingstone eventually.

There was a communal sigh of relief at this for the other members of the household did not have Mr Livingstone's apparently unlimited reserves of patience, his willingness to postpone the inevitable or his highly developed lack of curiosity.

But even then the waiting was not over.

First, Mr Livingstone needed to find a knife with which to open the envelope. And then he decided that the paper knife which had been produced was nowhere near sharp enough for the task. A second knife had to be fetched from the kitchen. And then Mr Livingstone suddenly remembered that he had in his pocket a small, silver penknife; a treasure which he had carried with him for most of his life.

And with the aid of the penknife the envelope was finally breached and the contents duly withdrawn and revealed.

'What does it say?' demanded Mrs Peterborough, who could hardly contain herself with the excitement of it all. She could not have been more on edge if the packet had been addressed to her.

'It appears to be from a firm of solicitors,' said Mr Livingstone.

There was widespread gloom at this announcement.

No one could remember ever receiving any sort of communication from a solicitor which had brought good news. To the residents of the former Twilight Years Rest Home, solicitors had always been the harbingers of doom; the senders of writs and threats and communications which were without prejudice and which demanded action by the morning of the 12th inst at the very latest, if terrible, unimaginable consequences were to be avoided.

But in this case the gloom was soon dispelled.

'I appear to have inherited a pier,' announced Mr Livingstone, after he had hurriedly scanned the documents he had been sent.

And if he had just announced that he had been invited to become an astronaut or to ride the favourite in the Grand National there could have scarcely been more surprise among the assembled company.

Chapter Two

'You've been left a what?' asked Mrs Merivale, who hadn't had her ears syringed for nine months and wasn't quite sure that she'd heard properly.

Quietly and confidentially, she rather thought she'd heard that Mr Livingstone had said that someone had left him a pear but that didn't seem very likely and she didn't mention this suspicion. Why, she reasoned to herself silently, would anyone go to all the trouble of involving solicitors and writing out a will and putting in Mr Livingstone's name as a beneficiary just to leave him a pear? Still, she thought, people did do such strange things that you could never really rule anything out these days.

'A pier,' repeated Mr Livingstone.

'Do you mean you're going to be a Lord?' said Mrs Merivale, pleased that she hadn't said anything about the pear. She thought that being a peer was definitely a rather good thing. She didn't in the slightest bit mind having a friend who was entitled to dress up in ermine and decorate his notepaper with a tastefully embossed little coronet.

'No, no,' said Mr Livingstone. 'I've been left a pier. One of those long thin things they have at the seaside. One of those things that enables you to leave the country without going to the trouble of going abroad.'

'Ah,' said Mrs Merivale, understanding at last, feeling a little foolish but now even more relieved that she hadn't aired her thoughts about pears and peers. 'Well, why didn't you say so?'

'Is your pier by the sea?' asked Miss Nightingale.

'It will be very nice if it is,' said Mrs Peterborough, who liked the seaside very much indeed and who was the sort of brave person who would take off her shoes and stockings, tuck up her frock and go for a paddle even if the temperature were close to freezing and the sky full of grey clouds. Paddling and eating whelks were, she believed, things you had to do when you were at the seaside, whether you felt like it not.

Miss Nightingale and Mrs Peterborough were both delighted when they were assured that, although no one was terribly sure precisely where Mr Livingstone's pier was situated, the chances were high that it was somewhere on the English coast and, therefore, almost certainly near the sea.

'That's where they usually put them,' said Mrs Torridge, speaking firmly and knowledgeably. 'They put them beside the seaside because that's where the seagulls always congregate.'

'Why's that?' asked Mr Merivale, who was, as usual, sitting next to his wife.

'I don't think I know,' admitted Mrs Torridge. 'I suppose they like the sea. That would be why they're called seagulls. Piers always have seagulls. Seagulls, candyfloss, kiss-me-quick hats and those lovely, soft ice creams served in cones.'

'I went fishing on a pier when I was seven,' said Mr Merivale. 'I can't remember where the pier was but it had dodgem cars at the end. I spent all day sitting on the pier with my legs dangling over the edge and when we went back to the boarding house for our tea, my shoulders were so badly burnt that I couldn't put my shirt on. The landlady wouldn't let me into the dining room without a shirt so I had to eat my dinner in our bedroom. She said that if she made an exception for me no one knew where it would end. I remember she made a speech about standards and my mother got very upset. She wanted to leave and find somewhere else but my father said we couldn't leave because we'd paid for the week in advance.'

'Did you catch any fish?' asked Mrs Torridge.

'No. I didn't. Actually, I don't remember ever seeing anyone catch any fish. To be frank, I didn't really take much interest in the fishing. I just liked sitting on the pier with my legs dangling down over the edge. It felt very daring. At one point, a chap pointed out that the end of my line was lying on the mud. The tide had gone out. I don't suppose that would have helped much with the fishing. I think the pier was maybe at Weston-super-Mare. The tide there goes out for miles.' He stopped for a moment, clearly thinking. 'Where do you think the sea goes when the tide goes out?'

'Maybe it comes in somewhere else,' suggested Mrs Peterborough.

'On the piers which I remember they always had a kiosk where you could buy little windmills which whizzed round and round in the breeze. Or if you blew on them,' said Mr Williams. 'I liked those very much.'

'And Turkish Delight in wooden boxes, and peppermint rock shaped like pebbles, and big shells which you could take home to use as an ashtray, and boxes of fudge with a photograph of the pier on the front,' added Mr Twist.

Mrs Caldicot closed her eyes and smiled. 'I liked the Turkish Delight the best. You opened the little, wooden box and there was a layer of greaseproof paper. You lifted up the paper and the cubes of Turkish Delight lay there in rows, all covered in icing sugar. There were always little piles of icing sugar in the bottom of the box and when you'd eaten the Turkish Delight you could wet your finger and dip it in the sugar.'

Some people, notably cynical millennials, the sort who are full to the brim with so many prejudices and so much narrow mindedness that there is no room for any imagination, do not believe that things were ever as they are now said to have once been, and that nothing could have ever been better than it is now. But Mrs Caldicot and her friends knew that what they remembered was nothing more nor less than the truth; for it was their history and it was their world before the Great God of Progress destroyed the past and invented the future.

'Who the devil has left you a pier?' Mr Hewitt asked his good friend Mr Livingstone. Mr Hewitt was having one of those rare days when his practical nature overwhelmed the side of him which leaned towards the fanciful.

'I appear to have had an Uncle Bertram,' said Mr Livingstone. 'I don't remember having had an Uncle Bertram but a firm of solicitors called Standfast, Angel and Barrowclough seem convinced that I did and they don't appear to be the sort of people who go in for practical jokes.'

He read a little more of the letter he had received.

And there was a good deal of it for, like most members of the legal profession, Standfast, Angel and Barrowclough were not keen on using one word when 27 could be just as easily employed.

In addition to the letter itself, which took up two pages of foolscap, a paper size which no one had seen for years, there was a plan of the pier concerned and a map of the town of Penmouth showing the pier's precise location. The pier, and a good sized portion of land at the landward end of the pier, had been carefully outlined in red ink so that there could be no doubt whatsoever about the location and extent of the property concerned.

'So, does it say where it is?' asked Ruth.

'It appears to be in a town called Penmouth,' replied Mr Livingstone, still studying the letter from the solicitors. 'And Penmouth seems to be in the county of Devon.'

Mr Roxdale said he thought he'd heard of Penmouth and Mr Twist said he thought it was in South Devon rather close to the well-known resort of Torquay. Mrs Torridge said she was absolutely sure it was in North Devon, possibly somewhere near Bideford, while Mrs Peterborough said she was pretty sure the solicitors had got it completely wrong and that Penmouth was in Norfolk, probably somewhere near Aldeburgh.

Mrs Merivale, keen to get involved, said she thought there was somewhere called Yarmouth on the Isle of Wight and asked no one in particular if the solicitors could have possibly made a mistake and misspelt both the name and the location of the pier. She said she had heard of something like this happening before. She said that a firm of solicitors had written to tell a neighbour of hers that she'd inherited a house in Stratford-on-Avon and the neighbour had been terribly disappointed when she'd discovered that there had been a slight typographical error and that the house was really in Stockton-on-Tees, doubtless a very nice place but quite not the same thing at all, especially when you've already set your heart on picnics on the banks of the River Avon and evenings spent at the Royal Shakespeare Theatre. Mrs Merivale said her neighbour had been so upset by the whole thing that she'd gone into a decline. She had never visited the house in Stockton-on-Tees but had instructed the solicitors to sell it on her behalf.

A little research, done by Ruth with the aid of the search engine on her mobile telephone, confirmed that Penmouth was a small West Country town, hardly much bigger than a village, which was situated in the southern part of the county of Devon and which sprawled comfortably at the mouth of the River Pen. The town had apparently once been a favourite resort with Victorians, especially those keen to escape London's heat and bustle during the months of July and

August and eager to avoid the capital's Christmas bustle, and the inevitable pea soup smogs, in December.

The town was, it seemed from the photographs that Mr Williams managed to find in an encyclopaedia he had taken from the bookshelf, more than adequately supplied with expensive, well-built homes in standard, solid Victorian stone and brick. These were interspersed with a collection of fine Arts and Craft houses, all furnished with fancy roofs, delicate wooden balconies, massive chimneys and all the other architectural folderols popularised by William Morris and his acolytes.

Mr Williams reported that according to the encyclopaedia, it was common during the reigns of Queen Victoria and King Edward for the mothers of well-off families, together with the children and the servants, to move to Penmouth while the husbands stayed in London and moved into rooms at their clubs for a few weeks.

And finally, Mr Williams reported, with no little sadness in his voice, that most of the grand houses had been converted into boarding houses or guest houses. The ones which hadn't been converted into boarding houses had been turned into flats and bed sitting rooms and were rented out to holidaymakers.

Still, Penmouth may have been way past its prime but, as Gertrude Stein would have doubtless said, a pier is a pier is a pier.

Chapter Three

Most of us have happy memories of piers.

They bring back childhood memories of bucket and spade seaside holidays; of sandcastles, of sunny days that seem to last for ever but never last quite long enough; of pink, sticky rock; of picnics on the sand; of using a simple hand line to fish for mackerel from the pier; of sudden, unexpected rainbursts and cheap plastic macs; of shops packed with colourful buckets and spades and beachballs and of fish and chips wrapped in newspaper.

For honeymoon couples of a certain age, the ones who chose to spend their honeymoons at the English seaside rather than somewhere foreign, distant and expensive, seaside piers bring back memories of strolling arm in arm into the sunset; of giggling at the archaic, and remarkably innocent, black and white pictures in the 'What the Butler Saw' machine; of huddling together in a shelter to escape from a sudden downpour; of buying matching Kiss Me Quick hats and finding the courage to wear them; of sharing a dodgem car on the funfair; of smiling at old aged pensioners slumped in their deckchairs, drinking tea from thick, white, china cups and trying to catch the crumbs while eating chocolate covered digestive biscuits.

And of quietly wondering what life will have to offer in the years to come; the years until they too are of an age to settle comfortably together; content to watch the world trundle by.

Those were simpler days.

A holiday away from everything meant just that.

You could, in those days, be much further away from your daily worries while sitting on a pier just a few hundred miles from home than you could today while sitting on a beach in the Bahamas or Bali.

Mr Williams, who had pulled an encyclopaedia from the bookcase, suddenly yelped with excitement. 'Did you say that your pier was in Penmouth?' he asked Mr Livingstone.

Mr Livingstone didn't hesitate. 'Yes,' he said confidently. 'Penmouth! And Penmouth is in Devon.'

When you've just become the proud owner of your first pier you damned well know where it is.

'Well, it's mentioned here in the encyclopaedia,' said Mr Williams. 'It seems that you're the new owner of a famous pier. The encyclopaedia says that a Dr Ignaz Hessyan recommended sea bathing at Penmouth in 1793 and it was as a result of a series of articles which the good Dr Hessyan wrote for the *Morning Post* newspaper that the town first became popular with holidaymakers. The encyclopaedia says that local hoteliers built a Winter Gardens and a Hydro and that the pier was built by a consortium of local businessmen in 1822. The Winter Gardens were turned into a hotel in 1934 and the Hydro is now a car park but the pier remains.'

And at this point the questions about the pier came thick and fast. Indeed, they came so thickly and so quickly that it was difficult to discern who had asked what.

'How long is it?'

'Does it have amusements?'

'Does it have one of those little trains that chug up and down carrying passengers from one end to the other?'

'Can we go fishing off the side and catch mackerel?'

'If it does have one of those little trains do you think I could drive it occasionally?'

And last, but certainly not least: 'When can we go and see it?'

But it was Mr Livingstone's next statement, culled from the First Epistle of Messrs Standfast, Angel and Barrowclough that attracted the greatest amount of attention, particularly from Mrs Caldicot who had, since opening her own communication from the Government, been wondering where she could find a house big enough to home herself, Jenkins and a dozen good companions.

'There appears to be a hotel stuck on the landward end of it,' announced Mr Livingstone with a mixture of surprise and delight.

'A hotel! How big is it?' asked Mrs Caldicot who was now doubly excited by Mr Livingstone's inheritance.

'My new best friend, the estimable Mr Roland Canterbury, of the equally estimable firm of Standfast, Angel and Barrowclough, has kindly enclosed a photograph and a plan,' said Mr Livingstone. He opened the plan he had been sent and studied it carefully. 'On the first floor there appear to be 20 bedrooms, an assortment of bathrooms, a kitchen and a room labelled BallR. On the ground floor there is a ticket office, a souvenir shop and a café selling fish and chips and cups of tea.' He looked across at Mrs Caldicot. 'There are enough rooms for us to move in and live there!' he said.

Mrs Caldicot looked at him to see if he was serious.

He was.

'Do you think so?' she asked, hardly daring to believe that their misfortune had already been counterbalanced by matching good fortune.

'Absolutely!' said Mr Livingstone, excitedly. 'We can all live on the pier! Can you imagine anything more exciting?'

'I think the BallR will probably be a 'ballroom',' said Mr Hewitt, who had been looking over his friend's shoulder. 'There's an asterisk and a bit here, at the bottom of the plan, which explains that it was formerly used by a local dancing academy.'

'Golly,' said Mrs Roberts, who was impressed. 'You've got your own ballroom.'

'I've never known anyone who owned a ballroom,' said Miss Nightingale, who was not alone in this.

'I've never known anyone who owned a pier,' said Mrs Peterborough whose absence of experience in this area was also not unique. Indeed, it was quickly agreed by the assembled company, that no one present had ever even known anyone who had known anyone who had owned a pier. All this made Mr Livingstone feel very privileged indeed.

'When I was a girl I met a boy on a pier in Brighton,' said Mrs Torridge. 'We were both 16 and we thought we were in love for ever. His name was Eric and he used a lot of Brylcream on his hair. Every day we sat side by side in deckchairs on the pier. I remember the deckchairs were made of faded green canvas. We ate chips, ice creams and cockles with loads of vinegar and we sat there all day long. We spent the entire holiday just sitting beside each other because we thought that was what people did when they were in love.'

'What happened to him?' asked Miss Nightingale.

'At the end of the week we both went home. Even though I was 16 and thought I was in love, I think I knew it was over. I'd been so happy that I cried and cried and cried all the way home. He worked in a warehouse in Bolton and I was still at school in Dudley. I sent him several letters but he wasn't much of a letter writer. In fact he could only just write his name, poor fellow. His sister had to read my letters to him and then write down his replies to send to me. It wasn't a terribly romantic way to conduct a correspondence and eventually it all sort of fizzled out. It was very sad at the time but it was a wonderful week.' Mrs Torridge stopped for a moment, deep in thought. 'It was the very best holiday of my life until that holiday we all had in Paris. The one when Mr Twist lost our money to those crooks and we all went busking to earn money for our food. That was the best holiday of my life. I enjoyed that very much indeed.'

Mrs Caldicot, who had been listening, looked across to where Mr Twist was sitting. She was relieved to see that he was talking to Mr Williams and hadn't heard what Mrs Torridge had said about him losing their money.

'Does owning a pier mean that you're very rich?' asked Ruth, who was not an avaricious girl, and not greedy for money for its own sake, but who, at the age of 18 going on 19, already knew enough about life to know that riches can often bring more fun, more adventure and more good times than poverty and who was, therefore, perfectly prepared to admit that if offered a choice of the two options she would, generally speaking, opt for the one involving riches rather than the one which didn't.

'I have no idea,' said Mr Livingstone, who was still rather overwhelmed by the whole thing and still striving to accustom himself that whereas he had, only that morning, woken up as a 70 something former Bomber Command hero and keen musician, but nevertheless entirely pier-less, he now appeared to be one of that very select group of individuals able to describe themselves as pier owners. This was quite an adjustment to make for a man who had not yet properly digested his breakfast bacon and egg. (Two slices of crispy bacon, egg slightly runny, served with two slices of white toast and a half pint mug of tea.)

The fact is that Mr Livingstone had reached an age when he preferred that surprises, if they had to come at all, to come a little later in the day and preferably not at mealtimes or within, say, three quarters of an hour of their conclusion.

'Good heavens!' cried Mr Williams, startling them all with the suddenness of his exposition. He held up the encyclopaedia he was studying. 'It says here that Penmouth was one of Jane Austen's favourite holiday resorts. She was enormously fond of the South Devon and Dorset coasts and she and her family were regular visitors. She was known to have visited Dawlish, Sidmouth and Teignmouth in Devon, and Lyme Regis in Dorset. And she visited Penmouth at least three times. The vicar of Penmouth was apparently one of her father's favourite pupils.'

'I've been to Lyme Regis,' said Mrs Peterborough. 'My parents used to take us there every summer. It's very pretty. We stayed in a cottage which had the lavatory at the bottom of the garden. It was full of spiders and I was terrified of them.'

'Jane Austen's father was a vicar,' continued Mr Williams, who was now quite excited. 'And he took in apprentice vicars from time to time – including one who later became the vicar of Penmouth. It says here that literary historians believe that Miss Austen's unfinished novel *Sanditon* was almost certainly based on her visit to Penmouth. Her last visit to Penmouth was in the late summer of 1816. She was already ill and the family hoped that a visit to her favourite seaside resort might help improve her health. She seemed to have made something of a recovery because she started work on *Sanditon* in January 1817.'

'I don't think I know that book,' said Mrs Caldicot who had been an admirer of Jane Austen and the Bronte sisters since she'd been a girl.

'She never finished writing *Sanditon,*' said Jenkins. 'She worked on it for a couple of months but died in the summer of 1817 – June or July I think it was. I don't think she completed more than around 50 pages.'

'It was July 18th, 1817,' said Mr Williams, reading from the encyclopaedia. 'Good heavens – the poor girl was only 41 when she died.'

They all agreed that this was no age at all. And this was perhaps not surprising for if Ruth and Mrs Roberts were excluded from the equation the average age of the people in the room was considerably closer to 80 than it was to 70.

'Who was Jane Austen?' asked Ruth.

'She was a writer,' explained Mr Williams. 'A very famous English writer.'

'She wrote…er…books,' said Mr Livingstone, who seemed not quite able to think of any titles.

'*Pride and Prejudice*,' said Mrs Caldicot. 'That was one of hers.'

'Oh!' said Ruth. 'I didn't know you meant she wrote films. I haven't seen it but my Mum watches it whenever it's on the television. It's all old-fashioned, isn't it? It's one of her favourite films. My Mum will be thrilled. Do you think Mrs Austen would have visited the pier?'

'No, I'm afraid she wouldn't have been able to, dear,' said Mrs Caldicot. 'She died over 50 years before the pier was built.'

'Golly!' said Ruth, clearly surprised. 'I didn't know they were making films then. The one my Mum was watching was in colour too. That's amazing. It's a pity she couldn't visit the pier. But do you think other famous people would have visited it?'

'Oh yes,' agreed Mrs Caldicot. 'There's a theatre at the end of the pier so all sorts of famous people would have performed there.'

'Pop groups?'

'Oh, quite probably,' said Mrs Caldicot. 'Almost certainly, I would say.'

'I've found it!' interrupted Mr Merivale, with considerable excitement.

While the others had been discussing Jane Austen's connection with the town of Penmouth, Mr Merivale had pulled a 1998 road atlas out of the same bookcase from whence Mr Williams had obtained his encyclopaedia.

Content in the knowledge that, although some roads might have been moved, closed, extended or added to, and that county boundaries may well have been moved or done away with altogether, there was a better than evens chance that wherever Penmouth had been in 1998 it had probably not moved very much, and was, indeed, most probably more or less in the same place now as it had been then.

Everyone, including Mr Livingstone, crowded round the map, anxious to see just where Penmouth was situated.

'Look!' said Miss Peterborough. 'It's right on the coast.'

'So it will almost certainly be near the sea!' said Miss Nightingale, excitedly.

'There, I told you it wasn't in Norfolk!' said Mrs Peterborough, whose memory had good and bad moments. Even Mrs Peterborough admitted that her memory wasn't all what it had been in its earlier days. If offered for sale, it would have had to be described with some caution, and some imaginative text, if strict advertising rules were not to be breached.

Chapter Four

Two days later, Mr Livingstone, accompanied by Mrs Caldicot, caught a train to Bristol where the solicitors Standfast, Angel and Barrowclough had their offices.

Neither Mrs Caldicot nor Mr Livingstone could remember ever having visited Bristol before though Mr Livingstone said he could remember flying over it during the War.

'There's an airfield nearby,' he said. 'We used it during the War though I seem to remember that it was often rather a foggy place.' He paused, and for a moment wandered back to the early 1940s. 'I remember that we used to think it was a silly place to put an airfield,' he continued. 'The fog meant that half the time we couldn't take off and the rest of the time we couldn't land.'

'I think it's a proper airport now,' said Mrs Caldicot. 'When we all went to Paris I remember looking at the brochure and seeing that they offered flights from Bristol Airport.'

'We had good fun on that trip,' said Mr Livingstone.

'We certainly did,' agreed Mrs Caldicot.

'I'm glad we went on the train,' said Mr Livingstone. 'That was quite an adventure in itself wasn't it?'

Mrs Caldicot laughed. 'I suppose it was a bit of an adventure,' she said. She remembered saying a silent prayer of thanks when they finally got through the customs post in London without being arrested.

An 'adventure' it certainly had been.

'Does Ruth still hear from that nice, French lad she met in Paris? The one with the accordion?'

'Oh yes. She and Jean-Jacques speak to each other every day and they're forever sending each other little messages on their telephones.'

Jenkins had given Mrs Caldicot a mobile telephone but she was allowing herself to become accustomed to new technology bit by bit and still wasn't entirely comfortable with the idea of being able to use the phone to write messages. It seemed odd to be able to make and receive telephone calls while out shopping. She hadn't said anything to Jenkins but to her it didn't seem entirely natural to be able to make telephone calls without a wire dangling from the telephone.

'I'm pleased about that,' said Mr Livingstone. 'That young chap was very good on that accordion of his,' said Mr Livingstone. 'Especially for a French person.'

Mr Livingstone thought for a moment. 'Doesn't it cost a fortune to telephone foreign parts?'

'Apparently not,' said Mrs Caldicot. 'They use some clever internet thing that means they don't have to pay a penny for their calls.'

'Good heavens!' said Mr Livingstone. 'Is that legal? I do hope it's legal.'

'Oh, I'm sure it is,' said Mrs Caldicot. 'Ruth's a good girl. She wouldn't do anything naughty. Jenkins says it's terribly easy to do. He's going to show me what I have to do so that we can talk to each other when he's in America.'

She frowned, suddenly very sad at the thought of her husband being away on the other side of the Atlantic. She hated it when they were parted but knew that sometimes it could not be avoided.

At the Temple Meads railway station, Mrs Caldicot and Mr Livingstone queued and took a taxi driven by a morose fellow who had a nose which would have been more at home on a larger head, and skin the colour of a very ripe tomato.

It turned out that the offices they were visiting were no more than a five minute walk from the station but the city's traffic system meant that the journey required a 20 minute drive.

Mr Standfast, Mr Angel and Mr Barrowclough, and whatever aides and assistants they had to help them with their work, laboured in a building which looked as if it had been built, painted and decorated in the middle of the 19th century, and then abandoned and left to its own devices. It may well have been much loved when it had been built, but since those long ago days the love had not always been generously bestowed and the building was, to be polite, beginning to show its age. The brickwork and stonework were crumbling and had been eaten away by acid rain and the whole structure looked as if it were held together only by the soot which had been deposited upon it by steam trains chugging into and out of the railway station. The building's wooden window and door frames, which had long since lost most or all of their paint, were grey and wrinkled with deep cracks, and appeared to be still in situ only because they didn't have the energy to go somewhere else.

A receptionist, whom Mrs Caldicot felt had probably been with the building since it was opened, sat behind a telephone switchboard which appeared to be dependent upon old-fashioned plugs and long wires. She was very tiny, shrunken almost, and constantly wheezed and coughed. She peered at them through rheumy eyes as though she were thinking of buying them and trying to assess their value. She was, thought Mrs Caldicot, a woman who had seen more than everything, several times, and was now quite beyond surprise, beyond horror and beyond despair. She was a strangely dignified ruin of a woman, beyond every imaginable emotion.

She was there, secure behind her switchboard and her memories, quietly comfortable and confident because when life holds no more terrors what is there to be startled by?

When Mr Livingstone had stated his name and his business, she directed them to a narrow, wooden staircase with a wobbly wave of a very weary hand. There was, she said without apology, no lift.

Mr Canterbury, the solicitor who had written to Mr Livingstone, had a small, rather dusty office on the fourth floor. The stairs were narrow, twisting and very badly lit. The only light came from very occasional small windows; so narrow that they reminded Mrs Caldicot of the slits built in castle walls so that the residents within could fire arrows at the marauders outside.

The staircase ended in a small landing; the floorboards of which were uneven, like pond water on a windy day, and which felt rickety and rather unsafe. Both Mr Livingstone and Mrs Caldicot trod delicately, and with considerable caution, lest they go through the creaking, unstable boards and unintentionally end up back on the floor below. In front of them there was a single door. The upper half of the door was glazed in the sort of opaque glass usually preferred when glazing bathrooms, and the glass had the name of the firm printed on it in gold, capital letters.

When there was no response to his knock, Mr Livingstone opened the door and they entered. The first person they saw was a skeletal woman in her mid to late sixties. She was the only occupant of the room and she was standing facing them, holding a bundle of files in her arms. She wore glasses, squinted and appeared to have had a cigarette stub permanently glued to her lower lip. She appeared to be a secretary of some kind, working in an office which was packed with files and tottering stacks of paper. The lines around her eyes suggested that the squinting was permanent and was a result of cigarette smoke rather than a need for stronger spectacle lenses. A plume of smoke curled upwards from the cigarette and, not surprisingly, the ceiling had that yellow hue that years of tobacco smoke can create. The woman wore a dress in a style that had gone out of fashion in the 1970s, and when she finally moved to put the files down on top of another heap of files, she shuffled about in a pair of fluffy, blue slippers. She also wore an old-fashioned flowered pinafore – the sort which hangs from the neck, ties behind and has a large pocket at the front. The pocket was clearly half full of something though Mrs Caldicot could not see what it was. The woman stared at them and opened her mouth but did not speak. The cigarette remained in place, stuck to the woman's lower lip.

Mrs Caldicot thought that the secretary looked as if she had always been the same age. She did not look like a woman who had ever been seven-years-old, skipping and cuddling dolls; never been 16, shy and giggling at boys; never been 22 and courting; never even been 29 worrying about her 30th birthday. She had, thought Mrs Caldicot, the look of a woman who been born wrinkled, short-sighted, squinting, wearing a shapeless cardigan and with a fag (never for her could it be called a cigarette) stuck fast to a lower lip. Mrs Caldicot did not think any of this in an unkindly or critical way.

The room was dominated by two large, grey filing cabinets upon which there were yet more files. There were files everywhere. This was not a paperless office. Mrs Caldicot couldn't help looking around to see if there was a fire extinguisher anywhere. There wasn't. An old-fashioned wooden desk bore an old-fashioned sit up and beg typewriter, a Bakelite telephone left over from a less hectic era, and more old-fashioned files and bundles of paper. There were no signs of computers, printers or other modern distractions. It was not the sort of environment where mobile telephones buzzed or vibrated. The secretary did not look like the sort of woman who was likely to be a fan of social media. The only sign of modern office equipment was an open box of carbon paper balanced on top of a dozen, thick cardboard folders.

It seemed incomprehensible to Mrs Caldicot and Mr Livingstone that the woman could possibly know the location of anything but, as if often the case, this proved to be an entirely baseless assumption. The moment Mr Livingstone announced his name, and the reason for his visit, and showed her the letter he had received, the woman lifted the box of carbon paper and half a dozen files and found a pink, cardboard folder which bore a label carrying the hand printed words: 'Estate of Bertram Livingstone Esq– Decd'.

Saying nothing but indicating with a wave of the hand that they should follow her, the woman led the way into an office where a huge man sat behind a monstrous desk paring his fingernails with the long blade of a large pocket knife. To the man's left there lay a large piece of greaseproof paper upon which lay part of a loaf of crusty bread, two tomatoes and the remains of a piece of cheese. There was also a bottle of port and an empty wine glass that, by the dregs within it, had clearly been used rather recently.

'This is Mr Canterbury,' said the woman, introducing the man behind the desk. She waved her hand in the direction of Mr Livingstone and Mrs Caldicot. 'These are the Estate of Bertram Livingstone deceased.' She then put the Bertram Livingstone file down on Mr Canterbury's desk. She had some difficulty finding a space not occupied by files, bread, cheese, tomatoes or port wine.

Mrs Caldicot rather suspected that Mr Canterbury probably brought his luncheon with him and ate and drank at his desk so that he only had to climb the staircase once a day. She didn't blame him. It was the sort of staircase that people climb when they want to take exercise and Mr Canterbury did not look the sort of man who thought much of exercise.

Mr Canterbury looked up, stopped what he was doing, carefully folded the blade back into his penknife and laid it down on his desk as though it were a treasured heirloom which, indeed, it may have been. He nodded at his two visitors, in acknowledgement of their presence. Mrs Caldicot thought he looked rather grand, very old-fashioned and intimidating.

Like the outer office, Mr Canterbury's room was full of paper.

Three of the four walls had shelves which were stuffed with row upon row of neatly bound law books and the carpet was pretty well covered with towering and unstable stacks of files, briefs and miscellaneous papers. Some of the piles of paper were tied together with the sort of red ribbon which lawyers traditionally prefer, and some were tied with what looked like common or garden string. There wasn't enough carpet visible to tell what colour it was or whether it had any sort of pattern. It was an office which would have made a perfect set for any film company looking to make a movie based upon one of the many novels by Dickens which features a lawyer or a legal office. Two upholstered chairs, which looked as though they had once been members of a dining room set, sat waiting for occupation.

'Come in and sit down,' said Mr Canterbury.

As Mrs Caldicot sat down, she thought that Mr Canterbury was even larger than huge; he was a man who clearly regarded food as something more than just fuel for the machine. It was impossible to see how tall he was for he did not lift himself out of his chair when they entered, but merely waved a hand towards the two chairs on the visitors' side of his desk. The front and top of his head were both bald but at the sides and back there were copious quantities of grey curls. He wore pince nez with a gold frame, a dark-grey pinstripe suit with a broad chalk stripe, a stiff, celluloid wing collar and a hand-tied, black bow tie. Mrs Caldicot thought he was probably in his 70s but although he could have been older he was probably not younger.

Mrs Caldicot, turning to thank the secretary for showing them into the solicitor's office now saw that the bulge in the pocket of the woman's pinafore was caused by two kittens. Their heads peered out, like baby kangaroos peeking out of their mother's pouch. Mrs Caldicot liked cats very much but when she moved to stroke the kittens, the secretary hurried away as though protecting them. There was no sign of the mother of the two kittens though there were plenty of places where she could have been sleeping.

Mrs Caldicot and Mr Livingstone both sat down.

'You're Mr Livingstone,' said Mr Canterbury to Mr Livingstone.

Mr Livingstone confirmed that he was indeed Mr Livingstone.

'Do we have any identification?'

Mr Livingstone produced the letter he had been sent and then rummaged around his pocket and offered, as supplementary evidence, the railway ticket he had used for the journey to Bristol. Mr Canterbury waved away the letter but accepted the railway ticket which he examined carefully.

'This does not have your name upon it,' the solicitor pointed out, unnecessarily.

'No, but it proves that I came from the place to which your letter was sent,' replied Mr Livingstone.

'Indeed it does,' agreed Mr Canterbury. He sighed, nodded and handed the used ticket back to Mr Livingstone. He then looked at Mrs Caldicot. 'And are we safe in assuming that you are Mrs Livingstone?'

'Not safe at all,' said Mr Livingstone. 'This is Mrs Caldicot.'

'Actually, my name is Mrs Jenkins,' said Mrs Caldicot.

'My apologies,' said Mr Livingstone, who still thought of Mrs Caldicot as Mrs Caldicot.

Mr Canterbury frowned and appeared to be a little confused. 'Are you cohabiting?' he asked Mr Livingstone. 'Do you live together?'

'Oh yes,' said Mr Livingstone. 'There are twelve of us, plus Mrs Caldicot and Mr Jenkins.'

'Twelve of you?'

'Plus Mrs Caldicot and Mr Jenkins.'

'And who, pray, is Mr Jenkins?'

'That's Mrs Caldicot's husband.'

'Her common-law husband?'

'No, we're properly married,' said Mrs Caldicot. 'We had confetti and cake and someone tied a horseshoe and some old tin cans onto the back bumper of Mr Jenkins's motor car. It took us ages to untie them all.'

'That was Mr Hewitt,' said Mr Livingstone.

'We thought it was,' said Mrs Caldicot, looking at Mr Livingstone.

Mr Canterbury sighed the deep sigh of a man who long ago realised that life regularly offers up far too many complexities for any man to hope to understand even a small proportion of them. 'Are we safe in assuming that Mrs Caldicot aka Mrs Jenkins is cognisant?'

Mr Livingstone stared blankly at Mr Canterbury.

'Mrs Caldicot aka Mrs Jenkins knows about the bequest? She is fully cognisant?'

'Oh yes,' Mr Livingstone nodded. 'Definitely.'

'And you are comfortable with her presence here today?'

'Oh yes, definitely. She is fully cognisant.'

'Excellent.'

'May I ask you something?' asked Mr Livingstone.

Mr Canterbury, seemingly surprised by this, frowned, blinked and nodded.

'Where are Mr Angel, Mr Standfast and Mr Barrowclough? I didn't see any sign of them having offices here.'

'Mr Angel passed away in 1951 and Mr Barrowclough ran away with the counter girl from Waverly's the tobacconists in 1962. We have no idea where he is now.'

'And Mr Standfast?'

'Mr Angel and Mr Barrowclough started the firm after the Second World War. They felt at the time that having three partners sounded more substantial than having just two. They felt that 'Angel and Barrowclough' made them sound like a chain of shoe shops or a provincial dentist. They wanted gravitas and so they invented Mr Standfast, using a name they took from a novel by John Buchan.'

'So now there's just you?'

'Indeed that is so. Apart from Miss Ball, whom you have met, and who is our secretary, we work alone. But we have always felt comfortable in working under the aegis of the original triumvirate. Does that satisfy your curiosity?'

'Absolutely,' said Mr Livingstone. 'Thanks very much. It just puzzled me. I hope you don't mind my asking.'

'Not at all. Not at all. We congratulate you, sir, on your perspicacity. You are the first person in two decades to have queried the absence of my partners.' Mr Canterbury shuffled his substantial bulk in his chair, looked down at the unopened file relating to Mr Bertram Livingstone, and then continued.

'As you will know from our letter to you, Mr Bertram Livingstone was your uncle. Did you know that you had an uncle?'

Mr Livingstone shook his head. 'I'm afraid I didn't know I had an uncle Bertram. I've never heard of him.'

'Mr Livingstone, your uncle, was, we think it is fair to say, an unusual man of slightly eccentric tastes and interests. We met him only once, when he drew up his will. He was a memorable man if not a particularly remarkable one. He never married or, as far as we are aware, had any relationships of note. He had few friends and told us that he had spent much of his life in an old caravan which was permanently ensconced, sequestered indeed, in a distant corner of the car park of 'The Wounded Soldier', a public house situated in the outskirts of a town called Walsall which used to be in Staffordshire but which is, we believe, now to be found in the West Midlands. One assumes, one hopes, that the town itself has remained static but that its apparent migration is a result of one of those boundary readjustments which bureaucrats are fond of making from time to time. Mr Livingstone paid for his parking spot by doing odd jobs in and around the licensed premises and his evenings were spent in the public bar of 'The Wounded Soldier' where he passed the time playing dominoes, cribbage and other games popular among those who found darts and bar billiards too energetic for their taste.'

'You seem to remember him well,' said Mrs Caldicot.

'We refreshed our memory by reading the file before we wrote to Mr Livingstone,' explained Mr Canterbury. 'And he was, as we have said, a memorable man. He told us that he won the Penmouth Pier in a game of dominoes some twenty three years ago. He then moved out of his caravan and subsequently lived on the pier until his death. He was a solitary man, something of a recluse we understand, and the pier was the only property of value he left behind. There was a small amount of money in a current account but sadly that has all gone in funeral and legal expenses and your uncle left nothing else in the way of chattels. He made a will in 1998, leaving all his worldly goods to his brother, your father, but sadly, as you are no doubt aware, the beneficiary of that will died in 1987 and it is to be presumed that your uncle did know of this sad event. If he ever did become cognisant then he did not choose to update his will. The result is that the pier comes to you, Mr Livingstone. You were his sole surviving relative and are therefore the sole beneficiary. The pier is yours, as it stands, without encumbrances.'

'Right,' said Mr Livingstone, who wasn't entirely sure what an encumbrance was but thought that on balance, and probably quite rightly, that it was undoubtedly a good thing that there weren't any. 'That's splendid,' he said. 'I've never owned a pier before,' he added.

'We would doubt if many people could say they have,' agreed Mr Canterbury. 'We would certainly say that we ourselves would fall comfortably into that category.' He looked at Mrs Caldicot. 'You, madam? Have you ever owned a pier?'

'No,' said Mrs Caldicot. 'No, I can't say that I have.'

'No, you can't,' said Mr Canterbury. 'Not unless you have.' He looked at the cheese on the greaseproof paper, opened a blade of the penknife he'd been using to trim his nails and cut off a decent sized chunk of cheese. He ate the cheese off the point of the knife.

It occurred to Mrs Caldicot that it was quite likely that Mr Canterbury never actually really stopped eating.

'You, Mr Livingstone are only the second person we have known who has owned a pier. Your uncle, of course, being the other. You are a rare beast, sir. We gather that many of the remaining piers around the coast of Britain are owned by corporations, charities or local councils. We doubt if there are half a dozen individuals in the country who can, if they feel the urge so to do, stand up and say 'I own a pier'. You, sir, are now one of them – even though it has to be admitted that your pier has, temporarily at least, fallen into desuetude.'

'What's that?' asked Mr Livingstone.

'A state of disuse,' explained Mr Canterbury.

'Ah,' said Mr Livingstone, wondering why solicitors liked to use words which no one else used. 'So if I wasn't mentioned in the will how did you find me?'

Mr Canterbury finished chewing his piece of cheese and then swallowed it before replying. 'We found you, sir, with considerable difficulty. We advertised in a periodical known as the *London Gazette* though why we do that we never know because in our experience nothing ever comes of it. We made the usual enquiries and eventually we employed the services of a private detective who specialises in researching family trees. We use the word detective and you might imagine a man in a grubby mackintosh, carrying a magnifying glass and a pistol but the reality is less romantic. The expert we hired is a spinster who spends her days ploughing through public records. She uses something called the internet though we have only the loosest notion of what that might be. Sadly, the expense of these endeavours utilised entirely the small cash bequest which you might otherwise have enjoyed alongside the pier.'

'And the Mr Livingstone who died was my uncle?'

'Yes, indeed. He and your father were brothers.'

'I didn't even know my father had a brother.'

'No, we had assumed that you were probably not aware of his existence just as we doubt that he was aware of yours. You would be surprised how many families there are where relatives do not know of each other's existence. We assume that your father and your uncle must have had a falling out when they were young. They then drifted apart and your father didn't mention that he had a brother when he met and married your mother.' Mr Canterbury poured himself a small port. He did not offer any to Mrs Caldicot or to Mr Livingstone. He sipped at the port. He then opened the drawer of his desk and took out a tin box. From the tin box he took a huge bundle of keys. The keys were all labelled. He looked through the labels, found the one he was looking for and put the remaining keys back into the tin box. He then put the tin box back into the drawer and closed the drawer.

'These are the keys to our pier,' he said, putting a bunch of keys onto the desk in front of him. There were many different types and sizes of keys. He did not, however, hand them to Mr Livingstone straight away. 'But you have to sign some papers before we can give them to you.'

He took the cardboard file that his secretary had given him and took out several pieces of paper which he pushed across the desk to Mr Livingstone. 'If you would be kind enough to sign these then we can complete the transfer,' he said.

He then picked up his penknife and cleaned the blade with a large, white pocket handkerchief. When he'd done this he started to pare his nails again. There really didn't seem to be anything left to trim.

Mr Livingstone signed the papers.

'Mrs Livingstone can witness your signature.'

'Mrs Caldicot,' said Mr Livingstone, correcting him.

Mr Canterbury frowned as though the relationship were still something of a puzzle to him. He examined the blade of his knife, wiped it on the handkerchief again, and then cut himself another piece of cheese. When he'd done this, he closed the blade of his knife and lay it gently on the desk before him.

'Mrs Jenkins,' said Mrs Caldicot.

'Are you sure you know each other?' said Mr Canterbury. He popped the cheese into his mouth and chewed thoughtfully.

'It's complicated,' said Mrs Caldicot.

'Everything always is,' said Mr Canterbury.

He picked up the signed and witnessed documents and handed the keys to the pier across to Mr Livingstone.

From the folder in front of him he then took a number of photographs. He reached across his desk and handed these to Mr Livingstone. 'There are one or two things about our pier of which you might like to be aware,' said the solicitor. 'First, the distal end of the pier rests upon a rocky island and it is there, upon that island, that the original builders created a large and rather ornate theatre. We believe that this sort of arrangement is considered quite unusual in the world of piers. The piece of rock is known as 'Stone Rock' and it is part of the freehold associated with the remainder of the structure.'

'Stone Rock!' said Mr Livingstone. 'I bet someone spent a lot of time thinking up that name!' Mr Livingstone had already been thoroughly excited by the whole business of owning a pier and could now hardly believe that he also owned a small, rocky island upon which a theatre had been built.

He had not admitted this to anyone, not even to Mrs Caldicot, but there had been a moment, well actually rather more than just a moment, when he'd wondered if there had been a mistake. Maybe the lawyer had mixed him up with another Mr Livingstone; an entirely different Mr Livingstone. Maybe the pier didn't exist. Maybe it was all an elaborate, practical joke. After all, thought Mr Livingstone, the many previous years of his life had not been marked with an abundance of good fortune.

'Precisely,' said Mr Canterbury. 'We would imagine that the name of the rock probably goes back to a time before the pier was constructed.'

'Does the pier have a name?' asked Mr Livingstone.

'It does. Indeed it does.' Mr Canterbury fiddled about with the papers in front of him. 'Ah yes, here we are. Its official name, the name on all the documents and, we believe, the name by which it is known locally, is 'The Pier'.'

'The Pier?'

'Precisely. The Pier.'

'That's the name? Just that?'

'It is.'

'Not The Palace Pier or The Grand Pier or something like that?'

'No, unfortunately not. Our pier is known simply as 'The Pier'.'

'They didn't spend a lot of effort thinking that name up either, did they?'

'We suspect not. Our pier was one of the very early first piers to be built and maybe the people who commissioned it felt no need to identify it in a more elaborate way. Work was started on it in 1874 and the pier was opened in 1877. It was designed by a man called Eugenius Birch, who was, we believe, the premier designer of Victorian piers. We gather that Mr Birch also designed piers in Brighton, Bournemouth and Blackpool.'

'Well that's a good start,' said Mr Livingstone. 'May I ask you a question?'

'Of course.'

'You keep referring to the pier as 'our pier'. Does that mean that you are a part owner?'

Mr Canterbury appeared to be quite startled by this. 'Oh, good heavens no! We use the first person plural in a purely legal sense. It is quite customary for members of the legal profession to unite themselves with their clients in this way. The pier was left to you and to you alone and all the delights and responsibilities associated with its ownership are yours and yours alone.'

'Oh, right ho,' said Mr Livingstone. 'Just got a bit confused, that's all.'

'Quite so,' agreed Mr Canterbury. He picked up another document. 'We believe you will find that the theatre built on Stone Rock is still in existence though we understand it is possible that it may be in need of a little cosmetic attention. On the other hand the wooden piles upon which the pier rests are, we believe, surprisingly sound. According to a report we have here, they were checked just three years ago and found to be perfectly solid and safe. The pier itself is 2,195 feet long and down the centre of the structure there runs a covered walkway which is equipped with numerous benches. It appears that at intervals of twenty yards or so there are vending machines and amusement machines of one sort or another. And according to the information we have before us, there is also a little train. It doesn't run on rails but there's a small engine and three open coaches.'

Mr Canterbury's eyes lit up when he mentioned the little train. 'These little trains can be quite enchanting,' he said. He closed his eyes for a moment. 'Quite enchanting,' he murmured. He was, thought Mrs Caldicot, talking to himself more than to them. For a while he said nothing, apparently lost in a reverie; a pleasant daydream. The daydream can't have lasted more than thirty seconds but it seemed like an age.

'At the proximal end of the structure,' continued Mr Canterbury at last, 'the spot where the pier joins the promenade, there is a large gatehouse which consists of two towers, each of which is three stories high. These towers are connected by a bridge-like structure which creates an archway – from the plan we have in front of us it looks rather like the Admiralty Arch in London though perhaps not quite as grand. The lower part of each leg of the arch is given over to commercial premises. On the left, as we look down the pier, there is a kiosk where visitors can buy sweets, postcards, ice creams, paperback books and tickets for the little train. On the right there is a small café which sells popular and appropriate comestibles such as fish and chips and cups of tea. The two upper floors of the archway and the towers provide accommodation, including a number of bedrooms, bathrooms and so on. We believe that when the pier was built, the gatehouse was designed to be run as a hotel.'

'And there's a ballroom,' said Mr Livingstone.

'Indeed so. We are pleased to see that you have studied the details we sent to you. We see from the documents we have that a previous owner specialised in catering for weddings, anniversaries and birthday parties, with the ballroom inevitably providing a suitable venue for dining and dancing and the bedrooms providing accommodation for those involved and their guests.'

Mr Canterbury pushed another small sheaf of documents across his crowded desk. 'There is one other communication we are obliged to share with you. As the executor of your uncle's estate we have to show you this communication.' He then reached into the file, took out a three page letter and handed it to Mr Livingstone. When he'd done that he tore a large piece of bread from the crusty loaf on his desk and popped that into his mouth.

'What is it?' asked a rather puzzled Mr Livingstone, accepting the letter as a man might accept a summons, a writ or some other unpleasant legal document. 'Is this something I need to worry about?'

'No, no, not at all,' said Mr Canterbury when he'd finished chewing the piece of bread. 'To save you time and effort we can tell you that the communication you are holding is a letter offering to purchase our pier from us.'

'Someone already wants to buy it?' said Mr Livingstone, thoroughly surprised by this completely unexpected turn of events.

'Indeed they do, indeed they do,' said Mr Canterbury. 'But we fear you might not find the offer to be irresistible.'

'I don't care what the offer is,' said Mr Livingstone. 'I've only just got my pier. Why would I want to sell it?' He looked at the long letter he had been handed. 'Who wants to buy it and what are they offering?'

'The agent who wrote to us did so on behalf of a property company and the offer, for the full freehold, is for £1.'

Mr Livingstone stared at him incredulously. 'Did you say £1?'

'We fear so. We gather that the pier has been losing money for some time and although we have not heard from them directly, we gather from a paragraph in the letter you are holding that the local council has some concerns about the ownership and management and is keen to see the pier developed in a way which, as they say, 'will reflect the needs of the town in these changing times'.' Mr Canterbury paused, picked up his penknife and opened the blade. He only ever opened, and used, the one blade. Once again, he used the blade of his knife to trim his well-trimmed fingernails.

'Crumbs!' said Mr Livingstone.

'But as I have already mentioned we have no reason to believe that the structure of the pier need be of concern. It appears that any problems relate more to the management of the pier.'

'So you don't think it's falling down?'

'No, no, not at all. You would find that a very expensive event.'

'Why would it be expensive if the pier fell down?' asked Mrs Caldicot.

'The council would doubtless insist upon you moving the wreckage from the beach and the sea,' Mr Canterbury pointed. 'Given the size of the structure and the weight of the materials involved, the costs would be very high. There would be some salvage value but not enough to cover the high costs of demolition and removal.'

'Who would be responsible for the costs if that happened?' asked Mr Livingstone.

'Oh that would be our responsibility,' said Mr Canterbury. 'As the owner of the pier we would be responsible for all those costs.' He coughed, remembering Mr Livingstone's question. 'Er, you would be responsible since you are the owner.' He rooted through the paper work and produced yet another document. 'Unfortunately, your uncle allowed the insurance to lapse and so the pier is not insured at all at the moment. In that regard we are exposed.'

'I'm responsible for all the costs if the pier falls into the sea?'

'Oh yes.'

'But I don't have any money,' Mr Livingstone pointed out.

'You have no properties? No savings?'

'No.'

'Then you need not concern yourself. You would simply declare yourself bankrupt.'

'They wouldn't be able to put me in prison or anything like that?'

'Oh, good heavens no. You would be bankrupt for one year and that would be the end of that. Under normal circumstances we would advise a client inheriting a property, particularly one as large and as complex as this one, to take out comprehensive insurance. But insuring a pier can be very, very expensive.'

'How expensive?'

'We are not insurance specialists but we would say that if you had an excess of £500,000 on your policy then the premium would be as much as £100,000 a year.'

'An excess of £500,000? What does that mean?'

'It means that you would agree to pay the first £500,000 of any loss – in the same way that house or motor car insurance policies often include an excess.'

Mr Livingstone laughed.

'Quite,' said Mr Canterbury.

'But if there's a problem and the pier falls down or something terrible happens to it I could just go bankrupt for a year?'

'Precisely.'

'That would be a bit cheaper than the insurance policy I couldn't afford.'

'Indeed it would.' Mr Canterbury paused for a moment. 'In some ways we are a perfect owner for a pier. If a rich man inherited a pier he could be made into a poor man by the running costs – the insurance alone being a major part of the costs. If a rich man inherited a pier which fell into the sea he would have to spend a large part of his fortune on recovering the debris, compensating the authorities and so on.'

'But I don't have any money so I'm safe from all these terrible things?

'Exactly!'

Mr Livingstone looked at Mrs Caldicot and smiled. She smiled back.

'One good thing has come from this communication,' said Mr Canterbury, touching the letter offering to buy the pier. 'The offer, valuing the pier at £1, has enabled us, as the executors of your uncle's will, to inform Her Majesty's Customs and Excise that there will be no tax to pay on the property. We cannot be obliged to pay more inheritance tax than our inheritance is worth.'

He stopped trimming his fingernails and wiped the blade. Mrs Caldicot knew what was coming next. As we get older our habits become irrepressible routines. Mr Canterbury pared his nails more than was reasonable. His nails could not possibly be growing that quickly. The nail paring was part of a complicated behavioural tic. He pared his nails before he ate. It was a ritual. Open knife, pare nails, wipe blade, cut cheese, chew, close knife. She sympathised. She knew all about rituals and routines. Our habits rust with age and become increasingly inflexible and unavoidable.

'I hadn't even thought of inheritance tax,' said Mr Livingstone.

'Most people don't,' said Mr Canterbury. He cut himself a small piece of cheese. When he had eaten the cheese he poured himself another glass of port. That too was part of the routine. 'The sad news is that our pier doesn't appear to be worth very much. But by the same token, this means that we won't have to pay tax on our acquisition. And so the sad news becomes good news.'

'But I can just ignore the letter from these people who want to buy the pier?'

‘Oh yes. We can keep our pier. The only real concern would be if the council decided that the pier was unsafe or an eyesore or in some other regard unsatisfactory. The structure reports I have seen confirm that the pier is in good condition. There is no need for you to worry on that score. However, councils have given themselves a good deal of power over property owners these days. And a pier, not being hidden down a side street as it were, is not the sort of property that is likely to be overlooked.’

‘Will it be possible for us to move into the accommodation at the entrance to the pier?’ asked Mrs Caldicot.

Mr Canterbury, who was sipping his port, raised half a pair of un-groomed eyebrows. He seemed surprised.

‘Our local council have just told us that they have decided to purchase our home,’ explained Mrs Caldicot. ‘They’re going to knock it down and put railway lines there instead.’

‘Oh dear!’ said Mr Canterbury sympathetically. ‘We take it that your property is in the path of this absurd new high speed railway the Government has decided to build?’

‘I’m afraid so.’

‘Then we fear there is no saving you from your fate. The Government has given itself extraordinarily draconian powers over the owners of homes and land which stand in the way of its various tentacle building operations.’ Mr Canterbury sounded disapproving. ‘But your pier is another kettle of fish, if you will pardon the rather inappropriate metaphor. We can’t imagine the Government will have plans to build a new railway line through your pier. That would be a most unfortunate case of ‘incidis in Scyllam cupiens vitare Charybdim’. And we can’t see them wanting to build an airport there either. So our only threat will come from the council – usually rather less of a threat than central government. If we get into trouble let me know and we will see if we can help. We have not, of course, seen the property ourselves but it is our sad experience that local councillors and their planning officers have a tendency to attempt to ride roughshod over the rights of local property owners and if they have some pet project in mind there will be no end to the devious nature of their machinations.’

‘Excuse me, said Mr Livingstone. ‘But what, er, was the incidis in Scyllam whatever?’

‘My apologies. The Latin phrase ‘incidis in Scyllam cupiens vitare Charybdim’ means simply ‘out of the frying pan into the fire’.

Mr Livingstone and Mrs Caldicot then thanked Mr Canterbury.

‘Meanwhile, mind how you go down the stairs,’ said Mr Canterbury, making it clear that the audience was over. ‘They’re rather steep. They used to be the only stairs in the building but now they lead only to my offices here on the top floor. The other floors in this building have all been modernised and are now all accessed by an elevator.’ He shuddered as though he found the very idea alarming.

‘So the receptionist downstairs works just for you?’ said Mrs Caldicot.

‘Oh yes. Ethel has been here since 1946. She tried to retire in 1990 but found retirement such a traumatic experience that two weeks later she asked if she could come back to work. We hadn’t found a replacement so we just treated the two weeks as though it had been a holiday. My secretary, whom you have also met, has been here since 1955 and Ethel still regards her as something of a newcomer.’

Mrs Caldicot and Mr Livingstone rose and thanked the solicitor again.

‘It’s been my pleasure. In our career we have dealt with many problems, many wills, many properties but we’ve never dealt with a pier before. We congratulate you on your good fortune. If you find you need legal help, advice of any kind, don’t hesitate to get in touch with us. We will be pleased to help.’

They looked back. They both felt that he meant it.

‘A first pier is always bound to be rather special,’ he said, with a boyish smile, as though he felt he needed to reinforce what he had said; to explain his genuine enthusiasm. ‘And to be honest we would very much like to know how things go.’

And with that final thought Mr Canterbury, now smiling to himself, opened his penknife and began, once again, to pare his already well-trimmed fingernails.

Chapter Five

Sitting in a railway carriage can be immensely frustrating when you're racing to a time sensitive assignation. The more urgent the journey the more the train seems determined to dawdle; stopping here a while, stopping there a while and wandering along as though it has all the time in the world. And, inevitably perhaps, if a journey is really important, and you have a vital appointment to keep, then the train will suddenly trundle to a halt and sit wherever it is; stranded in the middle of nowhere, alongside fields where cows chew their cud with all the time in the world or, tantalisingly, just a few hundred yards from the railway station itself. Naturally, there is never anyone to explain where you are, why you're there and how long it's going to be before you're the somewhere that you'd rather be.

But train travel is wonderful, peaceful and relaxing when you have all the time in the world, no appointment to keep and no connection to catch. There is, perhaps, no form of travel so peaceful and so relaxing. You can read, work, talk or simply look out of the window. All you really have to do is sit back and enjoy the view.

Mrs Caldicot and Mr Livingstone now had no appointments to keep and so their journey back home promised to be restful, charming and restorative. They would have time to look out of the carriage window at the rooftops, back gardens, kitchen windows and remaining branch line stations which Dr Beeching had missed or forgotten when he ill-advisedly took his axe to the railway network in 1963.

And they would have plenty of time to talk.

They each bought coffee, snacks and magazines at the railway station buffet.

Mrs Caldicot purchased a magazine called *Devon Days*, in the hope that she might learn a little something about the county wherein lay their new home.

Mr Livingstone bought one magazine called *Coach and Bus Weekly* and another titled *Airports of the World Monthly.*

'I didn't know you were interested in buses or airports,' said Mrs Caldicot.

'I'm not,' said Mr Livingstone. 'I know nothing about either of them.'

'But why...?' began Mrs Caldicot.

'Oh, I always like to buy magazines that will introduce me to new worlds,' explained Mr Livingstone. 'Have you ever noticed that the world seems to be divided up into little speciality groups? Some people live for football. They know an enormous amount about their favourite teams and players. Their heroes are all footballers. Other people live for horse racing. Their lives are dominated by their interest in horse racing. They live for horse racing in the way that the other people live for football. You get people whose lives revolve around ballroom dancing, carp fishing or stamp collecting but they never take much interest in one another's enthusiasms. The people who love boating on canals, and who are absolutely passionate about narrow boats, don't usually know much about bell ringing or model railways. I find all these little worlds quite fascinating.'

'Yes, I suppose that's true,' agreed Mrs Caldicot. 'I hadn't thought about it quite like that.'

'Well, I like to learn about other people's interests. And the easiest way to do that is to buy specialist magazines. Last week I bought one on keeping cage birds. The week before that I read one on sea fishing. I suppose you could say that my hobby is learning about other people's hobbies.'

Mrs Caldicot was quiet for a moment.

She found that she was always learning about her friends. Just the other day she had found that Mr Merivale had once competed in the Olympics. He had come fourth in one of the breaststroke swimming events so he hadn't won a medal. But he'd competed at the Olympics and no one could ever take that glory away from him. And now there was Mr Livingstone and his curious hobby of collecting information about other people's hobbies.

When the train arrived they climbed aboard, found a quiet table and settled down. Since it was neither going to work time nor going home time the train was almost deserted.

‘Well, what do you think?’ asked Mrs Caldicot, settling into her seat as their homeward bound train chugged rather reluctantly out of the station.

‘I haven’t had time to look at them yet,’ said Mr Livingstone. ‘But the *Coach and Bus* magazine looks pretty good. I’m not sure about the airports. It’s difficult to see why there would be a whole magazine devoted to airports.’

Mrs Caldicot laughed. ‘Not the magazines! The pier!’

Mr Livingstone took a big breath, looked out of the window for a moment and then turned back to Mrs Caldicot. ‘It’s all a bit daunting,’ he said. He took a cardboard container of coffee and a plastic packet from a small, paper bag. The packet had a label which announced that the contents, something which looked to Mr Livingstone rather like a sandwich, was actually not anything as mundane as a sandwich but was something called an International Hoagie. The smaller lettering on the label announced that the International Hoagie contained the following ingredients: ‘A razor cut slice of Palma ham with segments of Swiss Gruyere cheese and sun dried Spanish tomatoes flavoured with English pickle and French mustard’.

Mr Livingstone put the ham and cheese sandwich and the coffee down in front of him. He idly wondered where the coffee had come from. It seemed strange that they hadn’t told him. Columbia? Where else did they grow coffee beans? Java, of course. Brazil naturally. And Africa too. But which bits of Africa? Either way there was little doubt that they hadn’t been grown in England. So they were definitely foreign and therefore fitted comfortably into the international theme of his picnic. He took the keys to the pier from his jacket pocket and lay them down on the table alongside the sandwich and the coffee cup.

‘It’s a big bunch of keys,’ said Mrs Caldicot.

‘There must be a good many doors and locks,’ said Mr Livingstone. He picked up one of the keys. It was large, made of iron and slightly rusty. ‘What on earth do you think this is?’

‘I’ve absolutely no idea,’ said Mrs Caldicot. She paused. ‘Fancy you owning a pier!’

‘Not something I ever imagined I’d be able to say. ‘David Livingstone – Pier Owner’. It’s all pretty exciting isn’t it? I bet none of my school teachers ever thought I’d one day own a pier.’

'It is very exciting,' agreed Mrs Caldicot.

She was looking forward to the move to the seaside. It was another adventure and she was looking forward to it. Her life with Mr Caldicot had been rather short of excitement and she couldn't help thinking that she was now rather making up for lost time.

The truth was that Mr Caldicot, her former husband and partner on life's rocky road, now sadly deceased, gone and mostly forgotten, had not encouraged excitement. He always said that 'adventure' was frivolous and 'excitement' a distraction. His trousers were always held up with a belt and a pair of braces (or, as the Americans call them 'suspenders') and his idea of recklessness was going out of the house without tying a double knot in his shoelaces.

A lot had changed in Mrs Caldicot's life since her first husband had died.

In what she tended to think of as the old days, another time, Mrs Caldicot had often had 'thoughts'. She had imagined herself saying things but she had never actually found the courage to say them.

These days she didn't have anywhere near as many 'thoughts'. She felt able to say what she felt about things. Mr Jenkins, her new husband, known to one and all simply as Jenkins, was completely the opposite to Mr Caldicot. He always encouraged her to speak her mind, to say what was troubling her.

'A very different kettle of fish,' her grandmother would have said about him. The saying reminded her of Mr Canterbury. He'd used it too.

Another thing that was different was that Jenkins didn't mind taking chances. He had been excited by the prospect of their moving to Devon to help manage Mr Livingstone's pier. Like her, he had thought of it as a huge and invigorating challenge. 'Overcoming new obstacles keeps you young,' he sometimes said when they were having problems.

Thinking about Jenkins reminded her that he would be going to America within 24 hours. She'd have to help him with his suitcase when she got back home. Not that he needed any help. He was perfectly capable of packing a case. He wasn't going to fly to America and then find out he'd forgotten spare socks or his favourite brand of toothpaste. But she liked to help him. He let her pick out a tie and a shirt for him to wear when he was giving a speech or attending an important meeting. She liked that. It made her feel as though she were part of the 'him' that was going away. Mr Caldicot would have never allowed her to have a say in what tie he wore. As far as he was concerned, all she was good for was brushing the fluff off his blazer.

She was, she knew, going to miss Jenkins a lot when he went to America. Still, she thought, they'd try to get the pier sorted out for his return. All shipshape and Bristol fashion, whatever that meant. She liked to do things to show him that she had grown into the assurance and competence he'd found for her.

'I can't wait to get there,' said Mr Livingstone closing his eyes. 'I bet it's all brightly painted and red and blue. I can see it in my mind. Decorated with lots of flags and bunting and packed with holidaymakers all eating ice creams.'

'I'm glad you haven't lost your enthusiasm,' said Mrs Caldicot, who had always known that there would be more than a few snags to sort out. She thought she ought to warn him. 'We must remember that there are bound to be a few little teething problems to deal with when we get there.'

'Bring them on!' said Mr Livingstone with a boldness born more of hope than knowledge. 'My enthusiasm remains undimmed. What have I got to lose? Before that letter came from Mr Canterbury my worldly goods consisted of a tin box with a few medals in it, a couple of rather threadbare suits that had seen better days back in the 1980s, a collection of rather battered musical instruments and a rather inadequate pension.' He picked up the keys and held them aloft. 'Now I'm also the owner of a pier.' He thought for a moment. 'Or, rather, I'm part owner of a pier. We own it together. All of us.'

'Oh no...,' said Mrs Caldicot. 'It's your pier.'

'No it isn't,' insisted Mr Livingstone. 'We all share everything. You and Jenkins do far more than your fair share for the rest of us. If it hadn't been for you I'd still be in that damned Twilight Years Rest Home, drugged up to my eyeballs and eating liver and cabbage three times a week. And I know damned well that Mr Williams's photographs have helped pay our costs. No, we share the bad things and we share the good things. That's what friends do.'

In his earlier days, their companion Henry Williams had been a famous photographer who had worked in Paris. He had a fine collection of old negatives and for some time he had helped defray some of the costs of running the house which they all shared by selling off prints of the most famous of his pictures.

'Mr Williams won't be able to bail us out for much longer, I'm afraid,' said Mrs Caldicot rather sadly. 'He told me yesterday that a French internet company has managed to create some fake negatives and they've been making hundreds of prints and selling them. Apparently, they can do things like that these days. As a result of all the fakes being sold, the value of Mr Williams's negatives and pictures has fallen rather a lot.'

'Can't he do anything to stop them?'

'Apparently not,' said Mrs Caldicot. 'It seems that there are laws now which support the idea that 'copyright is theft'. I don't really understand it but Mr Williams looked into it and said it's all due to freedom of speech and human rights. I'm afraid there won't be much more money from Mr Williams's photographs.' She took the coffee and the plastic wrapped sandwich from her small paper carrier bag. 'He's very upset about it.'

'Poor chap!' said Mr Livingstone, genuinely sad for his friend. 'Still, we've got a pier! What is it they say? One door closes and another one opens? I know they say the pier isn't worth much but I bet we can make something of it.'

'I bet we can!' agreed Mrs Caldicot.

'Fancy offering me a quid for it!' said Mr Livingstone, rather disgustedly.

'That was very cheeky!' agreed Mrs Caldicot. 'They probably thought they could grab a bargain and make a lot of money.'

'Well, they've got another think coming!'

Mr Livingstone, who had been trying to open the sandwich package with his fingers gave up and took out his small, well-worn, silver penknife. Taking out the knife reminded him of the solicitor. 'That Canterbury is an extraordinary old chap isn't he?'

Mrs Caldicot laughed. 'Absolutely!' she agreed. 'But I must say I did rather like him. He reminded me of a character out of a novel by Dickens?'

'You're right! I knew he reminded me of someone. He was straight out of one of those long novels by Charles Dickens. Did you notice the way he kept paring his nails with his penknife?'

'And then he was using the same penknife to carve pieces of cheese from that huge block of Cheddar on his desk!'

'I'm glad he didn't offer me a chunk.'

'No, I was a bit worried about that too. Did you notice that he got almost tearful when he was talking about the little train on the pier?'

'Yes, I did! He seemed lost in memories. A very decent fellow, I thought.'

The two of them spent the rest of the journey looking at the details of the pier, for Mr Canterbury had given them maps, deeds and a surprisingly large amount of paperwork relating to the pier's structure and its history. When any building is the best part of a century and a half old there is bound to be a good deal of history associated with it and Mr Livingstone's pier was no exception. Some of the older deeds and mortgages were printed on vellum, a fine form of parchment which is made from the skin of a calf.

And the more the two of them looked at the details of the pier the more excited they got.

'It says here that during the War it was commandeered by the Navy,' said Mr Livingstone, reading one of the old documents. He seemed very proud of this. 'There are letters which say that the Navy took over the pier from 1941 to 1946 and that during that time it was closed to the public.'

'It'll be fun to move into the accommodation in that archway that Mr Canterbury talked about,' said Mrs Caldicot. 'Fancy us all living on a pier. There are enough rooms aren't there?'

'There are plenty of rooms,' said Mr Livingstone, unfolding a plan of the building. 'But I don't know what sort of condition they're in. I don't think anyone has lived there for a while.'

They talked more about the pier, learning as much as they could about its history and when they arrived at their destination (since they weren't in a hurry, the train was, inevitably, ten minutes early) neither Mrs Caldicot nor Mr Livingstone had opened their magazines.

Chapter Six

Mrs Caldicot and her colleagues had a meeting to discuss when they should move into the accommodation available on the pier.

'We don't have a lot of choice,' said Mr Twist, the former tax inspector. 'The Government has given us a few weeks before they send in the bulldozers. So unless we want to find ourselves scooped up and dumped in a landfill site we have to get out of here quite quickly.'

'We could tie ourselves to a tree,' suggested Miss Nightingale, who had always had a secret desire to be tied to a tree. This was not something she had ever mentioned before but this did seem a not inappropriate moment to float the idea.

'Oh no, I don't like that idea,' said Mrs Peterborough, wrinkling her nose. 'I'm too old to tie myself to a tree. Besides, I've never been any good at knots.'

'What if it rains?' asked Mr Roxdale. 'We'll be outside tied to trees and all getting wet!'

'I hadn't thought of that,' admitted Miss Nightingale, before quickly withdrawing her suggestion.

'Maybe Mrs Caldicot and Mr Livingstone should go and look at the pier,' suggested Mrs Merivale. 'They could check it all out, give the accommodation a once-over and then come back and let us know what the place is like.'

'But that seems a bit pointless,' said Mr Hewitt. 'We know that we have to leave here shortly and at the moment we haven't got anywhere else to go. Sending out a reconnaissance team isn't going to make any difference to what we do.'

Mrs Merivale, thinking about this, nodded and finally agreed with him. 'You're right!' she agreed. 'If we delay things then we'll be moving in a rush at the last minute. If we decide to move now then we can arrange to go to Penmouth at our own speed.'

'Shouldn't the people who are knocking down our house pay us some compensation?' asked Mrs Peterborough.

'They have said that they will be paying us,' said Mrs Caldicot. 'But we owe quite a lot to the bank so most of the money will go to them. And we won't receive our share of the compensation money for several months.'

'That's really not fair,' said Mr Twist. 'They should pay us our compensation before the bulldozers move in.'

'No, it isn't fair,' said Mrs Caldicot. 'But I'm afraid we're dealing with bureaucrats working for the Government. And they don't seem very sympathetic.'

'I've made several phone calls,' said Jenkins. 'But I can't get anyone to agree to send us our cheque for at least three months. There appear to be at least three layers of bureaucracy and all the compensation payments have to be authorised by something called the Residential Compensation Committee, a special subsidiary quango which is chaired by someone called the Comptroller of Financial Administration.' Jenkins sighed rather sadly. 'The committee meets every three months and I'm told that they've already got a backlog of claims. There is no way we're going to be receiving what we're owed for several months.'

'It's outrageous!' said Mr Hewitt. 'I bet they wouldn't like it if their homes were being knocked down.'

'I agree with you,' said Jenkins. 'It is outrageous. But it seems it's impossible to speed things up. You can't hurry a Government department if it doesn't want to be hurried.'

'Our other problem is that the amount we'll receive when the compensation payment finally does come through won't be sufficient to enable us to buy a new house,' Mrs Caldicot reminded them all. 'When we bought the Twilight Years Rest Home I was a year or two younger. The older you get the more reluctant the banks are to lend you money to buy property.'

'I think we should move onto Mr Livingstone's pier as soon as we can,' said Mrs Torridge.

'It's our pier,' said Mr Livingstone. 'It's only my pier if it falls into the sea.'

'Is it going to fall into the sea?' asked Mr Twist, looking worried.

'No, no,' said Mr Livingstone. 'I meant that if anything disastrous happens then it's my pier because I can just go bankrupt.'

'Our solicitor, Mr Canterbury, more or less suggested that it would be easier and cheaper for Mr Livingstone to go bankrupt than it would be for us to buy insurance,' explained Mrs Caldicot.

'I don't know what we're all worrying about,' said Mr Livingstone. 'Let's all move into the pier's hotel straight away!' said Mr Livingstone. 'It's where we are going to end up so why don't we just go there now?'

'Let's vote on it!' suggested Mr Williams. 'I propose that we all travel down to Penmouth and move onto Mr Livingstone's lovely old pier.'

And so they voted and it was decided, unanimously, that they would travel to Penmouth as soon as possible and that they would arrange for a removal lorry to transport their furniture and personal belongings.

'When do you have to travel to America?' Mrs Caldicot asked her husband.

'Early next week. So I'm afraid I don't think I'll be able to travel down to Devon with you.'

'OK,' said Mrs Caldicot in a very tiny voice. 'We'll try to get it all nice for when you get back.'

'It's only for three weeks,' said Jenkins, softly, though he thought three weeks sounded too much like a lifetime and would have been happy to have said, 'No, thank you' to the Americans if it hadn't been for the fact that Mrs Caldicot had made it quite clear that she thought he should grab the opportunity with both hands.

'Only three weeks,' repeated Mrs Caldicot.

She knew she would miss Jenkins terribly but couldn't help wondering what would happen in those weeks.

She had a feeling it was going to be a busy time for them all.

And, in a way, she was grateful for that.

Chapter Seven

Mrs Caldicot and Mr Twist went to the local railway station to find the cost of railway tickets. Mr Twist went with Mrs Caldicot since he was in charge of their money.

'We're enquiring about the cost of tickets to Penmouth,' said Mrs Caldicot, when she and Mr Twist finally reached the top of the booking office queue.

'You can telephone for information,' said a weedy little fellow with a grumpy looking face. 'We have a Railtime Hotline.'

'We tried that,' said Mrs Caldicot. 'But the phone line has been busy most of the morning. On the one occasion when it wasn't busy, it rang for fifteen minutes without anyone answering it.'

'They're very busy people,' sniffed Mr Grumpy. 'If it's just information you want you can find train times on our website.'

'A pre-recorded message on your telephone line suggested that we do exactly that,' said Mrs Caldicot. 'But unfortunately your website isn't working. I think the technical term is that it is feeling 'down'.'

'Feeling down?'

'That's what my husband says and he knows about these things. I can't see why a computer should feel down. But they do say that computers are almost human these days, don't they?'

'Get a bloody move on!' snarled a voice standing behind Mrs Caldicot. 'Are you going to be there all bloody day?'

Mrs Caldicot turned round and found herself facing a girl of about seventeen or eighteen. She had yellow hair, cut in the style which used to be compulsory for army recruits, and wore a dirty T-shirt and a pair of jeans with huge rips in the knees. She had two rings in her nose, a string of rings along the edge of each ear lobe and tattoos of knives on her neck. The knives were all dripping with blood.

'I'm just trying to get details of some tickets,' said Mrs Caldicot, sweetly.

'You're holding everyone up,' snarled the girl. 'Shouldn't you be at home having your incontinence pad changed?'

'Don't be so rude!' said Mr Twist, who was shocked.

'I wasn't talking to you old man,' said the girl.

Mrs Caldicot, who had turned back to the booking office window, repeated her request to Mr Grumpy.

'There's a pile of leaflets on the rack,' he replied.

'I'm afraid there isn't a leaflet for Penmouth,' said Mrs Caldicot. 'And the leaflets you do have are all out of date.'

'Not my fault,' said Mr Grumpy. 'We haven't had the new leaflets in yet. They'll probably be here sometime next month.'

'I'm afraid I can't wait that long,' said Mrs Caldicot. 'I just want to know how often the trains run to Penmouth and how much a ticket will cost. There will be thirteen of us travelling.'

'You need to speak to someone in Group Bookings,' said Mr Grumpy.

'And how do I get hold of them?'

'You ring the Railtime Hotline.'

'But they don't answer their phone!'

'Well, it's night time there. They probably won't be up yet.'

'Night time where?' asked Mrs Caldicot, confused.

'Somewhere in India I think it is. Or maybe it's the Philippines.'

'Who is in India?'

'Our call centre partners. The ones who answer the telephone for the Railtime Hotline,' replied Mr Grumpy.

'What the hell is going on up there?' demanded a voice from the back of the queue.

'It's this stupid old woman in front of me,' said the girl with the tattoos and the yellow hair. 'She doesn't seem to know what she wants.'

'I know exactly what I want,' said Mrs Caldicot, over her shoulder. She turned back to Mr Grumpy. 'Don't you have anyone to open one of the other windows?'

There were three other ticket windows in the booking office but they were all closed.

'They're all on their break,' said Mr Grumpy. 'We're allowed to have breaks you know.'

'But it's half past two in the afternoon!' said Mrs Caldicot. 'What sort of break are they having?'

'One of them is on an extended lunch break for personal reasons and the other two are having an early afternoon tea. It's a statutory requirement.'

'What sort of personal reasons require an extended lunch break?'

'He eats slowly. He's running in a new set of teeth.'

'Let's forget about the group booking,' said Mrs Caldicot. 'Can you please just tell me what time there is a train to Penmouth and how much a ticket costs?'

Mr Grumpy sighed. 'There's a big queue behind you.'

'I know there's a queue. If you just give me the information I need then I'll go and you can deal with the nice, young lady behind me.'

'Who are you calling a nice, young lady?' demanded the girl with the tattoos and yellow hair. 'I'll have the law on you!'

Mr Grumpy fiddled slowly with the keyboard in front of him. The screen in front of him remained blank. He pressed more buttons. Still nothing happened. 'My system is very slow today,' he said. He pressed the same buttons again. 'I think it's down.'

'There you are!' said Mrs Caldicot. 'I told you that your computer was feeling down today. Don't you have a printed timetable you can consult?'

'We should have brought a flask and some sandwiches,' whispered Mr Twist.

Mr Grumpy sighed and picked up a large, scruffy folder which had a label stuck to the front. The label contained the single word 'Trains' written on it in red ink. The folder, when opened, appeared to contain pages from a railway timetable.

'Where was it you said you want to go?'

'Penmouth in Devon.'

Mr Grumpy flicked through the pages in his folder and eventually found a page which seemed vaguely relevant. 'Ha!' he said with unconcealed delight. 'You've missed today's train.'

'I didn't want to travel today,' said Mrs Caldicot. 'I just wanted to know what time the train leaves.'

'How much longer are you lot going to be up there?' shouted a new voice at the back of the queue. 'What are you doing? Planning a revolution?'

'It's some old biddy and some old geezer,' shouted yet another voice.

'The train went at 11.47 today. That's the only train to Penmouth. But after next Tuesday it only runs on Mondays and Thursdays except at Easter.'

'And how much is a ticket?'

'What time do you want to travel?'

Mrs Caldicot was confused for a moment by this. 'The 11.47 I suppose,' she said.

'And what day do you want to travel?'

'One of the days when the train is running, I suppose.'

'That would be Mondays and Thursdays after next Tuesday.'

'Next Thursday then.'

'And when are you coming back?'

'We're not coming back.'

'So you just want a single?'

'Yes.'

'Not a return?'

'No.'

'A single for one for Penmouth next Thursday?'

'Yes, please.'

The blind at one of the other booking windows moved up a foot and another ticket collector peered out, saw the size of the queue and closed the blind again.

'Isn't someone going to open another booking window?' asked Mrs Caldicot. Behind her the queue was now so long, and snaking either out onto the street or in onto the platform, that the end of it was not visible.

Mr Grumpy turned and spoke to someone out of sight. They whispered for a while.

'My colleague doesn't like crowds. He gets nervous. He says he'll open his window when some of the people have gone.'

Mrs Caldicot started to say something and then realised there wasn't really any point.

'How will you be paying?' asked Mr Grumpy.

'Do you take cheques?'

'No.'

'Well, probably with a credit card.'

'I need to see it.'

'But I'm not buying the ticket today. I just want to know the cost.'

‘I can’t tell you that until I see proof of payment. It’s in my regulations.’

Mrs Caldicot opened her bag, took out her purse, found her credit card and showed it to Mr Grumpy.

‘Put it into the reader.’

‘The what?’

‘The card machine.’ Mr Grumpy pointed to a credit card reading machine fixed to the narrow ledge in front of Mrs Caldicot.

‘But I only want to know the cost of a ticket,’ repeated Mrs Caldicot. ‘I don’t want to buy one today.’

‘Has someone died up there?’ shouted a voice that Mrs Caldicot was now beginning to recognise. She turned round but saw nothing but dull, grey, stony faces. The girl with the tattoos and the yellow hair had disappeared.

‘I can’t do anything until you put your card into the machine,’ said Mr Grumpy.

Reluctantly, Mrs Caldicot put her credit card into the card reading machine.

‘Do you have a railcard?’ asked Mr Grumpy.

Mrs Caldicot said she didn’t have a railcard.

‘A student card?’

Mrs Caldicot said she didn’t have one of those either.

‘Are you travelling first or second class?’

Mrs Caldicot said she thought they would probably be travelling second class.

‘Are you travelling with a bicycle?’

Mrs Caldicot said she would not be travelling with a bicycle.

‘We have a special fare for people travelling with bicycles.’

Mrs Caldicot said that she thought that was doubtless very useful for people with bicycles and that she was very sorry that she would not be able to take advantage of the special fare because she did not have a bicycle.

‘A single, second class fare for one person will be £126.90,’ announced Mr Grumpy.

‘No, I want the price of a second class ticket, please,’ said Mrs Caldicot.

‘That is the price of a second class ticket.’

‘I don’t want to buy the train. Or even rent it for a special outing. I just want the price of one ticket to Penmouth.’

'That is the price of one ticket to Penmouth. Do you want to reserve a seat?'

'Does it cost more to reserve a seat?'

'Oh yes.'

'How much more?'

'Another £10 per ticket so if you have a single it's another £10 but if you have a return it's £20. And there's a £5 per ticket booking ticket price to add on but then you have to add that on even if you're not reserving a seat. Do you want to buy a ticket for the London Underground to go with your train ticket?'

'I'm not going via London.'

'Well you might be. Trains do get diverted sometimes – due to circumstances outside our control.'

'No, I think I'll leave that, thank you.'

'Do you want a car park ticket? You get a reduced price ticket if you buy your car park ticket when you buy your rail ticket.'

'No thank you. How much is a first class ticket?'

'You said you wanted to go second class.'

'I do but I'm just curious. How much is a first class ticket?'

'£276.45 for a single first class. And there are people waiting. If you want to buy a ticket you need to put your pin number into the machine.'

'I don't want to buy a ticket. I just wanted to know the price.'

'Of course, it would be cheaper if you were coming back.'

Puzzled, Mrs Caldicot looked at him. 'What do you mean 'it would be cheaper if I were coming back'?'

'I've given you the price of a single second class to Penmouth. If you wanted a return second class to Penmouth it would be cheaper.'

'How much cheaper?'

'It depends on when you're coming back.'

'I'm not coming back.'

'But when would you be coming back if you were coming back?'

'Does it make a difference?'

'Oh yes. If you come back within 30 days, it's cheaper than if you come back after 30 days. And if you come back the same day that you go then it's the cheapest of all.'

'How much is it if I come back within 30 days?'

'If you come back within 30 days then a return would be £122.14. If you come back after 30 days it would be £165.43 so that's not actually cheaper, is it?'

'And if I come back the same day?'

'Oh that's very cheap. That's only £101.21 for a return ticket. And it would be £99.14 if you caught a train going to Penmouth before 9.00 am.'

This still didn't seem 'very cheap' to Mrs Caldicot. It was also confusing. 'You said the only train to Penmouth was the 11.47.'

'That's right.'

'So how do I catch a train going before 9.00 am?'

'You can't, can you? And what time are you coming back?'

'Does that make a difference?'

'Oh yes. If you come back after 6 pm you can get a super saver day return fare.'

'How much is that?'

'That would be £98.43. But the only train after 6 pm is the 9.45 pm and you have to change four times on that train and so it doesn't get you in until 3.00 am and that's the next day so I'm not sure the super saver day return fare would count in that situation. I'd have to talk to my supervisor or you could ring the Hotline.'

'And speak to the man in India when he wakes up.'

'Or woman. Some of our partners in India are women.'

'So, the bottom line is that it's cheaper to buy a ticket there and a ticket back than just buying a ticket going there?'

'That's what I just told you. If you go and come back it's cheaper than if you just go.'

'That doesn't make sense.'

Mr Grumpy shrugged. 'I don't make the rules. I just work here.' He leafed through the folder in front of him. He seemed now to be quite taken by the seemingly unending possibilities. 'If you wait another month you can have our special seasonal price. It's only available for three months and you need to book at least a month in advance and there need to be at least three adults and one child or two adults and three children all travelling together. That would cost you £101.87 per person but one child goes free as long as he or she is under eight-years-old on the 1st May.' Mr Grumpy examined the folder a little more. 'The snag is that you have to catch the train before 11.30 am if you're going to take advantage of that offer.'

'And the earliest train is the 11.47.'

'Yes.'

'Has someone up there died, or what?' shouted an invisible woman near the back of the queue.

'Thank you very much, you've been very helpful,' said Mrs Caldicot, now totally confused.

'If you want tickets then come back before Sunday,' said Mr Grumpy. 'All our prices go up next Monday.'

'Right,' said Mrs Caldicot. 'I'll remember that.'

'If you're under 25 you can buy a railcard and get a discount on rail travel throughout Europe,' added Mr Grumpy. 'But the railcard is only valid for return tickets on trains which leave before 8.30 am on weekdays and Saturdays and before 8.45 am on Sundays.'

Mrs Caldicot removed her credit card from the machine and put it back into her purse. Then she put her purse back into her handbag. She and Mr Twist then left the booking office area. At least a dozen customers were now sitting on the ground, sprawled against the wall or leaning against cases and rucksacks. A youth with tattoos, earrings and a ponytail was playing a guitar and singing something tuneless and miserable. An empty coffee cup on the ground in front of him had a few coins in it.

'Those prices are absurd,' said Mrs Caldicot to Mr Twist. 'There are fourteen of us. It will cost a fortune to buy fourteen tickets.'

'We only need thirteen tickets,' Mr Twist pointed out. 'Your husband will be in America when we travel down to Penmouth.'

'Oh yes,' said Mrs Caldicot, who hadn't wanted to be reminded that her husband would soon be on a different continent. 'So how much does that come to?'

'£1,649.7.'

Mrs Caldicot stared at Mr Twist as if he'd gone mad.

'If we buy return tickets the total comes to £1,583.62,' said Mr Twist, who was very good at mathematics and could do quite complicated sums without a calculator or even a piece of paper and a pencil.

'I can't get over that. It seems madness that we pay less if we buy more tickets than we need.'

Mr Twist agreed with this.

The pair of them walked out of the railway station feeling bewildered to say the least.

As they walked away, a minibus drew up at the pavement and a horde of schoolchildren leapt out and rushed into the station.

'They don't need to rush if they haven't got tickets yet,' said Mr Twist drily.

The driver of the minibus, a woman in a blue anorak and a blue bobble hat, shouted something to the children, warning them not to run. She then pressed a button and the door hissed to and closed with a pleasant clunky sound.

'Excuse me!' cried Mrs Caldicot, tapping on one of the minibus windows. 'Could I have a quick word?'

The driver put on the brake and pressed a button. There was a hiss and the door swung open.

'I hope you don't mind my asking,' said Mrs Caldicot, 'but what sort of driving licence do you need to drive one of these things?'

'Just an ordinary driving licence,' said the woman. 'As long as the bus doesn't have more than 16 seats. If it has more than that then you need some sort of commercial licence.'

'Thank you very much!' cried Mrs Caldicot.

'Pleasure,' said the woman. She pressed the button again and the door closed. She then drove off.

'Maybe we could rent one of those,' suggested Mrs Caldicot. 'Then we could all drive down to Penmouth.'

'Great idea,' said Mr Twist. 'That way we could take more of our personal luggage. And I bet we'd save a fortune.'

They spotted a second hand car dealership on the other side of the road and wandered down to take a look. The dealership was decorated with faded union jack pennants which looked as if they had been out in the open for a few years. All the cars on display had advertisements painted on their windscreens in some sort of whitewash which, Mrs Caldicot assumed, could be washed or wiped off without too much difficulty.

'What can I do you both for?' asked a chubby little man in his forties. He wore a suit that he may have grown into but had certainly grown out of and his reddish brown hair was combed over his scalp in a vain attempt to disguise the fact that there was considerably more of the latter than the former. He wore a badge pinned to his lapel that had the word REG written on it in black marker pen. The word REG was written on a white, sticky label that had been fixed onto a child's birthday badge. Underneath the white label could be seen a red seven on a blue background with the words 'I am...' above the number and the word 'Today' below it.

'We wondered how much it would cost to rent a minibus,' said Mrs Caldicot.

'What size of minibus?' asked the chubby fellow. 'My name is Reg by the way. As in car registration. It's my real name, by the way.'

Mrs Caldicot introduced herself and Mr Twist. 'Suitable for carrying 14 people,' she then said.

'We don't do rentals,' said the chubby fellow.

'Well do you rent smaller vehicles?'

'We don't do any rentals at all. We don't have any call for them though that may be because we don't do them. But we've got a minibus I can sell you. It would be a much better proposition than renting one. A rental would cost you £200 a day including insurance.'

'Good heavens,' said Mrs Caldicot, though the price didn't seem all that bad. It would, she thought, be a lot cheaper to drive to Penmouth than to take the train. And there would be no need to hire taxis to take them all to the railway station. They would need three taxis and so that would be at least another £20 at each end.

'How much is the minibus you've got for sale?' asked Mrs Caldicot. She looked around the car lot but couldn't see anything that looked like a minibus.

'Well, let's have a look at it first and then we can talk about the price,' said Reg. 'We don't usually sell vans or commercial vehicles but we took this one in part exchange for a 1989 BMW. The BMW was a very nice vehicle – just three owners and less than 150,000 miles on the clock. I very nearly bought it myself.' As he chattered away he led them to a far corner of the lot where a rather sad for itself minibus was parked between an old Ford Zephyr and a Vauxhall of some variety.

'Oh,' said Mrs Caldicot when she saw it. She felt rather disappointed. It looked rather worn and battered.

'It was used to ferry around a boys' football team,' explained Reg. 'The bodywork isn't perfect but who cares about the bodywork on a minibus? The engine is perfect and the mechanicals are as good as new. It's got nine months left on the MOT and I can promise you that you won't find better value than this.' He opened the front passenger door so that they could see inside.

'Don't you lock the cars?' asked Mrs Caldicot, surprised.

'We lock the cars,' said Reg, with the emphasis on the word 'cars'. 'But who's going to steal a minibus? Joy riders want something with a bit of oomph – this does 0 to 60 in just under a minute!' He laughed. 'But you're not buying it to burn up people at the lights, are you?'

'No, I don't suppose we are,' agreed Mrs Caldicot.

'Does it have a button to enable the driver to open the front door on the passenger side?' asked Mr Twist who had been impressed by this facility on the minibus they'd seen at the railway station.

Reg looked at him and frowned.

'The driver presses a button and the door opens with a hissy sound,' explained Mr Hewitt.

'Oh no, you don't want anything like that,' said Reg firmly. 'Just something else to go wrong and drain your battery. Much better to have a door you open and close manually.' He closed the door and opened it again to illustrate this facility. 'And the windows are manually operated. You just wind 'em up and wind 'em down. Saves your battery. And imagine the mess you'd be in if your electrics failed with the window open when you wanted it up or vice versa the other way round.'

'Yes, I see what you mean,' admitted Mr Twist.

'This vehicle will get you where you want to go in fine style,' said Reg. 'New brake pads, new plugs, new windscreen wiper blades and nearly all the lights work perfectly. There's a couple of thousand miles left on the tyres.'

'How many miles has it done?' asked Mr Twist.

'Never tell a lady's age,' said Reg mysteriously. 'It's a good solid engine. There's a lot of driving left under that bonnet.' He winked. 'No, I'll be honest with you. I'm always up front with my customers. It's done 170,000 give or take a few hundred yards but these things have been known to do a million with no trouble. Just give her a little oil and water occasionally and she'll take you round the world and back again twice over. And there's £100 worth of rubber on those tyres. They've got more grip than a politician's handshake.

Look at those seats – that's real plastic that is! None of that leather rubbish or faux plastic they use on modern cars.'

'How old is it?'

'Just under 20 years,' said Reg. 'Another few years and it'll be a classic car taking pride of place in a motoring museum. If you take it I'll throw in three month's road tax. Who'll be doing the driving? Anyone under 25?'

'No one under 65!' said Mrs Caldicot.

'Marvellous. I'll throw in a year's insurance too. What am I saying? The boss will kill me when she finds out.' He laughed merrily and winked. 'That's the wife,' he confided. 'She looks after the books, I look after the sales side. She's a marvel with an adding machine. Thanks to her there's no VAT on any of our cars. Don't ask how she does it but it's all legal.' He winked. 'Well, almost.'

'What does it do to the gallon?' asked Mr Twist.

'Depends how you drive it,' replied Reg. 'Drive her gently, treat her like a lady, and you'll be able to drive from here to there without filling up your tank. But you won't want to be thrashing her, will you? You don't look the sort of fellow to thrash an old lady in the autumn of her lifetime. Why don't you take her for a spin? Try her out. The key's in the ignition.'

Mrs Caldicot climbed into the driver's seat and Mr Twist climbed into the passenger seat. Reg just stood beside the minibus and smiled up at them.

'It's huge!' said Mr Twist, looking behind him at the rows of seats. The interior of the minibus looked exactly like an old-fashioned bus but smaller and the design was definitely on the functional side of practical. 'You could get a football team in here!'

'The last owner did,' whispered Mrs Caldicot, reminding him of what Reg had told them.

'Oh yes!' said Mr Twist.

'Aren't you coming with us?' Mrs Caldicot asked, looking down at Reg the car salesman.

'No, no, you two just go for a little drive together. See how you get on with it. Talk it over with each other. I guarantee you'll want to buy it after ten minutes. You come back and we'll do a deal on a price. Just turn the key, take the handbrake off and away you go. It's a proper gear box – four forward and one reverse – and the brakes will stop her on a sixpence.'

So Mrs Caldicot drove off.

After one or two close scrapes, Mrs Caldicot found that she was coping with the size of the vehicle far better than she had expected. ‘People are very nice when they see us coming,’ she said. ‘They get well out of the way and leave me lots of room.’

Mr Twist, who regarded Mrs Caldicot as the closest thing he was ever likely to find to an angel, did not mention the fact that the minibus appeared to take quite a long time to slow down when the brakes were applied. It would, he thought, only stop on Reg’s sixpence if the sixpence were placed on the road a couple of hundred yards ahead.

Less than ten minutes after they had first climbed aboard, they decided they wanted to buy the minibus.

‘I wish we’d had one of these before,’ said Mrs Caldicot. ‘It’s perfect for us.’

‘If we buy it then we’ll have transport when we are in Penmouth,’ Mr Twist pointed out. ‘It might be useful to be able to get about the town.’

‘But where would we park? It’s very big.’

‘We could probably park it on the pier when we’re not using it.’

‘But they never let people park on piers.’

‘Mr Livingstone owns the pier. If we talk to him nicely I think he’ll let us park there.’

‘What did I tell you?’ asked Reg, when they got back and asked how much he wanted for the minibus. ‘Cracking vehicle, isn’t it? You could start your own little business with one of these. Put an ad in the local shop window and you’re up, up and away. Quick lick of paint and it’ll look like new. You could ferry wedding guests around from the church to the reception or take stag or hen parties off to the pub. There’s no carpet on the floor so the next morning you can wash it out with a hose pipe and a bucket.’

‘How much is it?’ asked Mrs Caldicot.

‘You’re a nice couple,’ said Reg.

‘We’re not actually…’ began Mrs Caldicot.

Reg held up his hand and winked. ‘You don’t have to tell me any secrets,’ he said. ‘When I first put this on the lot I was going to ask £2,500 for it but it’s not our sort of vehicle so for a quick sale I’ll let it go for £1,500. It’s worth twice that and you won’t find anything half as good at twice the price.’

Mrs Caldicot felt quite excited. She had no idea how much a minibus should cost but she had immediately worked out that at £1,500 the minibus was going to cost them less than the train fares. And if it costs £200 a day to rent a minibus then the purchase price wasn't much more than a week's rental.

'That's a bit more than our budget,' said Mr Twist, managing to look very disappointed.

'What's your budget?' asked Reg.

'We were planning to spend up to £1,000.'

'I'm giving it to you taxed and insured and it's got an MOT!' protested Reg, pretending to be shocked. 'I tell you what,' he said. 'Split the difference. Give me £1,250 and I'll throw in a free Sat Nav. One of those you plug into the cigar lighter. Brilliant. You'll never get lost again.'

And so they bought a minibus and drove it back home.

Chapter Eight

A few days later Jenkins left for his stay in America and the day after that Mrs Caldicot and the rest of what Ruth insisted on referring to as 'the gang' watched four apparently tireless removal men put their furniture and other belongings into two huge pantechnicons and set off on the long journey to Penmouth. The removal men were planning to sleep in their vehicles and to arrive in Penmouth early the following morning.

Once they'd waved goodbye to their beds, wardrobes, chairs and other essential bits and pieces, Mrs Caldicot and the gang packed themselves and their essential baggage into the minibus. The vehicle suddenly seemed to be considerably smaller than it had appeared when Mrs Caldicot and Mr Twist had first seen it. This was a result of the fact that instead of taking a single suitcase each, as had been agreed, the residents had crammed the minibus with a considerable array of personal belongings. Mr Livingstone insisted that his musical instruments counted as 'essential' and had to travel with him rather than with the beds and wardrobes. Mr Hewitt and Mr Roxdale decided that all their garden tools were also essential – though Mrs Caldicot did point out to them that there wasn't likely to be a garden on the pier.

In the end, Mrs Roberts and Mr Merivale had to climb the ladder fixed to the back of the minibus and put half a dozen suitcases into the massive roof rack on the roof. Once the suitcases were in situ, Mrs Roberts had to clamber onto the roof and tie the suitcases into place with an old clothes line which Mrs Merivale had found hanging on a nail in the outside lavatory.

Mrs Caldicot had intended to leave the house the minute the removal men had departed, and this intention had been generally accepted as ideal, but what with constantly rearranging the bags inside the minibus and then tying things onto the roof, things did not go quite as smoothly as had been generally hoped.

It has to be admitted that the delay came as no great surprise to Mrs Caldicot who had long ago come to accept that whatever could go wrong probably would go wrong.

As she once said to Jenkins, if she tried to define her life in terms of popular clichés it was definitely more about 'upset apple carts' and 'spilt milk' than it was about 'plain sailing' or 'a smooth ride'.

It was just after noon by the time they finally managed to lock the front door and hit the road for the first time.

And it was just after one in the afternoon when they hit the road for the second time, having returned so that Miss Nightingale could visit the lavatory one last time, Mrs Merivale could check that the gas was turned off and Mr Roxdale could fetch the bundle of peasticks which he insisted he could not possibly live without.

'Why are we bothering to check that the gas is turned off?' asked Mr Livingstone.

'There could be an explosion!' explained Mrs Merivale.

'But the Government is going to flatten the house,' pointed out Mr Livingstone.

But they'd had to go back so that Miss Nightingale could visit the lavatory and Mr Roxdale could fetch his peasticks so Mrs Merivale checked the gas anyway.

It took them several hours more than expected to travel to Penmouth and it was dark by the time the minibus trundled into the town.

There had been several reasons for the delay.

They had to stop four times to purchase coffees, teas and other fluids and they had to stop five times so that the assembled travellers could rid themselves of the fluids they had taken on board. They also found that the minibus had an almost insatiable thirst for petrol and oil. They had to fill the petrol tank twice, and the vehicle's need for oil was so great that they eventually bought half a dozen cans of engine oil and stuffed them under Mr Hewitt's seat.

And the satellite navigation device which Reg had given them proved to be rather more trouble than it was worth.

Mr Williams, the former photographer, whose experience with cameras had given him a rather optimistic confidence in his ability to deal with equipment of all kinds, said that he would accept responsibility for using the device to navigate their journey to Devon.

Sadly, either he or the device, which they had installed via the cigar lighter, proved to be flawed in some way and when they found themselves heading north on the M1 motorway, Mrs Caldicot announced that she would navigate with the aid of the little map of Great Britain which was printed at the back of her diary.

But, all these difficulties were forgotten as they drove into Penmouth, their new home.

'All we've got to do now is to find the pier!' said Mrs Caldicot.

'Let's just head for the sea,' suggested Mr Merivale. 'There's a brown sign over there marked 'Sea Front' and Mr Livingstone's pier is bound to be somewhere near the sea.'

Mrs Caldicot thought this a good and practical suggestion and so they headed for the Sea Front where, with unerring inevitability, they turned the wrong way and drove for two miles along a deserted promenade without seeing anything that looked remotely like a pier.

'I hope it hasn't been washed away,' said Mrs Peterborough. 'You do hear of it happening,' she added when she noticed her companions staring at her.

'I'll stop and ask someone,' said Mrs Caldicot who, being a woman, was not averse to asking directions from strangers.

This, however, was easier said than done for Penmouth seemed deserted and looked more like a film set for a movie about a post-apocalyptic Britain than a thriving seaside resort. Eventually, she pulled up alongside an elderly couple of flaneurs who were walking their dog, a small lively mongrel, and who had paused in their peregrinations in order to allow the creature to water a lamppost.

'The pier is the other way,' said the male half of the couple. He had a walking stick but carried it as though it were a weapon rather than a walking aid. He now waved it about as though indicating directions. 'But it's closed now,' he added.

'It's been closed for months,' said the female half, a stringy, gaunt looking woman. She spoke with relish, as though relieved to be able to pass on what she hoped was bad news. She looked the sort of individual who enjoyed sharing unhappiness. 'They say they're turning it into a conference centre,' she added. She did not seem enamoured of the proposal but then she did not appear to be a woman who was likely to be enamoured of anything much.

‘It’s not worth visiting,’ said the male half firmly. ‘It hasn’t been worth visiting since the 1960s. But they once had Gerry and the Pacemakers in the theatre at the end of the pier.’

‘We saw them,’ said the female half, as if her companion’s statement might need confirmation. ‘They were quite good. It was the best night I’ve ever had in Penmouth.’ She paused for a moment. ‘I’ve lived here all my life,’ she added.

Mrs Caldicot, thinking it a little sad that the woman’s ‘best night in Penmouth’ had been no better than ‘quite good’, thanked them both, turned the minibus round and headed back along the promenade. She wondered what on earth the woman had meant by claiming that the pier was going to be converted into a conference centre. Mr Canterbury had said nothing about a conference centre.

They found the pier at 9.47 pm precisely.

It was dark, unlit and rather depressing but none of that dampened their excitement.

‘Just look at that!’ said Mr Livingstone, who added he hadn’t been so excited since 1942 when he and the rest of his crew had dropped a large bomb directly onto a vital bridge in Northern Germany. This was quite a compliment to the pier for Mr Livingstone still remembered the sense of satisfaction he had felt as he had watched the bridge crumble into the raging river below.

‘We taught the Krauts a thing or two about precision bombing,’ Mr Livingstone always said when describing that glorious moment.

Mr Livingstone, who thought we’d been far too quick to forgive the Germans for starting two World Wars, still thought that ‘political correctness’ meant not spoiling your ballot paper when you voted.

There were double yellow lines and No Parking signs everywhere and consequently nowhere to park, so Mrs Caldicot bumped the minibus up over the kerb and onto a wide stretch of pavement. There were no signs forbidding parking on the pavement. Mrs Caldicot halted the minibus directly in front of the massive iron gates at the entrance to the pier. The minibus’s headlights showed two large signs – neither of which could be described as welcoming.

One sign said ‘PIER CLOSED’ and the second, even more forbidding than the first for it was printed in red and looked very angry, shouted ‘PRIVATE – KEEP OUT’. The gates were fastened with a massive chain and a suitably sized padlock.

‘Have you got the keys?’ asked Mrs Caldicot.

But her query was unnecessary for Mr Livingstone had already climbed down from the minibus and had pulled the ring of keys from his pocket. He was using the headlights to select the appropriate key for the padlock when the quiet of the evening was disrupted by the arrival of a police car.

'What you do think you're doing?' demanded a pasty faced young policeman who didn't seem to Mr Livingstone to be old enough to be in long trousers, let alone old enough to be allowed out after dark. He was clambering out of the passenger side of the police car as he spoke. He had spots and his flat, peaked hat was two sizes too big for his head. His uniform also looked as if it had been made for someone twice the size.

Mr Livingstone, who had found a suitable looking key but had not yet inserted it into the padlock, looked at the policeman. 'I think I'm opening this padlock,' he said. 'And aren't you supposed to say 'Allo, allo, allo' before you ask me what I think I'm doing?'

'Are you being funny?' demanded the very young policeman.

'Not particularly. Have you got a torch?'

'A torch? What do you want a torch for?'

'To shine on this padlock. So that I can see what I'm doing. Our minibus headlights aren't very good.'

'What do you think you're doing with the padlock?'

'I'm just trying to undo it. I want to open the gates. I want to open the gates so that we can drive onto the pier.'

'They don't allow parking on the pier.'

'Yes I do.'

'What do you mean 'Yes I do'?'

'It's my pier and I allow parking on it. For us anyway.'

At that moment two figures appeared on the other side of the gate. One of them, the tallest of the duo, was holding a broom and the other, inevitably the shorter, was not.

'Hey, clear off!' said the one with the broom. 'This is private property.' He waved the broom about menacingly. It was impossible to see him clearly but he had the voice of a man of years.

'Who are you?' demanded Mr Livingstone.

'I'm Pickering,' said the figure with the broom. 'If you don't bugger off I'll call the police.' He waved the broom belligerently but since he was on the other side of the still locked gate, the waved broom was of little consequence.

'I am the police,' said the youthful, spotty policeman, pulling himself up to his statutory five feet six and a tiny weeny bit inches, complete with helmet.

It had for him been a red letter day when the Chief Constable had announced that the Force was reducing the minimum height requirements for he had always wanted to work in crime in some way, to be a policeman or a crook, and he knew that his Mum wouldn't want him to be a crook like his Dad. She always said that one crook in the family was quite enough and what if they both got banged up at the same time and put in separate prisons? She would, she pointed out, be forever catching buses to see one and then the other. No, she was much happier about things when they reduced the height requirements and he could join the police. It didn't pay as well as crime but he got free uniforms and a boot allowance.

'I can't help that,' said Mr Pickering.

'This elderly gentleman says he owns the pier,' said the policeman. 'He wants to park his minibus on it.'

'The bloke what owned the pier is dead,' said Mr Pickering, the figure with the broom. 'He died months ago. I heard some big company from up London is going to turn it into a conference centre. The council's been round doing measurements and poking their noses into things.'

'The bloke who died was my uncle,' said Mr Livingstone. 'He left the pier to me.'

'What's your name then?'

'Livingstone,' said Mr Livingstone.

'That's the name of the bloke what's dead.'

'It would be. The bloke what's dead, as you so accurately put it, was my uncle. He left the pier to his brother, who was my father, but my father has been dead for some years so I inherited the pier instead.'

'Ah,' said Mr Pickering, who felt that this did put a different complexion on things. 'But can you prove that you're the new owner?'

'I've got the keys,' pointed out Mr Livingstone, holding up his bunch of keys.

'Anyone could have a bunch of keys,' said Mr Pickering.

'But these keys fit the pier,' pointed out Mr Livingstone.

'You might have stolen them,' said Mr Pickering. 'Or they might be them skeletal keys.'

'That's a good point,' said the policeman. 'Can you prove you are the owner?'

'Wait there a minute,' said Mr Livingstone. He climbed back onto the minibus and found the small suitcase in which he had packed his ukulele and his flute, all his socks and underpants and the paperwork relating to the pier. The ukulele and the flute were the only instruments he had which would fit into the suitcase. He had used the underwear and socks to pack around them. He left the ukulele and the flute, and the underpants and socks, and took the papers out of the case. He then climbed back down from the minibus and showed the papers first to the policeman and then to Mr Pickering. Both peered at the paperwork, frowned a good deal and announced themselves satisfied.

'They certainly look in order to me,' said the policeman who didn't have the foggiest idea what he was looking at, apart from the fact that there was a lot of it. He knew from experience that when there was a lot of paperwork then it needed to be taken seriously and that the people who had the paperwork were probably important. The driver of the police car, still in his vehicle, watched carefully. He was hoping that the suspects would decide to make a break for it. Realising the limitations of the minibus he had decided that he would give the fugitives a two minute start so that he'd have a chance to switch on his siren and speed along the promenade. If they headed east he'd be able to drive past the hotel where his girlfriend worked as a receptionist and she'd see him go speeding past and be terribly impressed.

'That's good enough for me,' said Mr Pickering who was labouring under the twin disadvantages of not having his reading spectacles with him and not having eaten enough carrots to be able to read in the dark. He didn't have the faintest idea what he'd been looking at. 'You'd better come in then.'

The policeman walked back to the police car, climbed in and slammed the door. The driver, who had kept the car engine running in the slender hope that the minibus might take off into the night, giving him an excuse to chase after it, sped off to fight crime elsewhere in Penmouth.

And so, at last, Mr Livingstone unfastened the padlock, unchained the gates and opened them wide to allow Mrs Caldicot to drive the minibus onto the pier.

It was now clear that the taller of the two figures, the broom handler, was a man of mature years. Critics (of the variety so commonly found on social media, unmistakeably trenchant and fearless in their comments, though, it has to be admitted, not always as resilient as might be expected when on the receiving end of trenchant and fearless comments) might well have dismissed him as being well beyond his best buy date and given him two stars and a thumbs down.

'Oh, you can't do that!' said Mr Pickering as Mrs Caldicot started to edge the minibus forwards.

'Why not?' asked Mr Livingstone, who was grinning happily because he was now standing on his pier. He hadn't been on a pier for decades and now here he was standing on one which he owned.

'It's not allowed,' said Mr Pickering.

'Who says?'

'Mr Livingstone never allowed people to drive onto the pier.'

'That Mr Livingstone has gone. I'm the new Mr Livingstone now,' Mr Livingstone reminded him. 'And I'm allowing Mrs Caldicot to drive onto the pier.'

'Who's Mrs Caldicot?' asked Mr Pickering.

'She's the lady driving the minibus.'

'Oh,' said Mr Pickering, absorbing this new piece of information and collapsing as quickly and as completely as a house of cards in a puff of wind. 'Oh, well I guess that's all right then,' he said.

The truth was that Mr Pickering was having considerable difficulty coming to terms with the change in circumstances which had been thrust upon him by life's eternal capacity to hurl around unexpected vicissitudes.

It seemed to him that life was moving far too quickly these days.

One minute he was happily working on the pier, operating the little train, changing light bulbs as and when they needed changing, and selling ice creams and Kiss Me Quick hats as and when such items were in demand. He was not a man who had a firm or fixed view of his responsibilities. He was not a man besieged by ambitions or expectations. He worked on the pier and that was that.

But the next minute a bunch of sour looking men and women in suits were swaggering about on the pier, poking their noses into rooms as if they owned the place which, for all he knew, they might well do, considering the way they'd walked in without introducing themselves. They were forever talking on their fancy mobile phones and taking pictures and they pointed at things a good deal. Closing the gates to keep out the bailiffs had at least succeeded in stemming the tide of sour looking intruders in suits. Mr Pickering didn't approve of people coming onto a pier in suits. Men who wandered onto a pier should wear open-necked shirts, preferably brightly coloured and worn outside their trousers. And women should ideally wear summer frocks or, failing that, the sort of clothes that made it clear that when they'd got up and dressed themselves they hadn't been planning on spending the day looking at spread sheets, pecking at a computer keyboard or ringing people up and selling them insurance.

And now a load of old folks had turned up and the woman who seemed to be in charge had driven a minibus straight onto the pier and parked it on the planking just as if they had a parking space booked; that was something which not even the men and women in suits had dared to do. They'd left their motor cars somewhere else and had walked onto the pier in little clusters, all with their plastic folders under their arms or their plastic briefcases in their hands.

There was no doubt about the fact that Mr Pickering sometimes found life a bit of a challenge.

Chapter Nine

Once the minibus was safely through the gates, and parked neatly next to one of those plywood boards with a hole in the top, brightly painted so that people could poke their heads through and have their photographs taken so that it looked, for all the world, as if they were a fat woman in a spotted bikini or a fat policeman with a raised truncheon, Mr Livingstone and Mr Pickering pulled the gates together and Mr Livingstone repositioned the chain and relocked the padlock.

Mr Pickering seemed relieved when the gate was firmly locked. He pulled at the chain a couple of times to make sure that the gate was indeed properly fastened. He had spent most of his life welcoming people onto the pier. But now he only felt secure when the gates were closed, chained and locked. It was, he knew, a rather sad state of affairs but what else can you do when a bunch of belligerent looking bald men with tattoos had taken to standing on the pavement outside, and threatening to remove goods to the value of whatever it was.

Only when the gates were locked did Mr Pickering introduce the second person who had been standing with him behind the gates.

'This is my granddaughter, Dorothy,' he said, introducing a girl of about sixteen to Mr Livingstone. 'She lives with me. She ran the café until Mr Livingstone passed on.'

Dorothy seemed to Mr Livingstone to be a nice young girl. She was the sort of old-fashioned girl he'd have been happy to have as a granddaughter. Indeed, she was the sort of old-fashioned girl most people of grandparent age would have been happy to have as a granddaughter. Her hair was brown and cut properly and she had no visible tattoos or bits of metal attached to her person. Mr Livingstone was a little old-fashioned and he couldn't understand why so many young people wanted to have rings put through their noses as though they were prize pigs or belligerent bulls. He had once suggested to Mr Hewitt that they buy a large magnet and stroll through the local town clearing the streets of youths who had so decorated their persons.

'Where do you two live?' asked Mr Livingstone, as Mrs Caldicot and the rest of the party climbed down from the minibus and stretched their legs.

'Where's the toilet?' asked Mr Williams who had been the first to climb down and who was now bending forwards very slightly and standing with his legs very close together.

'I need one too,' said Mr Roxdale.

'Me too,' said Mrs Torridge.

It quickly became clear that finding toilets (preferably in the plural) was the first requirement. Mr Pickering's granddaughter offered to show them the way to the lavatories behind the pier's café.

'We live on the pier,' said Mr Pickering, replying at last to Mr Livingstone's question. 'We've got a little flat behind the café.' He sighed. 'I expect you'll be wanting us to move on.'

'Do you know anything about the pier?' asked Mr Livingstone.

'I've worked on it since I was a lad,' replied Mr Pickering. 'It's a grand pier. A wonderful pier. And I've lived on it ever since after the War.'

'What do you do?' Mr Livingstone enquired.

'I drive the train and I'm the sort of odd job man. Any odd jobs that need doing, I do them. In between train rides I sometimes help out in the shop or the café. My Deidre and I lived and worked here. Deidre, my wife as was when she was still with us bless her, ran the café. Then when Deidre died three years ago, my granddaughter came here to live with me. Her parents had split up and she didn't get on with either of them. She's a nice girl; a good girl and now that Deidre has gone she's the only one who can handle the deep fat fryer. It's a bit on the temperamental side.'

'I'm definitely not going to throw you off,' promised Mr Livingstone who was impressed by the fact that Mr Pickering seemed to know things about the pier but more impressed by the fact that he clearly had a real affection for it.

'Is that a little train?' asked Mr Hewitt, who spotted the small train which took holidaymakers up and down the pier without them having to walk. Peering into the darkness he could just make out that the train was painted red and yellow.

'It is,' said Mr Pickering. 'That's Doris. At Halloween I dress myself up in a sheet and we call her the ghost train.''

'Doris?' said Mr Livingstone.

'That's what I call the train. Doris. I wanted to have the name painted on the front of the engine but he wouldn't let me. I don't know why. I just thought it would be nice. She's always seemed like a Doris to me. People give names to boats, don't they? And trains always used to have names. There was that Flying Scotsman. And the Golden Arrow and the Robin Hood. And the Devon Scot. Loads of trains had names. I don't suppose they give them names now. They probably don't even give them numbers.'

'Can I come aboard?' asked Mr Hewitt.

'You help yourselves,' said Mr Pickering, generously. 'We usually charge 25 pence each way and 50 pence for a return. It's been those prices since the year 2000. I kept saying to Mr Livingstone that we should put up the prices.'

'Who wouldn't let you?'

'Let me do what?'

'Who wouldn't let you paint 'Doris' on the front of the train?'

'Oh, that was Mr Simpkins.'

Mrs Caldicot and the others joined Mr Hewitt on the train. They waited for a few moments for Mr Williams, Mrs Torridge and Mr Roxdale to join them. There were three carriages and plenty of room for them all. Mrs Caldicot looked around and reckoned that the train could carry at least fifty people at a time. She did the sums in her head and quickly realised that if they put up the price a little then they could earn quite reasonable sums of money.

'How do I make it start?' asked Mr Hewitt, preparing to climb into the driver's seat.

'I'll drive it,' said Mr Pickering firmly, as he gently eased himself past Mr Hewitt, who was clearly keen to have a go at driving the train.

Mrs Caldicot, watching, thought that the small boy who resides within every grown man, and who sometimes seemed to be particularly dominant as far as Mr Hewitt was concerned, was in danger of taking over.

'It's not as easy as you'd think,' said Mr Pickering. He climbed aboard and sat in the driver's seat. Mr Livingstone sat beside him. Mr Hewitt sat behind Mr Pickering who then pressed a button and the train started. Once the train had started, Mr Pickering pressed the accelerator and the train moved forward slowly. 'It's got a battery,' the driver explained. 'So it's electric. We charge it up every now and then when the electricity has run out. We usually do runs up and down the pier every 30 minutes.'

'It doesn't look that difficult to start,' said Mr Hewitt.

'It's not the starting,' said Mr Pickering, bridling a little. 'It starts easy enough, as long as the battery is charged and I always keep it charged. It's the people walking about you have to watch out for. You could run people over.'

'But there aren't any people on the pier,' Mr Hewitt pointed out. 'We're the only people here. And we're all on the train.'

'That's as may be,' said Mr Pickering. 'You still have to watch what you're doing. You could crash. You could drive off the edge of the pier and land in the sea.'

'Quite right,' said Mr Hewitt, realising that, for the moment at least, Mr Pickering didn't want anyone else driving what he clearly thought of as 'his' train.

'Who is Mr Simpkins?' Mr Livingstone asked Mr Pickering.

'Why?'

'Mr Simpkins. You said a Mr Simpkins stopped you painting 'Doris' on the front of the engine.'

'He was the pier master.'

'Pier master? What's a pier master?'

'He's the chap what's in charge of the pier. A sort of manager. On a ship they have a captain and on a pier they have a master.'

'I didn't know that.'

'Not many people do.'

'Why wouldn't Mr Simpkins let you paint 'Doris' on the front of the train?'

'Dunno. It might have something to do with him being a bit of a mean bastard, I suppose.'

'Where is he? I'll have a word with him!'

'He left.'

'What do you mean 'He left'?

'He buggered off. Just upped and off when your uncle died. He said the pier hadn't got a future and he'd been offered a job by the council. They hired him to run a car park in the town centre. He said they were paying him a fortune because they valued him so highly so he just buggered off. I think they just wanted him away from here so that the pier wouldn't have anyone managing it. He took 48 boxes of Turkish Delight, 50 boxes of them little flags that kids stick in their sandcastles and a load of sticks of pink, peppermint, seaside rock. I don't know why he took the rock. It all had Penmouth running through the middle so unless he went somewhere else called Penmouth it wouldn't be much use to him. Unless he just liked eating it. Maybe he did. I can't eat the stuff myself. I used to eat a lot of it but then I lost my teeth and that was the end of my rock eating days. I never understand who bought them little flags we used to sell because there's no sand on the beach and you can't build sandcastles with pebbles, can you? We used to sell hundreds of those little flags on a nice day in the summer. The kids used to wave them. Mr Simpkins said he was owed some wages and something from his pension but he wasn't going to wait to get his money because he didn't think it would be forthcoming, that was the word he used, 'forthcoming', so he'd take it in kind. Just piled the boxes into the back of his car and off he went.'

'Oh,' said Mr Livingstone, rather started by this tale of woe. 'Well you can paint 'Doris' on the train. I don't mind. Who's left apart from you and Dorothy?'

'There's nobody else. Just me and Dorothy. Oh and the Fat Lady comes round most days to see if there's any news about the Pier reopening. And young Errol hangs about. He sometimes helps Dorothy with our shopping.'

'Who is Errol?'

'He's just a kid. He works for the council doing something or other. He likes the pier and he's taken a fancy to our Dorothy. He's a nice boy.'

'And the Fat Lady?'

'She's a lovely girl. Well I call her a girl but she's a grown woman. In her 30s I'd say though I wouldn't rightly know. She used to be bigger but she's lost a lot of weight since she lost her job. I suppose she can't afford to eat as much as she did before. She used to help out in the theatre when she wasn't being the Fat Lady. Selling ice creams and programmes, that sort of thing. We all mucked in and tried to help with those jobs.'

'How long has the pier been closed?'

'A month or two now. There were bills to pay but no one was paying them, so I locked the gates to stop the people getting in.'

'What people?'

'Bailiffs, they called themselves. They came in a van marked DEBT COLLECTORS in big, red letters. I think they do that to intimidate people and embarrass them. They were all big blokes and very threatening. They wanted to come in and take stuff because some bill or other hadn't been paid. So Dorothy and I locked ourselves in. Errol checked with somebody at the council and they said the bailiffs can't come in if the place is locked even if you owe them money. So we keep the place locked.'

'How long have you been locked in?'

'Oh, a month or two. Since old Mr Livingstone passed away and Mr Simpkins buggered off.'

'What do you do for food?'

'I've got a few pounds saved and our Dorothy climbs down after dark when it's low tide and runs along the beach to the supermarket. She buys what we need and then brings it back. Errol helps her.'

They had now reached the end of the pier. 'That's the theatre,' said Mr Pickering, pointing to a huge structure straight ahead of them. 'It's built on Stone Rock. They used to have good shows there.'

'I heard,' said Mr Livingstone. 'Gerry and the Pacemakers in the 1960s.'

'You remember, eh?' said Mr Pickering. 'That was a good night. Proper band they were. Not like the rubbish you see on the television these days. We nearly had the Beatles once. And we had that Cilla Black girl.'

'Shall we go back now?' said Mrs Caldicot, who was sitting behind Mr Livingstone. 'It's getting a little chilly.' She leant forward to speak to Mr Pickering. 'Do you know if there's anywhere we can eat? I'm starving. I bet everyone else is too.'

'I could ask Dorothy to do up some chips,' said Mr Pickering, turning the train around and heading back down the pier. 'And there may be a few bits of cod in the freezer.'

'That would be marvellous,' said Mrs Caldicot.

But long before they got back to the pier gatehouse they could smell the chips frying. Dorothy, guessing that the new owner and his friends would probably be hungry, had heated up the deep fat fryer and thrown in a large bag of potato chips and enough cod to feed a small army.

Chapter Ten

They all put on their coats and sat out on the pier, eating cod and chips and listening to the sound of the sea crashing against the pier's wooden piles.

Dorothy, Mr Pickering's granddaughter, and the only one who knew how to make the deep fat fryer work, found a crate of Dandelion and Burdock, presented in bottles not cans, and they celebrated the first hours of their new life with a series of cheerful and increasingly optimistic toasts.

'Here's to us and Mr Livingstone's pier!' said Mr Merivale.

'Here's to the best pier in England!' said Mr Twist.

'Let's drink to the brightest and most exciting pier in the world!' said Mr Roxdale, who was tired and felt a little emotional but meant what he said.

They all drank to this and, where possible, clinked bottles together to seal the toast.

'It's been a busy day,' said Mr Hewitt. He had remembered too late that fizzy drinks always gave him heartburn and wind. He tried to burp silently and succeeded in only one of those aims.

'A busy day and a brilliant day,' said Mrs Roberts.

There was a murmur as the others agreed with her.

'These are damned fine chips,' said Mr Hewitt.

'Damned good cod, too,' said Mr Roxdale.

'Plenty of salt and lashings of vinegar,' said Mr Livingstone, who, not without good reason, considered himself to be an expert on the subject of fish and chips.

'And no little, plastic trays,' said Mr Hewitt.

Mr Livingstone visibly shuddered. 'And no plastic forks,' he added sternly.

'I'm glad young Dorothy still wraps them in newspaper,' said Mr Roxdale. 'I always find interesting bits to read.'

'I only ever read a newspaper when I've got fish and chips,' confessed Mr Merivale.

'Didn't they make it illegal?' asked Mr Livingstone. 'Wrapping chips in newspaper?'

'It was that Common Market,' said Mr Hewitt. 'They passed some law about it. I think they were worried that they wouldn't be able to recycle the newspaper if it had bits of chip clinging to it.'

'What rubbish,' snorted Mr Livingstone.

'I think they allow it if you wrap the chips in plain paper before you put them into the newspaper,' said Mr Merivale.

'Well that's just plain silly,' said Mr Hewitt. 'That's wasting twice as much paper as they need.'

'I can't believe this is happening to me!' typed Ruth, who was not yet 19-years-old and had, in the short time since they'd arrived, sent a sequence of excited text messages to Jean-Jacques, the accordionist she had met in Paris, and to her best friend Denise who had, many months earlier, warned her that working for a bunch of old folk would be so dull that she'd die of boredom.

'We're on Mr Livingstone's pier,' she wrote to Denise. 'We've just had cod and chips, and drunk Dandelion and Burdock, and now we're going to sleep on Lilos in the pier ballroom. Mine is bright blue and has pictures of Donald Duck all over it. We got the Lilos from the shop because our beds haven't got here yet. Mr Livingstone owns the shop so he owns the Lilos so we didn't have to pay for them. We got stopped by two policemen when we got here and I thought they were going to arrest us. Dorothy, who is two years younger than I am and very sweet, says she'll teach me how to use the deep fat fryer and Mr Pickering, who looks even older than Mr Hewitt, has promised to teach me how to drive the train along the pier.'

'This is the best night of my life,' said Mr Livingstone to Mrs Caldicot, as they looked out over the sea. The light of a thousand stars, reflected in the water, sparkled and danced.

'Better than bombing that German bridge?'

'Oh, yes,' said Mr Livingstone. 'This is even better than seeing that Kraut bridge go down into the river.'

And he sighed the deep sigh of a contented man who knew that whatever travails and adversities lay ahead nothing will banish the magic of the moment.

'I'm very pleased,' whispered Mrs Caldicot, who was.

‘Who is going to be paying for the cod and chip suppers?’ asked Mr Pickering, of no one in particular. ‘Not to mention the Dandelion and Burdock.’

Mrs Caldicot took out her purse, asked him how much they all owed and handed over the money he asked for. Mr Pickering gave her the appropriate amount of change and then put the proceeds into the till. It seemed strange to Mrs Caldicot that they should have to pay to have dinner in what was, effectively, their own home but paying Mr Pickering seemed easier than trying to explain the new circumstances. He seemed like a man who felt that his capacity and yearning for surprise had already been more than satisfied.

They spent the night in the ballroom, sleeping on the plastic Lilos which Mr Pickering had found in a cupboard at the back of the shop and which he had inflated with a small foot pump. They had no blankets and so, since it was a little chilly, Mr Pickering turned on a small electric fire which Dorothy found in the café.

The new owner and his friends, exhausted after a long day and full of excitement about the future, wrapped themselves in their coats and slept peacefully.

They dreamt, variously and independently, of ice cream, candyfloss, the sound of seagulls, bunting fluttering in a summer breeze, men in deckchairs with knotted handkerchiefs protecting their bald heads from the sunshine and rows of smiling wives in summer frocks, all settled in deckchairs and all sipping steaming hot tea from white, china mugs.

Mr Hewitt dreamt of driving the small train and Mr Twist, who used to work for Her Majesty’s Revenue and Customs and who consequently worried a good deal about money, dreamt of hordes of happy holidaymakers handing over their 25ps and their 50ps to travel up and down the pier.

Chapter Eleven

They were awoken at 8.00 am the following morning by a good deal of tooting.

When Mrs Caldicot and the rest of the refugees from the Twilight Years Rest Home looked out of the ballroom window, fearful that Mr Pickering's awful bailiffs might be standing alongside their van, proclaiming shame and embarrassment for all who could read, they saw that instead of the bailiffs the two pantechnicons were there, parked on the pavement outside the entrance to the pier.

After Mr Livingstone had unfastened the padlock, opened the gates and greeted the removal men, they told him that they had got up at 4.00 am in order to finish their delivery without further delay. They admitted that they had done this not entirely out of a sense of generous good spirit but in the knowledge that if they finished unloading early enough they would be able to spend the day by the seaside; paddling, eating cockles and doing whatever grown men think of doing, dream of doing and actually do when they are released from the leash of daily toil and are well out of sight of employers and loved ones for the best part of a day.

By eleven that morning, the two huge removal lorries had been unloaded and the beds, wardrobes, dressing tables, kitchen whites, tables, chairs and other baggage and paraphernalia of 14 lives had been placed, if not precisely in their final positions, in an approximation that served well enough.

The drivers of the huge lorries then drove to a public car park where they left the vehicles neatly positioned on six car park spaces apiece. They handed two crisp £10 notes to the car park attendant who was on duty for the day and who, in return for this unofficial donation, promised to turn a blind eye to whatever bylaws had been broached. This chore completed, the removal men, as merry a band of workmen as you could hope to come across, returned to the pier on the promise of large helpings of cod and chips and unlimited supplies of Dandelion and Burdock in bottles and not in cans, thank you very much.

Only when the removal men had gone and some (but by no means all) of the boxes had been unpacked and clothes put away in wardrobes and so on, could Mrs Caldicot and what she now (thanks to Ruth) thought of as the gang, begin to explore the pier which Mr Livingstone had inherited and of what he was now, by common consent, considered to be the Pier Master. This was, without a doubt, a title he enjoyed just as much as any title within the gift of Her Majesty the Queen. 'I'm not just a peer,' he said proudly. 'I'm a Pier Master!'

Sadly, in the daylight, the pier was not quite what any of them had envisaged.

Mrs Caldicot had remembered the piers of her childhood as being always bright and busy and stretching out as far as the eye could see across a bright blue sea. They were always thronged with happy holidaymakers, children eating ice cream cones with chocolate flakes stuck into them, fathers in shirt sleeves, with braces or suspenders showing, women in cheerful summer dresses carrying raffia beach bags and looking pleasantly harassed and sunburnt. The only hazard was the occasional incontinent seagull.

There was, she remembered, always a busy theatre at the end of the pier, with posters displayed outside advertising names recognised from the wireless and the television.

And there were usually several small boats at a jetty at the end of the pier, ready to take tourists out to sea to fish for mackerel. Less intrepid fishermen lined the rails of the pier and dangled bits of twine in the water with plenty of hope but not much expectation. The one thing she remembered was that the people she saw on piers were always at peace with themselves and the world. There were many pipes being puffed and many dreams being enjoyed. Piers, she remembered, were always happy places – far away from the sometimes awful realities of the real world. When you stepped onto a pier, and felt the wooden planks beneath your feet, you left your bills and worries behind you and entered another world; a world where the sea breezes seemed to waft away all earthly trials and tribulations.

Sadly, the pier which Mr Livingstone had inherited was currently none of the things that Mrs Caldicot remembered.

Indeed, it has to be admitted that in light of Mrs Caldicot's memories, it was a distinct disappointment.

The pier itself looked rather ancient, which was to be expected since it was well over a hundred years old and had been standing with its feet in the sea for a long, long time. But it looked even older than its years and it looked sadly uncared for. The storm battered paintwork was faded and chipped and there was more rust to be seen than seemed entirely appropriate.

It perhaps did not help that the wind was howling in a very unseasonal sort of way, and that the rain was coming down in the sort of quantities which suggested that God was having an end of season sale.

It was, thought Mrs Caldicot, not the sort of weather anyone expected in the month of May. She felt sorry for the removal men who had such high hopes for their day.

And there wasn't a soul to be seen on the pier.

(Mrs Caldicot was initially startled by this but shortly realised that the absence of holidaymakers was, perhaps, not entirely surprising since the gates to the pier were firmly closed, chained and padlocked and decorated with large signs warning potential visitors that they were not wanted and should keep out and go away.)

It was, thought Mrs Caldicot, like meeting an elderly Cary Grant: wrinkled, bald, rheumy eyed and painfully arthritic. Still Cary Grant, but not quite what you'd expected or hoped for.

They spent the rest of the day pottering about, looking around, checking out the pier and sheltering from the rain. In the evening Mrs Caldicot and the gang sat in the café, together with Mr Pickering and his granddaughter Dorothy, and had chips and cod for their supper. (Mr Hewitt insisted that if they said it that way round it sounded as if it were a different meal to cod and chips. No one else cared very much what they called it as long as they had plenty of salt and vinegar at hand.) Outside, the storm had passed and the evening sky looked friendlier and more welcoming.

Mr Pickering, who told them that the pier had been closed for some weeks in order to keep out the bailiffs, explained that somewhere along the line the original Mr Livingstone, Mr Bertram Livingstone, had failed to pay a bill the council had sent and the council, showing all the mercy of a tom cat on the prowl, had pounced.

The bailiffs had been called in.

'Errol has been very helpful,' said Dorothy Pickering, rather proudly thought Mrs Caldicot. 'He did some research at the council offices and told us that the bailiffs can't break into a property and can't enter unless there is a door or window open. With the gates shut they have to stay outside. Errol told us to watch out because he said that they use a lot of tricks to gain entry. They ask to use the loo and then, when they're inside, they suddenly start taking away your stuff. Or they lie and say that they can charge £50 a minute for every minute they are kept waiting. The fact is that it doesn't cost anything extra to keep them standing around outside for hours and hours.'

Errol, who had joined them for their fish and chip supper, blushed but didn't say anything as he listened to Dorothy. He was a shy boy, younger than his years in many ways, and he spoke only to Dorothy, and then in whispers.

'They came this afternoon and we saw them outside and we didn't like the look of them one little bit,' said Miss Nightingale. She shuddered. 'They looked very menacing.'

'We were upstairs in the ballroom and we threw things at them,' said Mrs Peterborough. 'They had shaved their heads and had lots of tattoos. They looked like bullies.'

'What did you throw at them?' asked Mrs Caldicot, suddenly a little worried.

'We peppered them with coconut mushrooms and Pontefract cakes,' said Mr Livingstone. 'We checked the sell by dates and they were too old to eat or to sell. Oh, and we found some old dolly mixtures that had been nibbled by mice.'

'Sugar mice, sherbet pips and liquorice allsorts,' added Mr Hewitt. 'The boxes they were in had been kept somewhere damp so they didn't look very nice.'

'Oh and some fudge,' said Mrs Torridge. 'The box said it was extra creamy but sadly that had expired too. I tried a bit but it had gone hard.'

'And some pork scratchings,' added Miss Nightingale.

'Actually, I did taste one or two of the coconut mushrooms,' confessed Mrs Torridge. 'And to be honest I couldn't taste anything wrong with them. I think they put these silly dates on just so that people will throw stuff away and then have to buy more.'

'And a dozen pickled eggs which we found in a jar,' added Mrs Peterborough.

'What did they do?' asked Mrs Caldicot.

'They sort of went splat when they hit the pavement,' replied Mrs Peterborough.

'No, the bailiffs! What did the bailiffs do?' asked Mrs Caldicot. She didn't think the coconut mushrooms would do too much harm but she was a little alarmed at the idea of Mrs Peterborough hurling pickled eggs at the bailiffs. 'They didn't call the police, did they?'

'They hid behind their van and then they drove off,' said Mr Livingstone. 'I don't think they'll call the police.'

'One of them seemed to be crying,' said Miss Nightingale. 'He was hit on the head by a coconut mushroom. Two of the others were comforting him.'

'They'd look a bit silly if they complained, wouldn't they?' said Mr Hewitt. He drew an imaginary headline in the air: 'Bailiffs Run Away From Pensioners Hurling Coconut Mushrooms!'

'And there wasn't any evidence left when they'd gone,' said Mrs Torridge. 'The seagulls ate it all. Every last dolly mixture was gone in two minutes.'

'If they come back tomorrow we're going to throw blancmange at them,' said Mrs Peterborough. 'We found some blancmange powder and some dried milk, and Miss Nightingale said she thought there was enough to make three gallons of strawberry blancmange.'

'We can use soup ladles to hurl the blancmange,' said Miss Nightingale.

'And there's plenty more rotten fudge and six more boxes of out-of-date liquorice allsorts!' added Mrs Torridge, who had also tried the liquorice allsorts and had found them perfectly edible even though the date on the boxes suggested that they were nine months past the date when they could be safely consumed.

Errol, who was sitting next to Dorothy, leant a little closer to her and whispered in her ear. Dorothy listened carefully.

'Errol says that he heard people at the council offices talking,' said Dorothy. 'He said they were confident they'd get possession of the pier within a few days at the most.'

'Who said that?' asked an indignant Mr Livingstone.

Errol whispered to Dorothy again.

'Errol says he thinks they were people from the planning department,' reported Dorothy. 'He'll try to find out when he goes to work tomorrow.'

'How much do we owe the council?' Mrs Caldicot asked Mr Pickering.

'The original bill was for £5,743.60. That was for a tax bill that the council sent and that didn't get paid. But now there's a bailiff fee of £200 to add on so the latest bill we had said we owed them £5,943.6 altogether.'

Mrs Caldicot went quite cold and turned to Mr Livingstone. 'I suppose we'd better pay it,' she said.

Over the last year or two, Mrs Caldicot had learned a lot about dealing with people in authority. She had learned the hard way that one should never show weakness, fear or doubt of any kind when confronted by a policeman, a tax inspector or anyone with more power than they know what to do with. She knew that a uniform, or a position with a little status within any corner of a nation's bureaucracy, turns many individuals into bullies. And she knew that bullies thrive on fear.

But she had also learned that although there are times when it is best to stand up and fight, there are also times when you have to let the bullies win a round.

'I haven't got £5,743.60!'said Mr Livingstone. 'I can probably find the 60 pence but that's about it.'

'Let me see what I can do,' said Mrs Caldicot. She walked out onto the pier, took out the mobile telephone which Jenkins had given her, scrolled down the menu and pressed the CALL button when her husband's name appeared. She hated having to call him but could not think of anyone else to turn to. A few moments later, to her great relief, she heard his voice.

'We've got a problem,' admitted Mrs Caldicot after they'd exchanged private and loving greetings which have no place in this account. 'It seems that we owe the council some money and I think we will have to pay it. Bailiffs have been trying to get in and the council seems to be very aggressive.'

'How much do we owe?' asked Jenkins.

Mrs Caldicot told him.

'I'll ring the bank and move some money from my deposit account into our joint account,' promised Jenkins. 'You can let the council have a cheque. By the time they cash it the money will have cleared.'

'But how can we pay you back? We have to pay you back.'

'If you really insist on making it a loan then you can pay me back when the Government sends the compensation cheque they owe,' said Jenkins.

Mrs Caldicot wanted to cry but didn't. They talked for a few minutes about how Jenkins was getting on in America (very well but he really wanted to be with Mrs Caldicot and on the pier in Penmouth), about how he had decided to abandon his novel (it was, he said, the sort of novel best left in a box at the bottom of the wardrobe and he rather thought he might do some research and write a small book about Jane Austen's visits to Penmouth) and about how Mrs Caldicot was getting on in Penmouth (very well but she really wanted Jenkins to be on the pier with her and she thought that if Jenkins wrote a small book about Jane Austen and Penmouth it would sell very well in the shop on the pier) and finally they exchanged loving goodbyes and then turned off their phones.

Mrs Caldicot went back into the café, put her mobile phone back into her handbag and took out her cheque book. She then wrote out a cheque for the sum that they owed the local council.

'What are you doing?' asked Mr Livingstone, when he saw the size of the cheque Mrs Caldicot had written.

'Until we pay the council we can't open up the pier and start earning some money,' explained Mrs Caldicot.

'Oh no,' said Mr Livingstone, who looked very worried. 'I can't allow you to pay my debts.'

'But it isn't your debt!' insisted Mrs Caldicot. 'You own the pier but we are all living here now. And just as we did at the house, we will share our living expenses. Paying the council taxes counts as a living expense.'

When they'd all been living at what had formerly been the Twilight Years Rest Home the residents had all paid part of their pensions into a joint bank account so that bills could be paid. They kept money back for their own personal expenses. It was a system which seemed to work well.

Mr Livingstone looked at Mrs Caldicot. 'Maybe I should just sell the pier,' he said.

‘Mr Canterbury said that the people who offered to buy it offered only £1!’ she pointed out.

‘Maybe they’d pay that and also pay all the debts.’

‘I’m sure they won’t.’ said Mrs Caldicot. ‘But do you want to sell the pier?’

‘No, of course not!’

‘Well, I’m not going to discuss any such nonsense,’ said Mrs Caldicot firmly but kindly. ‘This pier is our new home. We’re here and we’re going to stay. I’ve written a cheque and paid the bill. That’s the way it is and that’s the way it’s going to be.’

‘That’s it, Mrs Caldicot!’ said Mr Hewitt, who was grinning. ‘You tell him!’

And so Mrs Caldicot put the bill and the cheque she had written into the weedy little envelope which the council had included with their bill and she gave the envelope to Errol to take to the council offices. She thought it would be a good idea to get the bill paid as quickly as possible – partly to ensure that the bailiffs didn’t come back and partly to prevent the council adding on any more expenses or charges.

‘Just pop it into the internal mailbox,’ she told the boy in a whisper. ‘Don’t let anyone there know that you delivered it.’ She smiled and winked at him in a kindly, motherly sort of way for he seemed a likeable, young fellow. He tried to wink back but it was more of a blink than a wink and he blushed bright red as he always did when people were kind to him. ‘And if you can find out why the council wants to control the pier, and why they think they’re going to be able to, that would be very helpful. Can you come and have supper with us again tomorrow evening?’

Errol opened and closed his mouth, rather like a goldfish, and nodded enthusiastically as a substitute for the words which were missing.

Chapter Twelve

After breakfast the following morning they opened the pier gates for the first time since the bailiffs had started their vigil outside the pier entrance. It seemed reasonable to assume that since the council had now received their money they would call off the dogs. Mrs Peterborough and Miss Nightingale were privately rather disappointed though they didn't say anything to the others. They had been looking forward to being able to hurl strawberry blancmange at large men with no hair and lots of tattoos.

The rain had gone and the sky was blue. It was a beautiful day and with the council tax bill paid and the pier gates open, Mrs Caldicot felt full of hope. They still had to deal with whatever else it was that the council was planning but it was now generally agreed that the pier, despite the rust and the signs of age, was looking wonderful in the sunshine. The paintwork, though chipped and faded, still managed to sparkle and shine and give every impression of having been given a thorough once over by one of those teams of Romanian car wash specialists who have taken over unused petrol station forecourts throughout England.

Mr Pickering, delighted at last to see the pier being prepared for action, removed the tarpaulin cover which he had put over the train when it had rained, and gave the woodwork a polish and the brass-work an energetic rub down with an oily rag.

His granddaughter Dorothy poured more chips and fish into the deep fat fryer (and made a note to tell her granddad, who had in the past been responsible for such things) that their supplies of both potatoes and fish were running rather low.

Miss Nightingale, Mrs Peterborough and Mrs Torridge continued to sort through the boxes of sweets and other delicacies which they had unearthed in the cupboards at the back of the shop as well as in some cupboards upstairs outside the ballroom. They had been asked by Mrs Caldicot to separate out the items which were within their 'sell by date' and could, therefore, either be eaten or sold, and those which were outside their 'sell by date' and would, therefore, have to be thrown away or (the preferred option of Mrs Peterborough and Miss Nightingale) stored to be used as ammunition should the bailiffs ever return.

Mr Williams, Mr Roxdale and Mr Twist who had moved some of the furniture around, and emptied quite a few boxes and trunks, were drinking tea in the café and making lists of things which had to be done, though preferably not immediately.

Mr and Mrs Merivale, who were good at this sort of practical stuff, and to be honest rather enjoyed it, were checking the bathrooms to see which taps were dripping and which light fittings needed new bulbs. Mr Merivale was carrying with him a wrench which he had brought and Mrs Merivale was carrying a large cardboard box full of spare light bulbs which she had discovered in a store room on the top floor.

And Mrs Caldicot, Mrs Roberts and Ruth were sitting together on a bench, each of them armed with a nice cup of tea with two biscuits on the saucer, and working on what Mrs Caldicot called the 'Plan for the Future'.

Mrs Caldicot had invited all the other members of the gang to join them but the general feeling had been that they were all happy to leave the 'thinking' and 'planning' to Mrs Caldicot since those were things that she was very good at. 'You make the decisions,' said Mr Livingstone.

And Mr Livingstone and Mr Hewitt, having opened the gates to the pier, were standing to one side, careful to keep out of the way so that they didn't get crushed in the rush, quietly waiting for the holidaymakers to flood onto the pier.

It is fair to say that they were excited.

'How many people do you think visit the average sort of pier in an average sort of day?' Mr Livingstone asked his friend.

'That's not something I've ever really thought about,' admitted Mr Hewitt. 'But, at a guess, I would say that you might expect 12 people a minute to wander onto a pier of this size.' If anyone had asked him where he had found this figure he would not have been able to provide any sort of sensible answer other than to say that it was a figure plucked out of the air and that one figure plucked out of the air is as good as any other.

'How many minutes are there in a day?'

‘Well, there’s 60 minutes in an hour and 24 hours in a day so the answer would be quite a lot but I suppose everything really depends on how many hours the pier stays open. What do you think the opening hours should be?’

‘Oh, I would have thought from eight in the morning until ten at night don’t you think?’

‘That sounds reasonable. How many hours is that.’

They stood and thought about this for a while and eventually Mr Livingstone found a piece of paper and a pencil and they worked it out and came to the conclusion that if they opened at eight in the morning and closed at ten at night then the pier would be open for 14 hours a day.

‘So, there are 60 minutes in an hour and the pier is open for 14 hours,’ said Mr Hewitt. ‘How many minutes is that?’

Some more calculations on Mr Livingstone’s piece of paper gave them several options: a total of 8,400 minutes, 840 minutes or 84 minutes.

‘Let’s take the middle figure,’ said Mr Hewitt.

‘That’s what I always do when I’m working things out,’ said Mr Livingstone. ‘I do it three times and take the middle one.’

‘That’s a very scientific attitude,’ agreed Mr Hewitt. ‘I bet that’s probably the way accountants do it.’

‘We must ask Mr Twist about that,’ said Mr Livingstone.

‘And what did we say, 12 people a minute?’

‘Let’s make it 10 people a minute,’ said Mr Livingstone. ‘That’s maybe more reasonable.’

‘And easier to work out.’

‘Definitely easier to work out.’

‘Multiplying by ten has got to be simpler. What does that come to then?’

They both thought for a while and then Mr Hewitt realised that all he had to do was put a nought on the end. ‘I reckon it’s 8,400 people a day.’

‘I agree with you,’ said Mr Livingstone, who was proud that he hadn’t even had to use his pencil and paper to do that sum.

‘Good heavens,’ said Mr Hewitt. ‘That’s quite a crowd. Can you get that many people on a pier?’

‘Oh yes, I would think so. And they won’t all be on at once, will they? Some will wander on and some will wander off again,’ said

Mr Livingstone. 'The next thing to do is to work out how much they're all going to spend. When we've done that we can work out our profit-loss thingy. Our financial objections.'

'Projections, I think it is,' said Mr Hewitt. 'Our financial projections.'

'No objection to that!' said Mr Livingstone with a grin.

'What are they going to spend money on?'

'Well, there's the train. They'll all want to go on that. And they'll mostly want to have return tickets. So that's 50 pence each for the train. And then they'll want teas and ice cream won't they?'

'Oh, I would think so. One ice cream each and a cup of tea each?'

'Definitely. And most of them will want a bag of chips.'

'And a stick of rock.'

'Possibly two sticks of rock. I think the average holidaymaker would need one stick for themselves and at least one to take home as a present.'

'And they'd need to buy a nice box of fudge for the neighbour who's been feeding the cat.'

'How much is that?'

'What?'

'A nice box of fudge?'

'I've no idea. Let's say £3. And £1 for a stick of rock.'

Mr Livingstone busied himself with his pencil. The piece of paper was actually a Eurostar train ticket which he had kept from their trip to Paris. And the pencil was one of those stubby things which really needed sharpening but which was so small that it would have been difficult to sharpen with a penknife and impossible to fit into a pencil sharpener.

'It might be more than £1 if it were a big stick of rock.'

'Let's keep it at a small stick of rock,' said Mr Livingstone, rather reluctantly. His piece of paper was rapidly getting filled up.

They stood in silence for a few minutes while Mr Livingstone tried to work out how much each visitor to the pier might spend.

'I make it £9.50 each,' said Mr Livingstone at last.

'Round it up to a tenner,' said Mr Hewitt.

'Fair enough,' said Mr Livingstone. 'They'd all want to buy a couple of postcards, wouldn't they?'

'So, what does that come to?'

Mr Livingstone did more work with his pencil. And then he frowned. 'It can't be that much!' he said. 'Can it?'

'How much does it come to?'

'It comes to £84,000,' said Mr Livingstone.

'Crumbs!' said Mr Hewitt. 'That's a lot of money.'

'Mind you, it's not all profit!' said Mr Livingstone sternly. 'We have to buy the stuff we sell.'

'But still,' said Mr Hewitt, who knew no more about running a pier than his companion and did not have the faintest idea how much a stick of rock cost when bought wholesale. 'Even if only £80,000 of that is profit that's not bad for a day, is it?'

'How much is that a year?' asked Mr Livingstone.

'Well, there are 52 weeks in a year and seven days in a week but I doubt if the pier would be as busy on some days as others.'

'What sort of days wouldn't it be busy?' asked Mr Livingstone, a little indignantly. He was a trifle disappointed by Mr Hewitt's pessimism.

'Well, very wet and windy days,' suggested Mr Hewitt. 'There probably wouldn't be very much business on very wet and windy days.'

'We could sell sou'westers and plastic macs,' suggested Mr Livingstone. 'No good selling umbrellas on a pier but sou'westers and plastic macs would do well.'

'That's a good idea!' said Mr Hewitt, impressed by his friend's business acumen. 'With those extra sales, the wet and windy days could well turn out to be even more profitable than the sunny days.'

'But let's forget about the sou'westers and those wet and windy days for the moment,' said Mr Livingstone. 'They'll make the sums too complicated and besides I don't know how much a sou'wester would cost.'

'We'll keep those days as our reserves,' said Mr Hewitt.

'So, let's say we have 50 weeks of good business,' said Mr Livingstone. 'That'll make it easier to do the sums.'

There was silence for a while as Mr Livingstone multiplied £80,000 by seven, for the number of days in a week, and then by 50 for the number of weeks in a year. This was the largest calculation Mr Livingstone could ever remember doing. He couldn't help wishing he had one of those calculator things. Both Ruth and Mr Twist had them. Mr Twist had one that was just a calculator while

Ruth had a mobile telephone which, to everyone's astonishment, could turn into a calculator, a torch, a calendar and a camera.

'What does it come to?' asked Mr Hewitt, impatiently.

'I make it £28,000,000 a year,' said Mr Livingstone frowning.

He paused and then repeated the calculation.

The two men stood for a moment, trying to comprehend a sum of this magnitude. It was the sort of huge sum of money they had previously only ever heard mentioned in reference to defence budgets and the salaries of television presenters employed by the BBC.

'With that sort of money you could probably buy a submarine,' said Mr Hewitt. 'Well a smallish one. Maybe a second hand one.'

'Why would we want to buy a second hand submarine?' asked Mr Livingstone, puzzled. If his friend wanted to buy a second hand submarine then he would not stand in his way. But he just wondered why he wanted one.

'I'm not saying we would want to buy any sort of submarine,' said Mr Hewitt. 'Just that we could if we wanted to.'

'I suppose we could,' agreed Mr Livingstone.

They stood in silence for a moment and contemplated the other things they could buy with £28,000,000. Mr Livingstone did more sums on the remaining corner of his bit of paper.

'The two of us could go on holiday in Spain for 4,000 years,' he said eventually.

'Why on earth would we want to do that? Especially now that you own a really nice pier by the seaside.' He paused. 'Would you say that it's by the seaside, on the seaside or in it?'

'Dunno. And I'm not saying that we'd want to; just that we could if we did want to.'

'I wouldn't want to go to Spain,' said Mr Hewitt. 'It's too hot and it's full of flies and foreigners.'

'I quite agree with you,' said Mr Livingstone who didn't much like the heat and was definitely not over fond of flies or foreigners though he liked Jean-Jacques and his father, who were French, and he very much liked the two Americans they'd met in Paris.

'How many of us are there?' asked Mr Hewitt.

'Well, there are 14 of us,' replied Mr Livingstone. 'So that's £2,000,000 each.' Although he actually owned the pier, Mr Livingstone would have never dreamt of not sharing his good fortune with his friends. 'But I think we should give a share to Mr Pickering and Dorothy and that young Errol.'

'That's still more than £1,500,000 a year each,' said Mr Hewitt. 'After a year we could all just retire. And sit on the pier and eat ice creams and ride up and down on the train.'

'Crumbs,' said Mr Livingstone very softly. 'It's a lot of money isn't it?'

Twenty minutes later, a tall man and a short dog wandered past them, looked around and then wandered off again. He didn't buy any rock, fudge or postcards. He didn't even buy a cup of tea or a bag of chips.

No one else came onto the pier.

'Maybe it's not really the season for piers,' said Mr Hewitt a few minutes later. 'Maybe this is one of the two quiet weeks we allowed for.'

'It's May!' said Mr Livingstone, looking up at beautiful, blue sky spoilt only by a few of those fluffy, white clouds which look just like cotton wool and which artists always regard as too unrealistic for their painted skies. 'It's springtime! It's a wonderful month for piers. It's just that people have got used to the pier being closed. Now they have to get used to our being open.'

They stood for a moment and enjoyed the spring sunshine.

'Do you fancy a cup of tea?' asked Mr Hewitt after a while.

'Sounds good to me,' said Mr Livingstone.

'I think I saw a tin of shortbread biscuits lying around.'

'Sounds better by the minute!'

And so the two almost millionaires abandoned their wait by the gates, wandered into the empty café and asked Dorothy for two cups of tea and a plateful of biscuits.

'I've just realised how brilliant this is,' said Mr Livingstone as he settled himself down.

'What do you mean?' asked Mr Hewitt.

'We can order tea and biscuits whenever we like and we don't have to pay a penny for them!' said Mr Livingstone.

'That's better than being a millionaire,' said Mr Hewitt.

And Mr Livingstone agreed with him.

Chapter Thirteen

'We need to decide what the pier is going to offer to make it attractive,' said Mrs Caldicot addressing the first meeting of the ad hoc committee convened to consider the future of the pier.

She still felt slightly uneasy at having this authority thrust upon her but Mr Livingstone had asked her if she would take charge of the pier's management and she was well aware that someone had to do it.

'I don't think I would make a very good Pier Master,' he told her. 'I feel that I'd make a better Pier Bosun or something like that so would you take charge of everything for me? I'm the sort of bloke who is better suited to taking orders than giving them.'

And so, with genuine reluctance, Mrs Caldicot had assumed control of the pier's management and was now the Pier Master. She had wondered if she should be known as the Pier Mistress but Mr Pickering had assured her that it would be more appropriate if she stuck to the traditional title. She had been relieved by this for she had felt considerably more comfortable sticking to the time honoured title.

Now she was sitting out in the spring sunshine, with Mrs Roberts on one side of her and Ruth on the other, and she had a small notebook open on her lap and a pen in her right hand. Both these items had been purchased from the stock of items for sale in the pier's surprisingly well stocked shop. The hard backed notebook she was using had a picture of the pier on its cover while the pen was decorated with a picture of the pier and the words 'A Present From Penmouth' overprinted on the picture.

In preparation for the forthcoming meeting, Mrs Caldicot had carefully printed the words 'Penmouth Pier' at the top of the first page of the notebook. You have to start somewhere, she said to herself.

'I gather from Mr Pickering that even before the gates were shut the pier wasn't doing very well,' began Mrs Caldicot. 'Indeed, he seemed to think that the pier had been losing money for months.' She whispered all this information, which she thought might be regarded as commercially sensitive, although there was no one within earshot.

'It's a wonderful pier but, at the same time, it does look a little seedy,' admitted Mrs Roberts, after looking around. There was no doubt that if peeling paint had been in vogue then the pier would have made a powerful fashion statement.

'Having those big iron gates closed and padlocked wouldn't have helped much,' said Ruth who felt very proud to be included in the discussion. She had thought she really ought to be helping Mr and Mrs Merivale upstairs. But she had offered her services and they'd both thanked her very nicely and said that they thought they could cope quite well and that they'd call her if they needed her. Besides, Mrs Caldicot herself had asked her to join the ad hoc committee convened to study the pier's future. She wasn't entirely sure what an ad hoc committee was but it was something she could look up later on her phone and she suspected that it was almost certainly something she could tell her best friend Denise.

'We need someone to tell us what young people look for in a pier,' Mrs Caldicot had said. 'You can give us a different viewpoint.'

'Let's make one list of the things we need to do and another list of all the amenities the pier has to offer,' said Mrs Caldicot. 'I know the pier needs a lick of paint here and there but I think our first task must be to get things up and running. The council isn't going to stop sending us tax bills, so we need to generate an income.'

In response to this thought, she picked up her pen and drew a line down the centre of the page. On the left hand side she put the heading 'Things to Be Done' and on the right hand side she wrote 'Amenities'.

The other two were silent for a moment and then the silence was broken by Ruth.

'What's an amenity?' she asked.

Mrs Roberts quietly blessed young Ruth for asking the question she herself had wanted to ask but had felt too shy to put into words.

There were times when Mrs Roberts felt very maternal and loving towards Ruth. She always liked her very much, was always fond of her, but there were moments when she wanted to give her a big hug and a kiss. She would not have done this, of course. You had to be very careful these days for such signs could easily be misconstrued and might lead to embarrassment and unwanted complications. Still, she could quietly bless her and so she did. And then, not quite content that this was enough, she took Ruth's hand and gave it a little squeeze. Ruth squeezed her hand back and they both smiled at each other and then, a little embarrassed, let their hands part again because although they were very fond of each other they were, after all, both very English and the English don't like touching one another unless it's inevitable or necessary.

'The amenities are the things the pier has to offer to people,' explained Mrs Caldicot. 'In a village the amenities might be, well,' she paused thinking, 'the village shop, the Post Office and the pub.'

'We've got a little train,' said Ruth. 'Is that what you'd call an amenity?'

'Exactly!' said Mrs Caldicot. She wrote down 'Little Train'.

'And a café and a shop,' said Mrs Roberts, now getting into the swing of things.

Mrs Caldicot wrote these down.

'Oh, and there's the theatre at the end of the pier!' said Ruth. 'They used to have pop concerts there.'

'And Mr Pickering said they put on Pantomimes in the winter and variety shows in the summer,' added Mrs Roberts. 'Most people love a nice panto, I know I do. Oh, and Mr Pickering said they used to have tea dances in the afternoons throughout the summer.'

'What's a tea dance?' asked Ruth.

'It's sort of, well, a dance where people also have cups of tea,' explained Mrs Roberts. 'They move some of the seats out of the theatre so that they can make a dance floor and they have a little orchestra which plays music and the women come in their best frocks and the men come in smart suits and they all sit at tables and drink tea and eat little sandwiches, cucumber and suchlike, and they have fancy cakes, those little ones covered with icing, and when they aren't eating or drinking they dance.'

'I'm not sure there'd much call for that these days,' said Mrs Caldicot who didn't think she'd ever been to a tea dance though she vaguely remembered that her Auntie Maude, her mother's rather wild younger sister, might have gone to one or two occasionally. 'What do you two think?'

'Probably not,' agreed Mrs Roberts. 'Not these days.'

'I don't think I'd want to go dancing immediately after drinking lots of tea and eating cakes,' said Ruth with a shudder. 'It might make me feel a bit queasy.'

'I think you're both right,' agreed Mrs Caldicot, thinking that Ruth's idea of dancing was probably rather more energetic than her own. 'There are lots of other things we can do with the theatre – plays and suchlike would be nice perhaps.'

And so they continued.

The list of amenities grew quickly and the list of things to do grew even more speedily.

Mrs Roberts pointed out that there was a weighing machine in the foyer to the café and then she remembered that although they didn't have a Fortune Teller to sit inside it, there was a booth half way down the pier that had the remains of the words 'Madame Mystery' painted on the front in large, red letters and the words 'Penmouth Pier's Fortune Teller' painted underneath in blue. 'If one of us dressed up a bit I'm sure we could open the Fortune Telling booth – though, like most things, the booth does need a lick of paint.'

Ruth asked if Mrs Caldicot thought that the row of Victorian slot machines could be made to work. She said there was one called 'What the Butler Saw!' and another which advertised a working model of King Charles having his head chopped off. Mrs Caldicot made a note of this and said she hadn't seen these machines but would ask Mr Williams to take a look because he seemed to be the member of their party most able to deal with complicated pieces of machinery.

Mrs Roberts said that if they were going to put on plays in the theatre at the end of the pier then perhaps they ought to get in touch with touring companies which went round the country putting on shows wherever they could find a suitable venue. 'Not Shakespeare though,' she said. 'I don't think people on holiday expecting to sit through one of those Shakespearean tragedies – all those witches and all that gloominess.'

And so it went on.

There were things that needed painting, things that needed mending and stock that needed sorting.

And, in addition to the theatre at the end of the pier, there were the side shows and booths which needed to be attended to.

'We need to decide who's going to do what,' said Mrs Caldicot, looking at the two long lists in her notebook. 'But for now I think we've earned ourselves another cup of tea.'

'Talking of the café, perhaps we could add some fresh items to the menu,' suggested Mrs Roberts. 'Young Dorothy makes marvellous cod and chips, I don't think I've ever tasted better, but maybe we would attract more customers if we extended our range a little. I don't think we should try anything too challenging, but cheese on toast, teacakes, crumpets, home-made sandwiches and so on might bring in a few more customers.'

Both Ruth and Mrs Caldicot agreed that this was a splendid idea and they quickly found themselves suggesting other simple dishes which could be added to the menu, and their own visit to the café was delayed.

'Naturally, we'd need to find someone to help Dorothy,' said Mrs Caldicot. 'She works very hard but if the café is going to be busier she would need another pair of hands.' She sighed. She wasn't looking forward to having to interview prospective waitresses. Still, it was something that had to be done.

After another half an hour of chatting, the three of them decided that they'd pretty well exhausted all the possibilities and their imaginations.

Leaving the other two sitting on the bench, in case they could think of anything else that could be added to their list of amenities, Mrs Caldicot went indoors to find the telephone book and look up the number for the secretary of the biggest local amateur dramatic society. Mrs Caldicot was, she knew, probably the only person in the country who still looked up numbers in the telephone directory. But some habits die hard.

The secretary of the dramatic society answered her telephone immediately.

'As you know there's a wonderful theatre at the end of the pier,' said Mrs Caldicot, having introduced herself, and explained that although Mr Livingstone was the new owner of the pier she was the Pier Master and in charge of organising events on the pier.

'Oh yes,' said the secretary, a lady called Mrs Upton. She sounded quite excited. 'In the past we've often hoped we would be able to use the theatre for one or two of our productions. At Christmas we always put on a pantomime and we do two or three other shows during the year – usually including a musical in the summer.'

'So am I right in thinking you would be interested in putting on a show in our theatre?' asked Mrs Caldicot.

'That would be amazing! But may I ask why you're inviting us when you could easily get professional theatre companies to put on a show. You have a wonderful theatre. It's one of the biggest and most beautiful auditoriums in the whole of Devon!'

'It's very simple,' explained Mrs Caldicot. 'We don't have the money or the expertise to put together a show ourselves. And we need to put on something as soon as possible. We want to get people coming onto the pier.'

'How would this work financially?' asked Mrs Upton.

'You would be responsible for selling the tickets and putting on a show of your choice,' explained Mrs Caldicot, making up the deal as she went along. 'We would then split the proceeds down the middle. You keep half and you give us half. The only condition is that you must have a show on the boards within a month.'

'Well, we have a show in rehearsal at the moment,' said Mrs Upton. 'We were planning to put it on in the village hall – that's the venue we normally use – but we'd obviously jump at the chance to put the show on in your theatre. That would be marvellous!'

'What are you rehearsing?' asked Mrs Caldicot, hoping desperately that it wasn't anything by Ibsen, Chekov or even Shakespeare.

'The Pirates of Penzance!' replied Mrs Upton. 'The opera by Gilbert and Sullivan. We're doing it as our annual musical production.'

'That will be wonderful,' said Mrs Caldicot, who loved all Gilbert and Sullivan operas. 'That would be absolutely perfect! And what better place to have an opera about pirates than on a pier!'

She put down the telephone and smiled happily. Things were beginning to fall into place. She went back outside and joined Mrs Roberts and Ruth who were now standing outside the café discussing whether or not they should put a fish stew onto the café menu.

'Time for tea and biscuits!' said Mrs Caldicot.

The others agreed immediately. Some decisions are easy to make.

Chapter Fourteen

But just as Mrs Caldicot, Mrs Roberts and Ruth were preparing to enter the café, a couple wandered onto the pier.

She was all curves; there were no straight bits at all.

He, on the other hand, was all straight bits; no curves.

She was five foot nothing.

He was six foot something and had about as much fat on him as the average telegraph pole.

She looked young enough to be able to remember her 21st birthday celebrations.

He was of the age when pensions become of practical rather than theoretical interest.

She had shoulder length brown hair that shone in the morning sunshine.

He didn't have enough hair remaining to fill a locket.

The pair, who weren't a couple in any sense of the word, but simply happened to be together at that moment, and who somehow managed to look lost but at the same time look as though they knew where they were, walked rather shyly up to where Mrs Caldicot, Mrs Roberts and Ruth were preparing to enter the café. Mrs Caldicot had paused for a moment and was writing down a list of the type of cakes the trio had decided the café should stock.

'We're sorry to bother you,' said the girl, not sure which of the three to address and so directing her enquiry to the three of them in turn, as though she were addressing a small audience. 'But we're looking for the new owner of the pier.'

'That would be Mr Livingstone,' said Mrs Caldicot. 'But I might be able to help you.'

'We used to work here,' explained the girl. 'On the pier,' she added, in case this might be necessary. 'And we wondered if you would still be needing us.'

When the girl spoke, every sentence finished as though it had a question mark at the end. It could have been an annoying habit but it wasn't. It gave her an innocence, a charm, a naivety, a shyness and a sense of genuine curiosity.

'What do you do?' asked Mrs Caldicot.

'My name is Miss Emerald Pettifer and I'm the Fat Lady,' said the girl. 'I used to be the Bearded Lady but I had electrolysis to get rid of the beard.' She paused, blushing lightly. 'I found it very embarrassing to have a beard. People used to make remarks.'

'I hope you don't mind my asking,' said Mrs Caldicot, rather hesitantly, 'but it seems relevant so I have to ask, would you please tell us how much you weigh?'

Miss Pettifer hesitated. 'Ten stone six pounds at the moment,' she said at last. 'That's 146 pounds,' she explained.

'Isn't that a little, er, on the light side for a Fat Lady?'

'I've been on a sort of involuntary diet. The pier has been shut and I didn't have a job. Not having a job made me depressed and besides, not earning any money meant that I couldn't afford the amount of food I needed to eat to keep up my weight.' She paused and made an attempt to brighten her voice. 'I could soon put the weight back on again.'

'Won't being so light make your work a little tricky?'

'I could wear lots of jumpers and things and I don't think anyone would really notice,' said Miss Pettifer. 'I'm quite plump in the face.' She puffed out her cheeks but this simply made her look as though she were blowing up a non-existent balloon. 'And I'm quite cuddly in the usual cuddly areas.'

'Wouldn't the customers expect you to be wearing just a bathing costume?'

'Oh no. I don't think so. Not these days. It would be considered very inappropriate. Sexist and fattist I think they'd call it. I think it would be all right if I just sat there looking plump; well a bit on the fat side really I suppose.'

'When you were the Fat Lady, you just sat there?'

'Yes, in a little booth. I did find it quite boring so I used to knit or read a magazine.'

'But is there still a market for fat ladies on piers?' asked Mrs Caldicot. 'Even if you put on quite a lot of weight there would probably be a lot of the customers looking fatter than yourself.'

'I suppose so,' agreed Miss Pettifer, rather sadly.

‘Did a lot of people pay to come and look at you?’ asked Mrs Roberts.

‘Not many,’ admitted Miss Pettifer with disarming honesty. ‘A few came when it was raining. I had a booth half way down the pier, next to the Fortune Teller booth. We both used to do quite well when it rained because there wasn’t anywhere else to shelter in the middle section of the pier.’

‘I don’t think we can just rely on bad weather,’ said Mrs Caldicot.

‘No,’ said Miss Pettifer. ‘I suppose not.’

‘Isn’t there anything else you can do?’ asked Mrs Roberts kindly.

‘Not really. I’ve never really tried anything else. I’ve always been a Fat Lady – except for a couple of years when I was the Bearded Lady.’

‘Maybe you could sit in the booth and be the Thin Lady,’ suggested Ruth who was such a kindly soul that she could not bear the thought of ‘letting anyone go to seek fresh opportunities’ as the saying goes. ‘We could repaint the sign on the outside of the booth.’

‘I don’t think I’m thin enough for that,’ said Miss Pettifer.

‘Well, let’s think about it,’ said Mrs Caldicot. ‘Why don’t you come and have a cup of tea with us?’ She turned and suddenly realised that the tall, thin man was still standing there. He was so thin that he was almost invisible. ‘I’m so sorry,’ she apologised. ‘I didn’t mean to ignore you…’

‘Oh that’s all right,’ said the tall, thin man. He seemed quite jolly, not all upset at having been forgotten. ‘People often don’t notice that I’m there.’

‘Are you with Miss Pettifer?’

‘No, not really. We just came together when we saw that the pier was open again. I live in a flat across the road and I telephoned Miss Pettifer when I saw the gates were unlocked.’

‘What did you do on the pier?’

‘I’m a silhouettist,’ said the tall, thin man with undisguised pride. ‘My name is Hyacinth Rowbottham and I’ve been a silhouettist all my life. My father was a silhouettist as was his father before him. I used to work on the West Pier in Brighton until it fell into the sea. I then wandered around the country until I ended up at the Penmouth pier. Mr Livingstone, the former pier owner was a keen supporter of my art. I did several silhouettes for him. Did you say that the current owner was a Mr Livingstone?’

'That's right. The current owner is the nephew of the owner you knew.'

'Ah,' said Mr Rowbottham with a nod and a smile.

'Excuse me for asking, and for being so ignorant,' said Ruth, 'but what exactly is a silhouettist?'

With a quite dramatic flourish, Mr Rowbottham pulled a pair of scissors out of one inside pocket and a sheet of black cartridge paper out of another. He then proceeded to snip away at the piece of black paper until he had produced a profile of Ruth that was quite uncannily accurate. When he had finished he handed the silhouette to her and put the scissors back into his jacket pocket.

'That's amazing!' said Ruth, genuinely astonished. She gazed at the silhouette of herself which she had been given. 'How on earth do you manage to do that?'

'It's an art,' said the man, with some pride. 'It is a disappearing art but an art nevertheless. Silhouettists used to be very popular in Victorian times but the widespread availability of the camera has rather taken away for the need for my work.'

'This is terrific!' said Ruth. 'I shall keep this for ever.' She immediately took a photograph of the silhouette with her mobile phone so that she could send a picture to Jean-Jacques and to her best friend Denise.

'Let's all go and have a cup of tea,' said Mrs Caldicot, who didn't really know why but who was beginning to feel very optimistic about the future. The others followed her into the café. Mrs Caldicot went up to the counter, gave their order and spoke to Dorothy for a few moments.

'So,' said Mrs Caldicot to Miss Pettifer and Mr Rowbottham when they were all settled at a table. 'We all live here, in the rooms up above, but we don't have any money, apart from our rather measly pensions, so we've got to make the pier earn our living for us. You haven't met everyone but there are 14 of us, plus Mr Pickering and his granddaughter Dorothy, whom I am sure you both know. However, even with 14 of us working we can't do everything by ourselves. So, would you two like to carry on working on the pier?'

Mr Rowbottham looked across at Miss Pettifer who looked back at him but didn't say anything. 'Well, I for one would be delighted,' he said. 'My previous arrangement was very simple. I worked on the pier and paid over half of my takings to Mr Livingstone, the older Mr Livingstone that is. In return I was the exclusive silhouettist on the pier.'

'And you were happy with that arrangement?'

'Oh very happy. On dry days I just wandered up and down the pier. If things were quiet I'd just do a silhouette of someone passing and get people interested that way. On wet days I worked in the foyer of the theatre. I'm never going to get rich but I made enough to live on and my overheads are pretty low – just a pair of scissors and a supply of black paper.'

Miss Pettifer looked at Mrs Caldicot and then at Mrs Roberts and Ruth. 'I realise that it's going to take me ages to put on enough weight to be a Fat Lady again,' she said, rather sadly. 'And to be honest I'm not entirely sure that I want to be a Fat Lady anymore. Being pointed out and sniggered at all day long can be a little dispiriting.'

'I can imagine,' said Mrs Caldicot. 'To be honest I don't think any of us would want you to be the Fat Lady anymore.'

'Do you think there might be something I can do?' asked Miss Pettifer, without much hope or confidence. 'I don't have any skills. All I know is how to be fat and that's not really a job requiring a great deal of skill.'

'Dorothy is going to carry on running the café for us,' said Mrs Caldicot. 'And although she's very young, I have asked her to be the manager. But we want to expand the café business and Dorothy can't do everything herself. I just spoke to her and she'd be very happy to have you working here as the waitress if that's something you'd be happy to consider.'

Mrs Caldicot didn't think she had ever seen anyone quite so pleased.

'Do you mean it?'

'Of course! Dorothy would be in charge. But you know her, don't you?'

'Oh yes, we get on well. I've known her since she first came here.'

With impeccable timing, Dorothy arrived at the table carrying a tray upon which there were six cups and saucers, two large teapots and a jug of hot water. 'Would you like some cake?' she asked. 'I hope you don't mind but when I knew we were opening properly I popped out to the supermarket and bought a box of little fancy cakes and a chocolate cake.'

'Oh yes, please!' said Mrs Roberts. 'You're an absolute angel.' Mrs Roberts loved nearly all sorts of cake, with caraway seed cake being the one possible exception.

'I'm going to be your waitress!' Miss Pettifer told Dorothy. She pushed back her chair and stood. 'So can I help you?'

'That's marvellous!' said Dorothy, clearly delighted. 'I've got the milk and the sugar ready on another tray but we need some cake and biscuits putting out on a plate.'

And so the pier now had a silhouettist and although the pier no longer had a Fat Lady the café had a waitress.

'It seems as though the Fat Lady booth is going to be empty,' said Mrs Caldicot to Mr Rowbottham. 'Would you prefer to work in one of the booths? You can wander up and down whenever you like, of course. But if the weather is bad you will have somewhere dry to work. And we can repaint the sign on the booth so that people know you're on the pier.'

It was now Mr Rowbottham's turn to look thrilled and it was clearly Mrs Caldicot's day to make people happy. 'Could I perhaps put some examples of my work in a glass case? And attach the case to the outer wall of the booth?'

'Of course you can!' said Mrs Caldicot.

'That would be marvellous,' said Rowbottham, who was perilously close to tears. 'My father used to have a booth on the West Pier.' He paused and wiped his eyes with a knuckle. 'A booth of my own!' he murmured.

Dorothy and Miss Pettifer then arrived back at the table. Dorothy was carrying a tray containing the milk and sugar and Miss Pettifer had a plateful of biscuits and little cakes, tastefully arranged and looking most attractive. There were also several slices of the chocolate cake on the plate.

Mrs Caldicot was delighted.

They had cake and biscuits and the café now had staff.

Chapter Fifteen

After dinner that evening (they were back to eating cod and chips after the excitement and adventure of experimenting with chips and cod) Mrs Caldicot, the gang of refugees from the Twilight Years Rest Home and Mr Pickering and his daughter Dorothy sat in the pier's café and discussed their future.

Miss Pettifer, the erstwhile fat lady and Mr Rowbottham, the accomplished silhouettist had both gone home walking on air.

It was still only 8.30 pm, rather earlier than Mr Livingstone and Mr Hewitt had planned to close the pier, but the gates were nevertheless locked and padlocked.

'I've got a list of things we need to discuss,' said Mrs Caldicot. 'But first would you all tell us how each of you got on today?' She turned to the Merivales. 'How did you two get on?'

'There were no great problems,' said Mrs Merivale. 'We replaced a dozen dead light bulbs and Mr Merivale put new washers on three taps. The rooms upstairs need decorating but they'll do for the time being.'

'They'll have to,' said Mrs Caldicot. 'Our main priority is to get the pier up and running – and to start bringing in some money. We've paid the last big bill from the council but I've no doubt they'll be sending us another tax bill before long. And there will be electricity bills to pay too.'

'Do you want us to take over the café and do the cooking?' asked Mrs Merivale.

This was a problem which had worried Mrs Caldicot for much of the day. The Merivales had been the housekeepers at the Twilight Years Rest Home and they had always bought the food and cooked the meals. Out of the corner of her eye, Mrs Caldicot could see that Dorothy was alarmed by Mrs Merivale's rather tactless enquiry.

'No, I don't think so,' said Mrs Caldicot immediately. 'We need you and Mr Merivale to look after our meals and to do all the housekeeping in our living quarters upstairs. There is an excellent kitchen attached to the ballroom and in future I think that we should keep the downstairs café for the pier's customers and we should eat our own meals upstairs in a section of the ballroom which we will turn into our dining room.'

Mrs Caldicot had rather hoped that this very practical solution would keep everyone happy. And, indeed, that was exactly what it seemed to do. Dorothy, who clearly enjoyed looking after the café, and who now had a waitress to help her, was obviously relieved. And the Merivales were delighted to remain in charge of providing sustenance for all their friends.

'How did you get on?' Mrs Caldicot asked Mr Williams, Mr Twist and Mr Roxdale.

'Not badly, not badly at all,' replied Mr Williams, answering on behalf of them all. 'We managed to sort out all the furniture and made sure that all the unpacked suitcases were in the correct rooms. We put all the kitchen stuff that we brought with us into the kitchen next to the ballroom.'

'And how did you ladies get on with sorting out the stock cupboards,' asked Mrs Caldicot, knowing that Miss Nightingale, Mrs Peterborough and Mrs Torridge had spent the day sorting through the cupboards in the stock room at the back of the shop and upstairs next to the ballroom.

'Oh we had a whale of a time!' said Mrs Peterborough.

'A marvellous time!' said Miss Nightingale.

'We made a list,' said Mrs Torridge.

There was then a short delay while the three of them looked for the stock list they'd made. In the end, Mrs Torridge found the list underneath the hat she was wearing. It was a sweet little hat made of navy blue felt and adorned with two artificial love birds and a large spray of what looked like gladioli. 'Silly me!' she said when she eventually found the list. 'I put it there for safekeeping.' She giggled. 'I always put valuable things under my hat and yet I still forget what I've done with them. Silly me, eh?' She giggled again.

'I remember where the list is now,' said Mrs Peterborough, who hadn't yet realised that Mrs Torridge had found her piece of paper. 'It's under your hat. You asked us to remind you that you'd put it under your hat so I wrote a message to myself on the back of my hand.' She held up her hand showed where she had written 'Mrs T's Hat' in red ink.

'Thank you,' said Mrs Torridge, who knew better than to get into a discussion with Mrs Peterborough.

'There were lots of boxes of liquorice allsorts,' said Mrs Peterborough. 'I brought one with me. I tried one of the little blue ones. They're my favourites.'

'Are they out of date?' asked Mrs Caldicot.

'I'm not sure,' replied Mrs Peterborough. 'There's no best before date on the box.'

'Does the box have anything printed on it?'

'Just the price. It says 2/11. That's two shillings and eleven pence isn't it? I remember shillings and pence. I understood shillings and pennies. They were proper money.'

'So the box was made before decimalisation,' said Mrs Caldicot, rather shocked. 'Golly. That almost makes them antiques. When did our currency change to decimals?'

'It was the 15th February 1971,' said Mr Twist.

'I think we'd better throw the liquorice allsorts away,' said Mrs Caldicot. 'What else did you find in the way of sweets?'

'We found a lot of Turkish Delight,' said Miss Nightingale.

'Sixteen large crates of it,' said Mrs Peterborough. 'And each box contains dozens and dozens of boxes of it. And they are large boxes, too! Those nice, little wooden boxes.'

Mrs Caldicot's heart began to beat faster. She loved Turkish Delight. 'Ooo!' she heard herself saying. 'I do like Turkish Delight.'

'Mr Twist reckons that's enough for each of us to have a whole crateful,' said Miss Nightingale.

'The crates were so big and heavy that we could hardly lift them,' said Mrs Torridge. 'And the good news is that they are all still in date.'

'But the bad news is that we have to sell them or eat them up quite quickly,' said Mrs Peterborough very earnestly. 'They all go out of date in another eight weeks.'

'I wouldn't have thought Turkish Delight would go out of date,' said Mrs Caldicot. 'It's mostly sugar so it ought to keep for years. I don't suppose we can sell it if it is out of date but I'm pretty sure it will be perfectly safe to eat.'

'I never understand that,' said Ruth. 'How can it be that a bar of chocolate that is perfectly safe to eat one day suddenly becomes dangerous at midnight?'

'I think they put a little radio receiver in each chocolate bar,' said Mr Roxdale. 'The receiver is probably hidden somewhere in the wrapper. At midnight on the allotted date a highly paid man in an office somewhere presses a button and sends a message to all the chocolate bars which are due to expire that day. The receiver then releases bugs or mould spores or something and the chocolate suddenly becomes inedible.'

'Crumbs!' said Ruth. 'You'd never know would you?'

'It's all done by the bureaucrats to increase waste and to force us to buy more stuff,' explained Mr Roxdale. 'They do it to give the sweet industry a boost.'

'Where did you hear that' asked Mrs Roberts.

'Dunno where I heard it,' said Mr Roxdale. 'I think it was in the *Daily Mirror*. But, anyway, it sounds true so it must be.'

'I know what you could do,' said Ruth. 'You could take the wrapper off the chocolate bar and put it in the rubbish, then when the message is sent to the little receiver it won't be able to make the chocolate go bad!'

'Don't you believe him, dear,' Mrs Roberts said to Ruth. 'I think he made that up.'

'No, I didn't. I read it somewhere,' said Mr Roxdale. 'If it wasn't in the *Daily Mirror* it might have been in the *Daily Mail*.' He stopped for a moment, clearly thinking. 'Or maybe I heard it on the radio.'

'Well, the next time I buy a bar of chocolate I'm going to remove the wrapper straight away,' said Ruth. 'Just in case the man in the office makes a mistake and presses his button too soon.'

'I think they do something similar with clothes,' said Mr Roxdale. 'They put moth eggs into a little capsule and then when you've had a jumper or a sweater for a year or so the capsule dissolves and the eggs are released into the wool.'

'Oh, that's just plain silly!' said Mrs Roberts. But she no longer sounded quite so sceptical. 'Where did you hear that one?'

'I probably did read that in the *Daily Mail*,' said Mr Roxdale. 'They have some good stuff in there. Or maybe it was the *National*

Enquirer. I sometimes buy that so that I can keep up with what's going on in the world.'

'Well, all that is as maybe,' said Mrs Caldicot who was now not at all sure what to believe but who was quite taken with the thought of all that Turkish Delight waiting to be enjoyed. 'Perhaps we should bring the boxes out before we forget all about them,' she suggested. 'We should share it all out. We'll never be able to sell that much Turkish Delight in the next few weeks so we might as well eat some of them ourselves.'

'I heard that Turkish Delight is very good for you,' said Mr Roxdale. 'It's full of stuff like iridium and strontium.'

'Did you read that in the *Daily Mail* too?' said Mrs Roberts.

'Might have been,' said Mr Roxdale, frowning in thought. 'Maybe it was in the paper that was wrapped round my chips last night.' He shrugged. 'I don't know where I read it but I just sort of know this stuff. It must be true if you read it in a newspaper.'

'He knows all sorts of strange things,' confirmed Mr Livingstone. 'It's a gift.'

'Some people can ride a bicycle without holding on, some people can swim under water, I just absorb useful information,' said Mr Roxdale. 'It's a skill I've acquired since I got older and it seems to be a natural thing.'

'Mr Hewitt and I did some financial projections,' said Mr Livingstone, changing the subject. He was excited about the work they'd done together. He pulled his scruffy piece of paper out of his pocket. 'We worked out that we should make around £28,000,000 profit this year. That's between £1,500,000 and £2,000,000 each.' He paused, clearly awaiting cheers of delight. Instead, there was silence. It is difficult to cheer, or to say anything, when your mouth has fallen open in shock.

'May I ask how on earth you got those figures?' asked Mr Twist, the accountant and former tax inspector. He tried not to sound as surprised as he sounded.

'Ah, it was all damned clever stuff,' said Mr Livingstone. 'We made an estimate of the number of people expected to come onto the pier each day, worked out what we thought they'd spend and then multiplied the total by the number of days in a year.'

'We didn't include February 29th, because that only comes round once every four years, and we didn't include anything for the sale of sou'westers and plastic macs,' said Mr Hewitt.

'That sounds very impressive,' said Mrs Caldicot who couldn't think of anything else to say. She glanced across at Ruth and saw that although the teenager deputy housekeeper had her eyes closed, her lips were moving. Mrs Caldicot, who knew Ruth well, guessed that the teenager was working out how she would spend her million pound windfall. She thought about saying something to Ruth about not taking Mr Livingstone's projections too seriously but stopped herself. After all, she thought, we're all entitled to have wonderful dreams when we're 18-years-old.

'So how many people a day did you reckon would come onto the pier?' asked Mr Twist.

Mr Livingstone consulted his piece of paper. 'We estimated that 8,400 people a day would visit the pier.'

'What did you base that on?' asked Mr Twist.

'It was just an estimate,' said Mr Livingstone defensively. 'It might turn out to be less than that.'

'But it could just as easily turn out to be more!' Mr Hewitt pointed out, his sudden optimism undimmed. 'It could be much, much more than that.'

'How much money did you estimate we would make each day?' asked Mrs Caldicot.

'£80,000,' replied Mr Livingstone, after consulting his slip of paper.

'That's nearly £10 per visitor isn't it?'

'Yes! That's it. That's what we thought. And we didn't even count any income from the theatre.'

'Or the sou'westers,' added Mr Hewitt. 'That'll be jam on the cake.'

'Was that the gross income or the profit?'

'Oh, that was our profit. We allowed a bit for the cost of buying the things we sell.'

'How much is a bit?' asked Mr Twist.

'Our estimated gross income was £84,000 so we knocked off £4,000 for the cost of buying the stuff we sold.'

'Though rides on the little train wouldn't cost anything,' said Mr Hewitt.

'That's right. So the profit figure might be a bit higher.'

'I think your figures might be a teeny weeny bit optimistic,' said Mrs Caldicot, who didn't want to be a wet blanket but who didn't want the rest of the gang getting too excited and then being terribly disappointed when they weren't all millionaires within a year. She turned to Mr Twist who was, as usual, in charge of the accounts. 'How much did we take today?'

Mr Twist pulled a notebook out of his pocket and opened it. 'We took £3.25 today,' he announced. 'That was comprised of two items purchased in the shop: a notebook and a pen. The notebook was sold for £2.00 and the pen for £1.25.' He held up the notebook he was holding. 'I had this notebook before we got here,' he added.

'I bought the pen and the notebook,' said Mrs Caldicot. She held up the notebook and the pen she was holding. 'I bought these from the shop.'

'So we were just £83,996.75 down on our projected income for the day,' said Mr Williams.

'Well, actually, it's not quite that good,' said Mr Twist. 'Because we are assuming that today's income of £3.25 was entirely profit whereas, of course, the notebook and the pen which we sold had to be taken out of stock.'

'I don't think we should be too downhearted,' said Mr Livingstone. 'There are bound to be good days and not such good days.'

'We sold some train tickets!' said Mrs Peterborough. 'I nearly forgot about those.'

'How much did that come to?' asked Mrs Caldicot.

'Oh we didn't charge for them,' said Mrs Peterborough. 'We were too busy sorting out the sweets.' She looked around in the silence which followed this admission. 'Sorry,' she whispered.

'If we make approximately £168,000 profit tomorrow then we'll be back on target!' said Mr Williams, exhibiting an air of optimism previously only displayed by Mr Livingstone and Mr Hewitt.

'Absolutely!' agreed Mr Hewitt. 'As Mr Livingstone said, there are going to be good days and bad days. That's business for you, isn't it? All we need is a nice coach party of rich tourists and we'll be back on target.'

'They'll have to be very rich,' muttered Mr Twist who was an unwilling adherent of Mrs Caldicot's brand of mild scepticism.

'Oh, and I forgot! We found a lot of rock,' said Miss Nightingale suddenly.

'Oh yes, thirty six boxes of rock,' said Mrs Torridge, examining her list. 'We forgot about that, didn't we? There didn't seem to be a sell by date on the rock but we think there might be a small problem with it.'

'Oh dear,' said Mrs Caldicot, who was still worrying about what Mr Roxdale had said about Turkish Delight. She wondered whether the ingredients he had mentioned meant that Turkish Delight was good for you or bad for you. 'What's the problem?' she asked.

'How do most people spell 'present'?' asked Mrs Torridge.

'As in 'A Present from Penmouth'?'

'Exactly, as in 'A Present from Penmouth'.'

'Well, I'd spell it p-r-e-s-e-n-t,' said Mrs Caldicot, rather nervously. 'But I could be wrong. I was never terribly good at spelling.' She decided she didn't care about the Turkish Delight ingredients. If you listened to the experts you'd never eat anything because you could always find someone to say that something was dangerous.

'That's definitely how I'd spell it,' agreed Mr Williams.

And with the exception of a few dissenters it was generally agreed that Mrs Caldicot's suggestion was pretty well the accepted spelling.

'Well, that's not what it says on our rock,' said Mrs Torridge. She took a stick of rock out of her handbag and handed it to Mrs Caldicot.

'It says 'A P-r-e-s-c-e-n-c-e from Penmouth', said Mrs Caldicot, reading the stick of rock.

'Well at least they spelt the name of the place properly,' said Mr Twist with a hollow laugh.

'How much of this rock is there?'

'A lot,' said Miss Nightingale.

'A very lot,' said Mrs Peterborough.

'At least one cupboard full,' said Mrs Torridge.

'I remember them ordering that,' said Mr Pickering. 'It was that Simpkins, him who used to be the Pier Master and who is now running a car park for the council. He ordered a new supply of rock and spelt the word 'Present' wrong on the form they sent. It wasn't the fault of the people who made the rock. They just did what they were told. We spotted it when it came in but it was too late to do anything about it.'

'It seems a pity to throw it all away,' said Mrs Roberts. 'There must be hundreds of pounds worth of rock if there is a whole cupboard full of it.'

'There was £7,000 worth of it,' said Mr Pickering. 'That's a lot of rock. There's more than one cupboard full of it. That Mr Simpkins made me cram it into cupboards all over the place. He wanted to throw it all into the sea but I told him we couldn't do that because it would take years to dissolve.'

They all sat in silence for a while wondering what they could do with £7,000 worth of misspelt rock.

'We could sell it as special rock,' said Mrs Caldicot, breaking the silence at last.

Everyone looked at her.

'We use the word 'presence' in funny ways,' she said. She was thinking aloud but she felt there was a germ of an idea struggling to get out. 'We say that 'we make our presence felt' and that we are aware of a 'presence' in a room. So why don't we sell the rock as being very, very special rock. If you take a stick of our rock home with you will be taking a 'presence' from Penmouth; a memory from the town where you enjoyed your holiday.'

There was silence for a while as people tried to understand what Mrs Caldicot was saying. Some people got there quicker than others. Some people never got there but were happy about the suggestion that they could sell the rock and that instead of being utterly useless it had now become a very special sort of rock.

'We could charge more for special rock!' said Mr Twist, excitedly. 'It's a unique type of rock so it should have a special price. People would pay a premium to have a stick of this rock! And when they ate it then they would have the presence within them.'

'Do you know what he's talking about?' Mr Livingstone asked Mr Hewitt in a whisper.

'Not got the foggiest notion,' admitted Mr Hewitt. 'But I think Mrs Caldicot and Mr Twist just turned £7,000 of rubbish into something profitable.'

'Brilliant!' said Mr Livingstone, whispering back with enthusiasm. 'And I don't think people took us seriously when we talked about us all becoming millionaires!'

'They didn't have the vision we have,' said Mr Hewitt.

Mr Livingstone nodded his agreement. 'Not everyone has our young, vibrant outlook on life,' he said.

'You're right there, Mr Livingstone,' said Mr Hewitt. 'I don't want to start feeling old before my time.'

'Very good attitude, if I may say so,' said Mr Livingstone. 'I don't mind growing old, it's one of life's little inevitabilities, but I do think it's a mistake to grow up.'

'Terrible mistake,' said Mr Hewitt. He pulled a face and shuddered.

Mrs Caldicot, who had overheard this conversation, smiled to herself. Mr Livingstone's next major birthday milestone would be his 80th and Mr Hewitt had celebrated his 90th birthday a year or two earlier.

She couldn't help remembering when she'd first met them at the Twilight Years Rest Home. They had both been heavily drugged with tranquillisers and sleeping tablets and had spent their days asleep or sitting on their beds. The transformation, since they'd abandoned their pills, had been startling. She now realised, for the first time, that maybe the word 'old' doesn't measure how far you are from the start but how far you are from the end. And that if you accepted that definition, rather than the one more customarily accepted, then Mr Livingstone and Mr Hewitt, and the rest of the gang, were still in the prime of their lives.

'Now, what else was there?' asked Mrs Caldicot, putting those unhappy memories away in a deep, dark place. 'Can anyone think of anything else?'

'If you think that we need a pier photographer then I would be happy to volunteer my services,' said Mr Williams. 'If people wanted their picture taken I could snap them at the beginning of the pier and then give them the finished photo when they left. I'd just need someone to help with the developing and printing while I stay on the pier and take the pictures.'

‘Oh yes!’ said Mrs Roberts, excitedly. ‘I think that’s a marvellous idea. I always used to love having my picture taken on holiday. I’ve got a lovely snap of me and Mr Roberts in my keepsake box.’

‘I think that’s brilliant!’ agreed Ruth. ‘Everyone has a camera on their phone these days but I think they’d still love to have a proper photo to take home.’

‘Are you sure you wouldn’t mind doing that?’ said Mrs Caldicot to Mr Williams. She knew that Mr Williams had once been an immensely successful photographer, whose pictures had been shown in galleries in London and Paris.

‘I’m definitely sure!’ said Mr Williams. ‘It’ll be fun.’

‘Well, that will be marvellous,’ said Mrs Caldicot. She looked down her list of things to do. ‘The final thing we need to talk about,’ she said ‘is that we need an official Fortune Teller. There is a Fortune Teller’s booth available and we can’t have a pier without a Fortune Teller. I am told by Mr Pickering that the booth was one of the most successful items on the pier. Sadly, I gather that the previous incumbent had to leave unexpectedly.’

‘Unforeseen circumstances?’ asked Mr Williams.

‘I fear so,’ agreed Mrs Caldicot. ‘The result is that we urgently need to find a replacement.’

‘Where on earth do you find a Fortune Teller?’ asked Mr Twist. ‘We can hardly telephone the local Labour Exchange and ask them to send along a selection of suitable candidates.’

‘We could put an advert in *Exchange and Mart*,’ suggested Mr Livingstone.

‘But what are we going to offer in exchange?’ asked Mr Hewitt.

‘Good point,’ agreed Mr Livingstone. ‘I don’t have the foggiest. How much misspelt rock could you swap for a Fortune Teller?’

‘Where did the last Fortune Teller come from?’ Mrs Caldicot asked Mr Pickering.

‘She just sort of turned up one day,’ replied Mr Pickering. He looked at his grand-daughter. ‘Do you know where she came from?’

‘I’ve no idea,’ said Dorothy, blushing at being asked to contribute to the conversation. ‘I think I remember her saying that she used to work in a travelling fair.’

‘Maybe one will just turn up!’ said Mr Livingstone.

‘There must be one somewhere who, even as we speak, realises that there is a vacant post for a Fortune Teller on Penmouth Pier!’ said Mr Hewitt.

‘I don’t think we can rely entirely on serendipity!’ said Mrs Caldicot, whose vocabulary had expanded since she’d been married to Jenkins.

‘What’s that?’ whispered Ruth to Mrs Roberts.

‘I don’t know dear,’ Mrs Roberts whispered back. ‘Maybe it’s some sort of agency for Fortune Tellers.’

‘Like if you want to hire an actor you go to Equity and if you want a musician you go to the Musicians’ Union?’

‘That’s it. But for Fortune Tellers you go to Serendipity.’

‘Ah,’ whispered Ruth. ‘Thank you.’

And so another harmless myth was born.

‘Do you need a licence to be a Fortune Teller?’ asked Mrs Torridge.

‘I don’t think so,’ said Mrs Caldicot with a frown. ‘Not yet anyway.’

‘Do you have to have training?’

‘I wouldn’t have thought you needed that either.’

‘Certificates?’

‘Not yet, though I’m sure they’ll bring in training, examinations and certificates when they get round to it.’

‘If no one else is doing it then we could run courses for Fortune Tellers,’ said Mr Livingstone.

‘There wouldn’t be any point in having an examination for Fortune Tellers, would there?’ said Mr Williams. He looked around at the puzzled faces. ‘If you were any good then you’d know all the questions beforehand wouldn’t you?’

‘If you don’t need training or a certificate or a licence then I think I’d like to try it,’ said Mrs Torridge.

Everyone looked at her.

‘I’ve got a nice silk scarf to go over my head,’ she said. ‘And I’ve got some big, gold hoop earrings. They’re a bit tarnished but they’ll polish up nicely. All I need is an upturned goldfish bowl and I’ll be ready to go.’

‘Do you really think you could do it?’ asked Mrs Caldicot, a little surprised.

'Oh yes,' said Mrs Torridge, with surprising confidence. 'And it would save us bringing in someone from outside.'

'It certainly would,' agreed Mrs Caldicot.

'Do you think it would count as my being something in show business?'

'Definitely,' said Mrs Caldicot.

'I once nearly joined an amateur dramatics society when I was younger,' said Mrs Torridge. 'It was organised by our vicar but there was a disagreement about what play we should put on. The man who was going to direct the play wanted to put on 'Macbeth' and the society's leading actor preferred 'Charley's Aunt'. They came to blows and the vicar was so shocked that he disbanded the society. I didn't care two hoots what they put on but I was very disappointed. I rather fancied the boy who was the Assistant Stage Manager. His name was Reggie and he was also one of the leading lights in the choir. He was in all those church things. I seem to remember he was a Brown Owl in the Boy Scout troop. Did they have Brown Owls in the Boy Scouts? Or was that in the Brownies?'

'I'm not sure,' said Mrs Caldicot. 'But I think that being a Fortune Teller would definitely count as a branch of show business.'

'Oh, that's good. Then I would very much like to give it a try.'

'Splendid,' said Mrs Caldicot.

'I wouldn't tell people anything nasty,' said Mrs Torridge firmly.

'You mean stuff like 'You will meet a tall, dark, handsome stranger but he'll be the undertaker',' said Mr Livingstone.

'Or you'll meet a tall, dark, handsome stranger who will be the judge sentencing you to ten years hard labour,' suggested Mr Hewitt.

'Stop it you two!' said Mrs Caldicot.

'I'll only tell people nice things,' said Mrs Torridge. 'I want to make them happy. Folk who visit a Fortune Teller on a pier are probably on holiday. They want to hear nice things. They'll hear enough bad things when they're at home – gas bills, noisy neighbours, leaky taps. They come away to the seaside to escape from real life for a while.'

'I think that's a splendid sentiment,' said Mrs Caldicot.

'Will you do my fortune for me?' Ruth asked Mrs Torridge.

'Of course I will, dear. You can be one of my first clients.'

'But you won't tell any of the others what you see, will you?' whispered Ruth.

'Of course not, dear. The Fortune Teller's booth is like the confession box or the doctor's consulting room in the olden days.'

'Thank you,' smiled Ruth.

'Perhaps I should do an audition?' suggested Mrs Torridge. 'Like actors and actresses do for the films? I could sit in the booth and one or two of you could come in and cross my palm with silver and I could tell you your fortunes.'

'I think you should tell people to cross your palm with a fiver,' suggested Mr Twist. 'Tell them you want paper money. If you tell them you want silver some mean bugger will put a five penny piece in your palm.'

'Well, if they try that then they darned well won't get a nice, jolly fortune,' said Mrs Torridge sharply.

Chapter Sixteen

Half an hour later, just as they were all preparing to retire for the night, there was a tapping on the door to the café.

Mrs Merivale had not yet got their new upstairs kitchen sorted out so they were still sitting in the café where there were teapots, milk and other essential ingredients for a comfortable evening. It was so dark outside that no one could see anything.

'Do you think it could be a ghost?' asked Miss Nightingale. 'If it is then I hope it's a friendly one.'

'Maybe it's burglars,' said Mrs Peterborough.

'Do you think they've come to steal our rock?' asked Mr Hewitt.

'I don't think burglars usually knock,' said Mrs Caldicot.

'Maybe the burglars round here are very polite,' suggested Mr Livingstone.

'Oh dear, maybe it's a spirit who's angry because I said I wanted to be a Fortune Teller,' said Mrs Torridge.

'Don't be silly,' said Mr Twist comfortingly.

There was another tap on the door.

Almost everyone froze.

The solitary unfrozen exception was 16-year-old Dorothy who had been sitting next to Ruth. The two girls were rapidly becoming good friends. Dorothy loved to hear Ruth's stories about her adventures with Mrs Caldicot in Paris and Ruth loved to hear about Dorothy's adventures on the Penmouth Pier.

Dorothy, who clearly had a good idea who was there, jumped up and went to the door. 'It's Errol!' she cried, peering through the glass and letting him in.

'Errol!' cried everyone with delight born of relief, that he was neither a ghost nor the world's politest burglar.

Errol, surprised and rather warmed by the unexpected and rather effusive response to his arrival, blushed deep red. He was carrying two carrier bags.

'I've brought you some more potatoes,' he said, putting the bags down on the floor. 'I'm sorry it's so late but I had to climb up twice because I could only carry one bag at a time.'

'You climbed up onto the pier from the beach?' asked Mrs Merivale.

Errol nodded.

'You're soaked!' said Dorothy, suddenly realising that the young man's trousers were drenched.

'The tide was coming in when I got here,' said Errol. 'It's a high tide tonight so it will come right up to the top of the beach.

Dorothy explained to him that they were no longer under siege, that the bailiffs had gone away and that Errol could now visit the pier during the daytime.

'You can come in through the main entrance,' she told him.

Errol, who was a boy with a strong sense of the romantic, and who had rather enjoyed imagining himself to be an improved version of Spiderman, with perhaps a touch of the Scarlet Pimpernel thrown in, just for the devil of it, was slightly disappointed by this news.

'Go and get the boy a spare pair of trousers,' said Mrs Merivale to her husband. 'I'll put the kettle on and make him a nice hot cup of tea.'

'Put extra sugar in it for him,' said Mr Merivale. 'Sugar is good for shock. He'll be in shock if he's been climbing up piers in the dark.' He said this as though he had some experience of the sort of shock likely to be engendered by climbing up piers in the dark. He then hurried off to fetch a pair of his trousers.

Mrs Merivale tottered quickly into the café kitchen and filled the kettle.

'I'll have one if you're boiling the kettle,' shouted Mr Roxdale.

And then everyone wanted a cup of tea. And Mrs Roberts and Ruth rushed off to help Mrs Merivale find all the necessary cups and jugs and pots and so on.

And Mrs Caldicot decided that it would be nice to have a box of Turkish Delight with her cup of tea.

So Miss Nightingale, who knew where to find the Turkish Delight, asked Mr Livingstone and Mr Hewitt to go with her to protect her from wandering ghosts, ghouls and cowering, timorous beasties and to help her carry the stuff back to the cafe.

'There won't be any ghosts out there,' insisted Mr Livingstone. 'The gates are closed and padlocked.'

'Ghosts can probably pick locks,' pointed out Mr Hewitt. 'Or slip through the gates.'

And so they accompanied Miss Nightingale.

Fifteen minutes later, Errol was wearing a pair of dry trousers and sipping an over-sugared cup of tea. He had a box of Turkish Delight on his lap. Everyone else also had a cup of tea (though not all containing quite so much sugar) and their own box of Turkish Delight.

'So,' said Mrs Caldicot, speaking to Errol, when she'd finished chewing her third cube of Turkish Delight. 'Did you manage to find out anything about the council's plans?'

Errol nodded and swallowed a chunk of Turkish Delight. 'I was doing some photocopying and I heard some of the bosses talking in the corridor,' he said. 'They were laughing about how they'd get control of the pier and talking about how much money they were going to make.'

'There you are,' said Mr Livingstone. 'They've worked out that they can make £28,000,000 a year from the pier! I knew my sums were right!' He pulled out the piece of paper on which he had scribbled his sums and waved it about as though it were all the proof anyone needed.

'Maybe they've got another plan,' said Mrs Caldicot gently. 'Let Errol tell us what he heard.' She turned to the boy. 'Who did you hear talking?'

'There were three of them. One was Mr Chapman who is something very important, one was Ms Schmidt who is the head of the ES Department. I don't know who the third person was. I couldn't see her and I didn't know her voice. She might have been from outside.'

'Did they see you?'

'They may have. But they wouldn't take any notice of me. I'm just a sort of office boy so I'm just sort of invisible to them. Even if they see me they always sort of talk over me as though I weren't there at all.'

'But the two people you saw and recognised were senior members of staff?' asked Mrs Caldicot.

'Yes, definitely. Mr Chapman must be terribly important because he shouts at people quite a lot and no one seems to like him except Miss Havering. He's quite ancient. I think he must be at least 40.'

'Who is Miss Havering?'

'That's his secretary. I caught her sitting on his knee once. They were very embarrassed. Mr Chapman said they were testing his chair to see if it would take the weight of two people but I don't think he was telling the truth because why would she jump off and go all red if that was all they were doing?'

'And Ms Schmidt?'

'She's quite old too. I would say she's probably at least 25 or so. She may be older.'

Mrs Caldicot smiled to herself. She could remember that when she was his age she too thought that 25 was quite old. Mind you, when she was seven she thought that 16 was quite old. Everything is relative. Now that she was old enough to regard grey hair, wrinkles and wonky joints as mere badges of honour, earned in the fight of life, she thought that 60 was very young, 70 just approaching middle age and 80 merely heading for maturity.

'What's the ES Department?' asked Mr Twist.

'That's the Department of Equality, Diversity and Sensitivity,' explained Errol.

'What on earth is that?'

'It's the department in charge of equality, diversity and sensitivity,' said Errol who seemed as puzzled as everyone else. 'They took over the Environmental and Social Governance Department and the Regulatory Compliance and Regulatory Oversight Department about six months ago. It's now just about the biggest department in the building. They take up the whole of the third floor and even the planning department only takes up half a floor. They've even succeeded in pushing the Health and Safety Executive Officers into a Portacabin in a corner of the car park. The Health and Safety department used to have all the power but I heard the Chief Executive say that these days they're a spent force. He said that these days everything is all about Equality and Sensitivity and that Health and Safety are yesterday's issues.'

'How on earth can you remember all those names?' asked Mrs Roberts, who was terribly impressed.

'I had to distribute all the new notepaper, visiting cards and identity tags,' explained Errol, rather prosaically but entirely sensibly. 'Ms Schmidt, who is in charge, had 100,000 visiting cards printed for herself.'

'Did you hear any more of what Mr Chapman and Ms Schmidt were talking about?' asked Mrs Caldicot.

'Oh yes,' said Errol. 'They told the third person…'

'…the one you couldn't see?'

'That's right, the one I couldn't see. They told her that they hadn't expected the new owner to turn up at all. They said they thought that having the bailiffs outside would frighten him off and that the offer to buy the pier would be accepted.'

'They damned well didn't frighten me off!' said Mr Livingstone indignantly. 'When you've dropped bombs on Germany you don't get frightened off by a bunch of ninnies working for the council.'

'Did you drop bombs on Germany?' asked Errol, clearly awed.

'I certainly did,' said Mr Livingstone proudly. 'Lots of them.'

'Golly! From an aeroplane?'

'From a Lancaster Bomber. The best flying machine ever invented or flown.'

'Were you a pilot?'

'No. I was in charge of dropping the bombs.'

'Wow. That's even better. Did you see them explode?'

'Definitely!'

'Would you like more tea?' Mrs Merrivale asked Errol. She had stood up and was holding a huge teapot, poised above his cup. She thought that Errol was perhaps a little young to hear about Mr Livingstone's bomb dropping exploits.

Errol shook his head. 'No thank you.' Dorothy took his cup off him and put it onto a nearby table. She was very proud of him. To her he seemed to be a cross between James Bond and the tiny actor with the too perfect hair who played the spy in the Mission Impossible movies.

'I'll have another cup, if there's one going,' said Mr Hewitt. 'I'll have to get up three times in the night but who cares. I'll probably have to get up three times anyway.'

Mrs Merivale filled his cup, and several other cups.

'I think someone from the council is coming round to see you this week,' Errol said to Mrs Caldicot. 'They said something about people coming round tomorrow or the day after. They laughed about that. They said that whoever was coming would frighten the daylights out of you all.' Errol said this as though he knew it could not possibly be true.

'Huh!' said Mr Livingstone who was clearly angered by this. 'They won't get in. We'll lock the gates and throw bits of Penmouth Pier rock at them. This is no time for hurling coconut mushrooms or blancmange. Bring out the rock!'

'No, we can't do that,' said Mrs Caldicot. 'For one thing we won't have any customers if we keep the gates shut. And for another we need to know what the council is planning.'

'Quite right!' agreed Mr Livingstone immediately. 'Thank heavens you're in charge, Mrs Caldicot.'

'I wonder what they are planning,' muttered Mrs Caldicot, more to herself than to anyone else.

'Do you think they could be planning to try to close us down for some legal reason?' asked Mrs Roberts.

'It seems very likely,' said Mrs Caldicot. 'But it's certainly good to know that they're planning something. It's always better to be prepared.'

'I did hear something else,' said Errol.

Everyone looked at him, waiting.

'I think they're planning to turn the theatre at the end of the pier into some sort of conference centre and the rooms above the café and the shop into offices. And they want to put windmills and solar panels on Rock Stone and along the pier itself.'

'We already sell windmills!' said Mrs Peterborough.

'I don't think Errol is referring to those pretty, little plastic ones,' said Mrs Caldicot.

'No, they were talking about those big electricity generating windmills. I think they want to make the conference centre and the offices all environmentally friendly and carbon neutral. I heard the woman I couldn't see say that they could get special grants if they put up solar panels and windmills.'

Mrs Caldicot, who was now beginning to understand just what they were up against, turned to the young James Bond. 'Thank you, Errol,' she said. 'You've been very helpful. You're marvellous.'

Errol seemed pleased with Mrs Caldicot's remark but he also looked embarrassed, as though there were something else he ought to say.

'What is it?' asked Mrs Caldicot, who guessed that Errol had a confession he wanted to make.

'I'm glad it's been useful, me being able to find out stuff,' said Errol. 'But I've been thinking of giving up my job for some time. I really hate working for the council. And because I don't have any qualifications I've got no chance of being promoted. I did apply for a better job when one became vacant but they told me they wouldn't even consider me. So I really want to leave.'

'Well, that's good,' said Mrs Caldicot. 'It's good that you've made up your mind.'

'But I won't be able to help you with any more information,' said Errol.

'Oh, don't worry about that!' said Mrs Caldicot immediately.

'Do you know anything about photography?' asked Mr Williams suddenly and quite unexpectedly.

Errol looked across at him.

'I'm the new pier photographer,' said Mr Williams. 'I need someone bright and keen to help with the printing and developing of the pictures. Is that something you'd be interested in learning about?'

Errol's eyes lit up. 'A job here? On the pier?'

'Yes,' agreed Mr Williams. 'It's not at all glamorous. You'd be stuck inside most of the time. You'd come out and pick up films from me, take them into the dark room, when we've got one set up, and then develop and print the pictures.'

'Oh crumbs yes!' said Errol.

'You'd be working here on the pier!' said Dorothy, who was clearly delighted that Errol would be working on the pier. 'That's fantastic!'

'What do I have to do to get the job?' asked Errol.

'Want it,' replied Mr Williams. 'That's all. If you want it then the job is yours.'

And so Mr Williams found the assistant he needed. And Errol found the job he wanted.

Chapter Seventeen

The original intention had been for three of the gang members to be the guinea pigs for Mrs Torridge's trial run as the pier's new 'Fortune Teller'.

But it soon became clear that this wasn't such a good idea.

'I'll feel rather embarrassed,' confessed Mrs Torridge. 'These are all my friends. They know me and I know them. There needs to be a little bit of mystery about the whole thing.'

Mrs Caldicot agreed with her. 'How about we do it this way,' she suggested. 'Instead of you seeing real people whom you know, I come into the booth and pretend to be a couple of different people. I will explain who I am pretending to be and you then tell me my fortune.'

Mrs Torridge agreed that this was a much better plan.

And so, as soon as Mrs Torridge was settled in her booth, with her headscarf wrapped neatly around her hair, a pair of gold earrings dangling from her ears and, in the absence of either a crystal ball or an upturned goldfish bowl, a glass mixing bowl in front of her as a temporary substitute, Mrs Caldicot entered the booth and sat down.

'What's your name, dear?' asked Mrs Torridge.

'My name is Sandra,' said Mrs Caldicot. 'I'm 24-years-old and I'm here on holiday with my boyfriend. I work in a pharmacy and my boyfriend is a van driver.'

'Do you have a big family?'

'Just me and my mum. My dad died a few years ago. My mum lives by herself and I live with my boyfriend.'

'That's nice, dear. How long are you here for?'

'Just a week.'

'How long have you and your boyfriend been together?'

'Fourteen and a half months.'

'Do you want to get married?'

'Yes. It would be very nice. I think it would suggest real commitment.'

'Does he think the same way?'

'I don't know. I was hoping you could tell me that.'

Mrs Torridge bent her head and studied the mixing bowl very intently. 'I'm afraid I don't think he does,' she said. There was a long pause as she continued to study the mixing bowl. 'But don't you worry, my dear. I can see you with six husbands – one at a time, of course. All of them far more handsome and far richer than the man you're with at the moment.' She paused and thought for a while. 'One of them will be a man whose name begins with a J. Do you know anyone whose name begins with a J? A John, a Jim, a Jack? Something like that. Or maybe his surname begins with a letter J. It could be Jones, perhaps.'

Mrs Caldicot started laughing. She couldn't help herself. 'I'm sorry!' she said. 'That was wonderful. What made you think of all that?'

'I felt sorry for the girl,' said Mrs Torridge. 'She knows exactly how long she's been with this fellow and she clearly cares for him a good deal. But either he doesn't know that she wants to get married or he does know and he doesn't want to marry her. Either way, he sounds like a rat and a loser and I don't think the relationship is going to last, so I thought I'd give her some silly hopes and something mad to tell her friends in the pharmacy where she works. She's bound to know someone whose name begins with the letter J. Everyone does.'

'How do you know she had friends at the pharmacy?'

'Because she said she didn't have many relatives but she had a dozen postcards and a dozen sticks of rock in her bag,' said Mrs Torridge. 'The cards and the rock were clearly for her pals. And they were probably for pals she'd met at work.'

'That was marvellous,' said Mrs Caldicot, who was enormously impressed with the extent of Mrs Torridge's imagination.

Mrs Torridge fiddled with her scarf but looked very pleased with herself. 'Try me with another!' she said. 'Be someone else.'

'OK,' said Mrs Caldicot, thinking hard.

'Who are you now?' asked Mrs Torridge, impatiently.

'My name is Bunty and I'm a 45-year-old housewife. I have two children, one aged 26 and one aged 23. They both live at home and show no signs of leaving. I do all the cooking and washing for both of them. They both have good jobs and they give me £20 a week each towards the housekeeping.'

'What sexes are the children, Bunty?'

'Oh, er, the 26-year-old is a girl and the 23-year-old is a boy. My husband is a plasterer. He's the only man I've ever been with. We got married when I was 19. He is 47-years-old. He spends most evenings in the pub, his Saturdays watching football and his Sundays cleaning his car. We hardly ever go out. I watch a lot of television. I want to know what my future holds.'

Mrs Torridge peered into the glass mixing bowl and turned it round, explaining that she just wanted to get a better look at Bunty's future.

'I see you out shopping, doing some routine chores,' she began, 'and you have just dodged one of those nasty Greenpeace chuggers. As you hurry along out of his reach you don't look where you are going and you bump into a tall man in Arab clothing.' Mrs Torridge turned her mixing bowl round once more, and peered into it before continuing. 'You drop one of the bags you are carrying and the contents spill onto the pavement. The tall man stoops to help you pick up the things you've dropped. When everything is back in the bag, the man invites you to have a coffee with him. You go along and you talk together. He is very well-spoken, clearly an educated man. He is obviously attracted to you. He is witty, charming and attentive.'

'Good heavens!' said Mrs Caldicot. 'I think I'll be feeling a little flushed by now.' She took out an imaginary handkerchief and mopped imaginary perspiration from her very real brow.

'You talk to the tall Arab for the best part of an hour and a half and you suddenly realise that you're going to be late getting home to empty the washing machine and to prepare dinner. The Arab asks if he can take you home in his limousine. And so you agree. On the way home, he asks if you really have to go back to your humdrum life. He points out that you are little more than a slave to these people, someone to sort their laundry and put meals on the table.'

Mrs Torridge paused and turned the mixing bowl again.

'What happens?' asked Mrs Caldicot. 'What do I do? Do I go home and empty the washing machine or do I drive off into the sunset with the tall man in the limousine?'

‘The picture is fading,’ said Mrs Torridge. ‘I think maybe you need to cross my palm with another five pound note!’

‘You can’t do that!’ cried Mrs Caldicot.

‘Can’t I? Do you not think I should?’

‘No, no, you mustn’t do that!’ said Mrs Caldicot laughing. ‘It’s a clever idea but you really can’t do that. Now tell me, what happens to Bunty?’

‘The tall man asks you to go back to his country with him. He wants you to be one of his most important wives. He promises that you will sit on soft cushions all day and eat unlimited quantities of Turkish Delight. Anything you want will be yours. Box sets of all the best Netflix programmes will be yours at the flick of a finger. You will never again wear anything bought from Walmart, one of the pound shops or a charity shop. You will wear dresses designed by the world’s most famous couturiers. Your lingerie will be silk, designed for your body and hand-made by skilled seamstresses. You will have a box of jewels so heavy that two men are needed to carry it. You will have no chores to do – no cooking, no washing, no ironing, no shopping. You will be his plaything, his toy, there only to entertain him when he returns from his long camel rides in the desert. You’ll be one of his top ten wives and your only responsibility will be to please him. When he goes abroad to stay in smart hotels in wonderful and exotic places such as New York, St Moritz, Paris or Manchester then he will take you with him…’

‘Manchester?’ said Mrs Caldicot. ‘I’m sorry to interrupt but did you say Manchester?’

‘Oh yes,’ said Mrs Torridge. ‘I read in a magazine that Manchester is now considered very fashionable, very exotic. They’ve got an indoor shopping centre, a new library and a marvellous one way traffic system.’

‘OK,’ said Mrs Caldicot with a nod. ‘OK. So Manchester is on the list of wonderful and exotic places that he will take me to if I agree to be one of his most important wives. But do I accept his invitation? Do I leave my parasitic, useless family and allow this tall, handsome man to take me away from the tedious drudgery of my pointless daily life?’

Mrs Torridge turned the mixing bowl yet again and studied it intently. ‘I can’t see that far ahead,’ she said, sadly. ‘I can only take you so far into the future. You have to make a choice. I can see you struggling with your dilemma. Do you stay with your husband and your two children or do you go? Only you can decide. It is your life and future and you must make up your own mind. All I can do is give you an advance peek into the future.'

'Phew! Bunty is now going to have to go and buy herself an ice cream,' said Mrs Caldicot with a broad grin. She stood up.

'Do I pass?' asked Mrs Torridge anxiously? Do you think I make an acceptable Fortune Teller?'

'You are an absolutely marvellous Fortune Teller!' said Mrs Caldicot.

She could not believe just how much Mrs Torridge and the others had changed since they'd stopped their tranquillisers and sleeping tablets.

And she couldn't help wondering just how many people who appeared to have dementia could be cured of their symptoms merely by taking them off their damned tablets.

'You are brilliant,' said Mrs Caldicot. 'But we have to get you something better than that glass mixing bowl to peer into! It's got measurement markings all up the side – a quarter of a pint, half a pint, three quarters of a pint and a pint.'

'Mr Merivale said he would find me something more suitable,' said Mrs Torridge. 'Do you remember that he used to work in the film industry? He and Mrs Merivale did the cooking for the film crews?'

'How could I forget?' asked Mrs Caldicot. 'Mr and Mrs Merivale were famous for their bacon sandwiches.'

'I remember all those big film stars coming to our garden party,' said Mrs Torridge. 'Michael Caine, Joan Collins, Peter O'Toole, Pierce Brosnan, Glenda Jackson, Judi Dench – they were all there.'

'And how could I possibly forget that?' laughed Mrs Caldicot. She'd always been a huge fan of Michael Caine.

'Well, I asked Mr Merivale to help me and he said he has a friend who is a props man who owed him a favour. He called his friend, using the telephone, and the props man said he had got a proper crystal ball which they had used in a film on which he'd worked. Mr Merivale asked him to send it to me and so he's put it in the post. It should be here tomorrow. The proper name for it is apparently an orbuculum so I think that's what I shall call it. My orbuculum!'

‘You’re going to be a huge success!’ said Mrs Caldicot, and she meant it.

‘It’s going to be great fun,’ said Mrs Torridge, who looked happier than Mrs Caldicot had ever seen her look. ‘And I can do it all sitting down, which is nice.’

Mrs Caldicot smiled at her.

‘I never knew there could be so much whoopee in life,’ said Mrs Torridge.

‘I don’t think any of us realised that either,’ said Mrs Caldicot, smiling at Mrs Torridge and wondering where on earth she’d learned such an unusual word.

‘Well, it’s clearly never too late to start having whoopee!’ said Mrs Torridge firmly. ‘And I’m going to have a good deal of it. As much as there is available.’

Chapter Eighteen

There were three people waiting for Mrs Caldicot when she left the Fortune Teller's booth.

'Oh dear!' said Mrs Caldicot. 'Has something terrible happened?'

'No, I don't think so,' said Mr Roxdale, who was the first in the queue. He thought for a moment. 'No, I don't think anything terrible has happened – not that I know of.' He looked at Mrs Roberts and Ruth who were standing patiently behind him. They shook their heads. 'But Mr Merivale and I have started painting the railings along the side of the pier and we think we will need some more tins of white paint.'

'I expect you will,' said Mrs Caldicot, who hadn't known about their plan to paint the railings but who thought it was a very good idea. 'Do you have any idea how much paint you'll need?'

'Well, we started off with two tins of white paint which Mr Pickering found in a cupboard,' said Mr Roxdale. 'And we've used one of those up completely.'

'How much railing did you manage to paint with that tin?'

'About seven feet,' said Mr Roxdale.

'Can you remember how long the pier is?'

'I asked Mr Livingstone and he says it's 2,195 foot long.'

'So if a gallon of paint is enough for seven feet of pier how many gallons will you need for 2,195 feet of pier?'

'It sounds like one of those sums they give you at school,' said Mr Roxdale.

'Let's pretend a gallon is enough for 10 foot of pier,' suggested Mrs Caldicot. 'That will make things a little easier.' She frowned for a moment. 'It seems an awful lot,' she said. 'But I make it to be 219 gallons. More or less.'

'That is a lot of paint,' agreed Mr Roxdale. 'But unfortunately, we'll need at least twice that much.'

'Why?'

'There are railings down both sides of the pier.'

'Oh dear. Yes, of course there are. So we need twice as much paint?'

'I'm afraid so.'

'That's, er, 438 gallons of paint.'

'Approximately,' agreed Mr Roxdale. 'But even that won't be enough.'

'Why on earth not?'

'Because the railings are going to need two coats of paint.'

'So that's nearly 1,000 gallons of paint?'

'I'm afraid so. And then when we've finished both sides for the second time we will probably have to start again.'

'It will be like painting the Forth Bridge?'

'Exactly! Just like painting the Forth Bridge,' said Mr Roxdale. 'Except, of course, that this is the Penmouth Pier.'

'Oh well, never mind,' said Mrs Caldicot. 'We must keep the pier looking smart. Maybe if you ring a local paint company they could deliver a few dozen cans of paint to keep you going.'

'And some brushes?'

'And some brushes,' agreed Mrs Caldicot.

Mr Roxdale, surprisingly happy for a man just starting out on a never-ending painting job, tottered off to report to Mr Merivale.

'Who's next?' asked Mrs Caldicot, looking first at Mrs Roberts and then at Ruth.

'You go first,' said Mrs Roberts to her assistant.

'Dorothy and I found a machine for making candyfloss!' said Ruth, the excitement bursting out of her. 'We need to order some syrup before we can find out if it works. Can we do that, do you think?'

'Does the machine look as if it might work?'

'Oh yes! Dorothy says it was working last year. Apparently candyfloss is very popular and the machine makes lots of money.'

'Then you should certainly buy some syrup and try it out!' said Mrs Caldicot who was beginning to realise that there was rather more to being a Pier Master than she had originally thought.

Ruth scampered off to set in motion the process of making the candyfloss machine work again.

'We could call our candyfloss 'artisan candyfloss',' suggested Mrs Caldicot to Mrs Roberts. 'That would give it a modern sort of image and attract those nice, young millennials who love spending their money. They seem to rather like the word 'artisan' though I really never quite know what they mean by it or why they are so taken with it.'

'I don't know what it means, either,' confessed Mrs Roberts. 'Do you think we could say that our rock was artisan rock?'

'Oh, I think so!' agreed Mrs Caldicot.

The two of them watched Ruth hurrying down the pier.

'Sometimes I think of Ruth as a young woman, almost ready for a husband, a washing machine, a toaster and a family, and sometimes I think of her as a young girl still enjoying dolls and likely to pull a skipping rope out of her pocket ,' said Mrs Roberts.

'She does look as though she's about to start skipping with delight,' said Mrs Caldicot.

The two of them watched, just in case Ruth actually did start to skip.

They were slightly disappointed when she didn't.

'I'm afraid I have a bit of bad news,' said Mrs Roberts. 'Do you remember speaking to someone from the local dramatic society?'

'Of course I do,' said Mrs Caldicot. 'They're going to put on 'The Pirates of Penzance'. And they're excited about doing it in our theatre. I'm looking forward to it. Do they want to fix up some dates for their rehearsals?'

'I'm afraid that if you want to see their production you'll have to go to their old theatre,' said Mrs Roberts. 'Someone rang today to say that they wouldn't be performing in our theatre after all.'

Mrs Caldicot, astonished, just stared at her friend. 'Did they say why?' she asked eventually.

'It was very strange,' said Mrs Roberts. 'I asked the woman who called why they wanted to cancel and she simply kept saying that they couldn't use our theatre after all.'

'Did she say 'couldn't' or 'wouldn't'?'

'She definitely said 'couldn't',' said Mrs Roberts. 'So I asked her why not and eventually she rather shamefacedly confessed that they had been told by the council that if they performed in our theatre then they would lose their grant. Apparently they receive an annual grant from the Arts Council and without the grant they wouldn't be able to continue.'

'Really? That's why?'

'The woman sounded very embarrassed and she said she thought they owed it to us to explain why they wouldn't be using our theatre but that they hoped we would understand. She said that the bit of the Arts Council that hands out the grants always checks with local councils first to make sure that a recipient is approved. So the council can easily stop the grant simply by withdrawing their approval.'

'But why on earth would they do that?' asked Mrs Caldicot more to herself than to Mrs Roberts.

'It sounds as if the council doesn't like us very much,' said Mrs Roberts. 'They want to stop us earning any money.'

'I hate to sound paranoid but it definitely sounds to me as if the council is trying to put us out of business,' said Mrs Caldicot. She thought for a moment. 'Do you remember what young Errol said about the council having plans for the pier?'

'I do.'

'Well maybe this is part of their plan. Maybe they just want us to fail so that they can buy the pier and turn it into a site for windmills, solar panels and businessmen holding conferences.'

'Golly!' said Mrs Roberts, bristling. 'The little beggars!'

Mrs Roberts could, when pushed, be almost as determined as Mrs Caldicot herself.

'Well, we'll see about that!' said Mrs Caldicot, looking at her friend.

'Oh, I forgot to ask,' said Mrs Roberts. 'How did Mrs Torridge's audition go?'

'She did brilliantly! Amazingly well. She's going to be a huge success – a wonderful Fortune Teller.'

'And with any luck we'll have Ruth's candyfloss machine turning syrup into money!' said Mrs Roberts, attempting to lighten the disappointment over the cancellation of The Pirates of Penzance.

'We'll fix up something for that theatre!' said Mrs Caldicot quietly and determinedly.

'I bet we will!' thought Mrs Roberts, smiling to herself. 'I bet we will!' she said out loud.

She had got to know Mrs Caldicot very well, and if it came to a showdown between Mrs Caldicot and the local council then her money was well and truly on Mrs Caldicot.

Mrs Caldicot, who had heard her, looked at Mrs Roberts and smiled.

Chapter Nineteen

By the second day of their residence on the pier, things seemed to be going tolerably well.

The pier was already beginning to look far more attractive and word had got around the town that the pier was once again open for business. Locals came to see exactly what was happening and holidaymakers came because going for a walk along the pier is what everyone likes to do when they're at the seaside to have a good time.

There was still the question of what to do with the theatre, of course, but the painting of the pier railings was continuing apace and Mrs Torridge's crystal ball had survived a journey through the postal system and had been installed, in pride of place, on the table in the Fortune Teller's booth. The candyfloss machine was up and running and, to the particular delight of Ruth, who was put in charge, was churning out vast quantities of 'artisan candyfloss'. Ruth was also in charge of the ice cream stand which had been cleaned up and stocked with all the necessary supplies.

Mr Rowbottham, the Pier's Traditional Silhouettist was constantly snipping away with his scissors and said that he had never been busier. He was delighted with his new booth and had already arranged to have samples of his art framed and fixed in a suitably eye-catching position.

The café was doing good business, with the two young members of staff producing seemingly endless cups of tea, toasted teacakes, buttered crumpets, sandwiches, Welsh rarebits, and the pier speciality, fish and chips.

The shop was up and running too, with Mrs Peterborough and Miss Nightingale in charge of selling postcards, fishing lines, paperback books, tickets for the little train, tickets for the deckchairs, bars of chocolate and the Penmouth Pier's speciality – sticks of peppermint rock with the words 'A Presence from Penmouth' running through each one in red.

The Pier Master was, of course, aware of all this activity and pleased with the way things were progressing.

If only Jenkins were with her, thought Mrs Caldicot, then her joy would be unconfined and her cup would be full to overflowing.

But, sadly, Jenkins was still in America, lecturing students. And somehow his absence increased her natural sense of wariness. When he was around she always felt safe, as though nothing too serious could go wrong.

She did not feel the untrammelled confidence of Mr Livingstone and Mr Hewitt as they stood at the entrance to the pier and counted in the customers.

Imbued with the sort of unnatural confidence that should, at their ages, have warned them that they were enjoying the calm before the storm, the two wise men of Penmouth Pier both felt that they and the pier had safely navigated the potholes which life had excavated in their path.

'The mirage appears to have water in it,' said Mr Livingstone, for once dipping a toe into the waters of poetic licence.

'True, true,' replied Mr Hewitt, determined not to be outdone. 'The beginnings of a wonderful rainbow can be seen forming behind the clouds.'

And just then, inevitably perhaps, a bunch of be-suited men and women from the council turned up.

There were seven of them: four women and three men.

In terms of ages, sizes and colour they were a pretty mixed bunch. This was no accident. Two were white, two were black, two were brown and one was oriental. Six were walking and one was in a wheelchair. All wore suits and had little pink and green ribbons pinned to their clothing, presumably to denote their solidarity with some cause or other. Several of them also wore badges upon which were printed slogans promising allegiance to Greenpeace, Friends of the Earth and an organisation called Save Our Glaciers.

They came onto the pier as though they were an invading force; a conquering army come to take charge of newly vanquished peasantry. The six who were travelling by foot all strutted. The one in the wheelchair merely scowled, as though upset that she too was denied the chance to strut. They all looked to be in their twenties or early thirties.

Mr Livingstone, looking at the invaders, thought that the pier was perhaps being visited by the annual outing of the entire readership of *The Guardian* newspaper. He found this a depressing prospect.

But if his poetic mood had not been shattered he would, perhaps, have realised that dandelions had appeared on the pristine lawn of Penmouth Pier.

The woman who was clearly in charge was short, wore a black trouser suit and black, low-heeled shoes, and had her hair cut very short, in the style once favoured by squaddies and football hooligans and now popular among lesbians and militant feminists. She wore no jewellery and no make-up. She introduced herself to Mr Livingstone and Mr Hewitt as Ms Schmidt.

As Errol had rightly surmised, when he had described her, she was probably in her mid-twenties, though she looked considerably younger, and she had the sort of arrogant, lopsided smirk that is so common among young people who are blessed with a diploma in something obscure, too much power and an absurdly exaggerated view of their own importance.

After examining her carefully, Mr Livingstone decided that she actually looked about 16 and that if she had turned up in a pub and asked for half a shandy, any wise barman (or barmaid) would have insisted on seeing her birth certificate before he (or she) had consented to serve her anything quite that strong.

'I need to see the owner of the pier immediately,' said Ms Schmidt, addressing Mr Hewitt. 'Fetch him to me.'

She spoke in what was clearly the voice she used when addressing older people, halfwits and serfs; somehow managing to turn up her volume control while at the same time increasing the bass levels.

Mr Hewitt, who was not easily bullied and too old to be intimidated by anyone not carrying a rocket launcher, looked at her and frowned.

'Who are you?' he asked, surprisingly politely.

'I am Ms Schmidt.'

She repeated this piece of information as though she expected the announcement to be greeted with expressions of awe and a good deal of bowing and scraping.

'Yes, you said that bit. But who are you?'

‘Do you work here?’ demanded Ms Schmidt, irritated. ‘I need to see your team leader,’ she added, without waiting for a reply to the first question.

‘I’m not in a team and I don’t have a leader.’

Ms Schmidt, clearly frustrated by Mr Hewitt, looked around and turned her attention to Mr Livingstone. She was beginning to redden with irritation and frustration. She looked around from time to time at the group standing just behind her and was clearly embarrassed to have them witness her failure to intimidate. ‘What is your name? Are you employed here?’

‘They’ve got tickets for the train in the shop,’ said Mr Livingstone. ‘And I have to tell you that they are very good value. A nice ride up and down the pier will calm you down.’

‘I don’t want to ride up the pier and I don’t need to calm down!’ snapped Ms Schmidt. ‘I’m a very busy person. And so are my colleagues. We don’t have time for joy rides.’

‘There are a lot of you,’ observed Mr Livingstone, ‘so if you ask nicely they’ll probably give you a group discount.’

Ms Schmidt stared at Mr Livingstone. ‘Are you insane? Demented? Or just old and stupid?’

‘I don’t think so; not that I know of. But you can never really tell, can you? These things are all relative, don’t you think?’

‘Who are you?’ asked Mr Hewitt once more. ‘Why are you here if you don’t want to have time for joy?’

Ms Schmidt turned her attention back to him. ‘I am the Directrice General of the Department of Equality, Diversity and Sensitivity for Penmouth and the surrounding district!’ She made this announcement clearly expecting Mr Hewitt to be awestruck.

‘Is someone in your position allowed to be disparaging about a person because of their age?’ asked Mr Hewitt.

‘My department is only concerned with gender and race discrimination,’ said Ms Schmidt. ‘There are no important, regulatory guidelines relating to age.’

‘Well that’s disgraceful,’ said Mr Hewitt. ‘There’s far too much ageism about these days.’

‘I decide what is an ism and what isn’t an ism,’ said Ms Schmidt firmly. ‘My Department is fully integrated and compliant with all the relevant legislation.’

'So now we know who you are. But who are all these people?' asked Mr Hewitt, waving a hand in the direction of Ms Schmidt's entourage.

'Mr Zygimantas and Ms Gostautas are my senior assistants,' said Ms Schmidt. 'Mr Zygimantas has a degree in Social Deviance from the University of Dresden and Ms Gostautas has a degree in Graduate Studies from the University of Dusseldorf. Our role is to ensure that community diversity is strictly monitored in all locally centred employment situations. And I have been empowered by our Deputy Chief Executive and our senior Planning Department Manager to make sure that the Penmouth Pier is satisfying the requirements of the relevant legislation.'

As she said, all this this she pointed to two of the invaders, to illustrate that one was Mr Zygimantas and one was Ms Gostautas. Neither Mr Livingstone nor Mr Hewitt had the foggiest idea which of the two was the genuine male article and which wasn't.

One of the pair was a very short, tubby, white person of about 40. He (or possibly she) wore a three piece suit in a shade of brown which would have enabled him to spill dark chocolate down his lapels and waistcoat without leaving any discernible evidence of the mishap. His (or possibly her) hair appeared to have been cut by the same ruthless barber who had mangled Ms Schmidt's scalp. The suit he (or possibly she) wore had been made for a smaller man (or possibly woman) or, at least, a man (or possibly woman) who had been smaller when the suit had been purchased. Underneath the suit, he (or possibly she) wore a bright yellow shirt and an orange and purple tie. He (or possibly she) had a plastic identification tag slung around his neck. The tag contained what appeared to be a starkly lit police photograph of someone wanted for murder, rape, arson and serious crimes against the State. Apart from the fact that he (or possibly she) did not have metallic teeth filed to a point, he (or possibly she) looked like one of the actors (or possibly actresses) who plays second assistant baddie in a James Bond movie.

The other man (or possibly woman) appeared to be younger, possibly no more than 20 or so, and had probably not been Made in England. He (or possibly she) wore heavy boots, which seemed strangely out of place, and a cheap, ill-fitting suit in a shiny, electric-blue material which was neither silk nor satin but appeared to be made out of something man-made and indestructible. The suit trousers were four or five inches too short, suggesting either that the suit had been bought off the peg and made for a much shorter man (or woman), or had been made by a tailor with a wicked sense of humour. He (or possibly she) wore a black shirt and a white tie and the combination made him (or possibly her) look like a cheap gangster in an early Martin Scorsese movie. His (or possibly her) head was completely shaved though anyone who examined his (or possibly her) scalp could clearly see the extent of the premature bald patch which had almost certainly triggered the enthusiastic use of a razor and which suggested that he was a he (and probably not a she). There were plenty of small cuts and scabs and a few curious tufts of hair, all of which suggested that he (or possibly she) did the shaving himself (or possibly herself), used a blunt razor and without access to a suitable mirror. He (or possibly she) also had a plastic identification tag slung around his (or possibly her) neck. The tag contained a photograph of a younger version of the man (or woman) who looked as if he were wanted for murder, rape, arson and serious crimes against the State.

Only if you examined the two photographs very closely would it have been possible to see that each man had his own photograph entombed in plastic around his neck.

Both men glared at Mr Livingstone and Mr Hewitt. Mr Hewitt thought they looked as if they ought to have worn collars and been on leashes.

'Congratulations,' said Mr Hewitt. 'That's probably very nice for you all. Do you have any English employees in your Department.'

'Of course not!,' said Ms Schmidt, who appeared to have been last in the queue when God was handing out senses of humour and not in the room at all on the day when irony was being distributed though, like most Germans, she would have probably laughed a good deal if she'd seen a fat man slip on a banana skin and land on his bottom. 'My department is thoroughly diverse and multinational. We do not employ English people, heterosexual people, white people or old people.'

Mr Livingstone sighed and turned to Mr Hewitt. 'You wouldn't think we'd won the War, would you?'

'You may think you won the War,' said Ms Schmidt, with what could only be described as a smirk, 'but we have definitely won the peace.'

‘Which part of Germany are you from?’ asked Mr Livingstone who didn’t much like Germans and couldn’t understand why successive British Governments kept apologising for having bombed so many German cities. It had, after all, been the Germans who had started the War and the Germans who had begun bombing cities and killing civilians. In Mr Livingstone’s eyes, the Royal Air Force had just ended up being better at everything, including bombing, than the Luftwaffe had been. British politicians always seemed to like apologising, thought Mr Livingstone. Bomber Command, of which he had been a proud small part, had been demonised after the War and even the Dam Busters were, in certain quarters, still regarded with more embarrassment than pride.

‘They have sown the wind and they shall reap the whirlwind,’ had been the crew’s favourite saying whenever Mr Livingstone had climbed into a Lancaster bomber and set off on another bombing raid.

‘I am from Hamburg,’ replied Ms Schmidt.

‘I know Hamburg quite well,’ said Mr Livingstone. ‘And I’ve been to Dresden and Dusseldorf. But only from the air.’

‘Why only from the air? Why are you not landing?’

‘We were bombing the shit out of them at the time,’ explained Mr Livingstone. ‘They were a lot flatter when we left than when we arrived and so dropping in for tea didn’t seem a particularly good idea.’

‘I don’t think you’re allowed to say that!’ murmured Mr Hewitt.

‘Oh dear, aren’t I? said Mr Livingstone. ‘Never mind, I’ll try not to say it again.’

Ms Schmidt scowled. Mr Zygimantas and Ms Gostautas did not seem to understand, which was perhaps fortunate.

‘What is the ‘shit out of them’ meaning?’ asked Mr Zygimantas, looking very fierce.

‘You really do have to stop saying stuff like that,’ whispered Mr Hewitt to his friend. ‘I think that one wants to take a bite out of your leg.’

Mr Livingstone raised a pair of elderly eyebrows.

‘That bit about bombing the shit out of them seems to have upset him,’ explained Mr Hewitt.

'Oh sorry,' murmured Mr Livingstone. He cleared his throat and tried again. 'We were bombing them at the time,' he said, turning to Mr Hewitt. 'Is that better, do you think? I left the word 'shit' out.'

Mr Hewitt just grinned at him and turned to Ms Schmidt. 'Who are all the other people with you?' he asked, indicating with a nod the remainder of Ms Schmidt's extensive entourage. It did sometimes occur to him that his very good friend Mr Livingstone could occasionally give the boundaries of tact a bit of a run for their money. On those occasions, he usually tried to deflect the conversation onto less troublesome ground. 'Or are they your bodyguards?'

'These are my Deputy Assistant Administrative Assistants,' replied Ms Schmidt very earnestly. 'They are here to observe and to take notes.'

The Assistants, none of whom seemed to understand precisely what was being said, did understand that they were being talked about and so they all nodded their heads slightly, reminding Mr Hewitt of those little dogs which were fashionable with a certain type of motorist a few years ago. The dogs, he remembered, would sit on the parcel shelf and nod their heads as the cars drove along. They would nod with exceptional enthusiasm whenever a pothole was encountered. He wondered what had happened to them all and if they had yet become valuable collectors' items.

'You remind me of Napoleon,' said Mr Livingstone to the short, tubby fellow (or possibly woman) in the brown suit. Mr Livingstone had never worried overmuch about upsetting people in authority and, occasionally to the alarm of his friends, appeared to have stopped worrying entirely about political correctness when he had passed his 75th birthday.

The man (or possibly woman) in the brown suit looked at him, frowned and seemed puzzled. 'Who is this Napoleon of which you are spoken?' he (or possibly she) demanded in a thick Eastern European accent.

Except that it was now clear that he was definitely a 'she', and Mr Hewitt thought it seemed not unreasonable to assume that they had at last identified Ms Gostautas.

'Napoleon Bonaparte. The French leader whom Wellington defeated at Waterloo,' explained Mr Livingstone. 'How many

Napoleons are there?' He sighed. 'The not-tonight Josephine fellow,' he added, in a final attempt to explain.

'Oh,' said the woman in the brown suit, trying to decide whether this was an insult or a compliment. She finally appeared to decide that it was a compliment for she thanked Mr Livingstone, though she did not smile as she did so.

'Just in size and shape,' said Mr Livingstone, clarifying his earlier remark. 'Short and rather tubby. And foreign, of course.'

'Very short, really,' said Mr Hewitt, amplifying his friend's judgement. 'Definitely on the approaching stout side of tubby. And certainly foreign.'

'Why do you all have your hair cut so short?' asked Mr Livingstone, turning to Ms Schmidt. 'Is it because someone told you it looks nice or is it because you all have nits?'

'Nits? What do you mean, 'nits'?' demanded Ms Schmidt.

'You know, the eggs you get with head lice. People used to shave their heads if they had lice. But you don't really need to do that these days. If someone told you that they do then they were wrong. You can buy shampoos and stuff to get rid of head lice.'

'I don't have nits or head lice!' shouted Ms Schmidt.

'That's good,' said Mr Livingstone. 'I'm very glad you managed to get rid of them. They can be very annoying and embarrassing in social situations. Still, it's nice that you don't have them now because it means you and your two pals can all let your hair grow.'

Ms Schmidt, who looked as though she were about to burst into tears, though of frustration and rage rather than sadness, sucked in enough air to inflate one of those balloons which carry four people in a wicker basket and then blew it all out again. She turned on her heels and marched away, closely followed by her companions. The click clack of shoes on the pier's wooden planking was accompanied the sound of the wheelchair's tyres and electric motor.

'I'm not entirely sure that went entirely as planned,' said Mr Hewitt.

'For us or for them?'

'Well, I think it went OK for us,' said Mr Hewitt. 'We exhibited our usual good humour and gentle, welcoming nature. But I'm not sure that it went entirely as planned for them.'

'I didn't much like them, myself,' admitted Mr Livingstone. 'They seemed in a hurry to me. I never trust people who are in too much of a hurry. No time to look at the world.'

'People in too much of a hurry never get anywhere,' said Mr Hewitt.

'If they had souls then they had souls without music,' said Mr Livingstone.

'They were all millennials, you see,' said Mr Hewitt. 'Millennials are a different breed. They're not like us. They're all hysterical and prissy and smug. They all remind me of the kids who were prefects when I was at school.'

'Millennials remind me of the worst sort of teenagers,' said Mr Livingstone. 'Not teenagers like Ruth, Dorothy and young Errol – they're good kids. But judgemental, narcissistic 14-year-olds who think they know everything and that their opinions are the only ones worth having.'

'They're all a bit self-righteous and self-obsessed,' said Mr Hewitt, warming to his theme. 'They think they're entitled to wealth, fame and respect without having to work for any of it.'

'Whingers too,' added Mr Livingstone. 'They're all professional victims – always looking for new ways to be offended.'

'They think they're liberal and open minded but they're more bigoted and prejudiced than Himmler and Goering.'

'And they hate us older folk.'

'Dunno why. They'll be old themselves one day.

'Not bright enough to have worked that out yet,' pointed out Mr Livingstone.

'I saw a piece in my paper the other day about when the internet thing stopped working for an hour or two. One of them was complaining that he was in a café and couldn't buy a cup of coffee because his phone wouldn't work.'

'What did his phone not working have to do with not being able to buy a coffee?' asked Mr Livingstone, puzzled.

'The millennials buy stuff with their phones. They don't use money anymore.'

'You're kidding!'

'No, really. It's true. And they don't drink proper coffee. They have it with loads of foam and something like nutmeg all over it.'

'Yes, I saw them doing that in the coffee shop at the railway station when we went up to see the solicitor. I think it's cinnamon they put on their coffee though I can't for the life of me imagine why.'

'I like a few cloves in my apple pie and apple sauce with a pork chop but why would you put cinnamon into coffee?'

'No idea. No idea at all.'

'But it's not nutmeg?'

'They may well put nutmeg in it as well. For all I know they probably put in a few drops of paint stripper and a handful of rabbit droppings. Doesn't make any sense at all to me.'

'Anyway, this chap who couldn't buy his cup of coffee with his phone became hysterical and said it was the end of the world. He said it was the apocalypse. The millennials were all sending each other little messages about it on their telephones.'

'They're all spoilt, that's the problem,' said Mr Livingstone. 'They were all brought up to think they are special.'

'I think it's the drinking water.'

'The drinking water?'

'I read that some doctor says our drinking water is full of hormones. It's made the fish go all odd and it's doing the same thing to youngsters. '

'Where do the hormones come from?' asked Mr Livingstone, puzzled.

'It's from all those drugs that people take – especially the contraceptive pill. Apparently the women pee out the hormones and then the sewage goes into the rivers, and the water companies take drinking water out of the rivers but they can't get the hormones out because they're dissolved.'

'Good God! I'm glad I don't drink water. I've never understood why people put it into whisky.'

'Probably doesn't matter to people our age. But these millennials have been brought up on it. And they're always told to drink more water. So they're full of hormones. It mixes them all up. Makes the women aggressive and turns the men into wimps.'

'That makes sense. A doctor said that?'

'Yes. And now the millennials all think they're special and entitled to everything they want.' Mr Hewitt paused for a moment. 'I wonder what that lot today wanted – that German woman and her millennial chums.'

'Dunno,' said Mr Livingstone. 'No idea. I heard the kraut in charge say they were looking for the owner.'

'I don't think you're allowed to call them krauts.'

'Really? Why not?'

'No idea. I think they regard it as offensive.'

'Oh, do they? Well, the kraut said they were looking for the owner.'

'Good luck with that,' said Mr Hewitt.

'I hope they're not going to be trouble,' said Mr Livingstone.

'I wouldn't think so.'

'The funny thing was that they all looked as if they wanted to be somewhere else.'

'You're right. I've met a lot of people in my life who always wanted to be somewhere else. It's a recipe for misery.'

'I have always wanted to be where I am and I've always thought that a blessing. During the War, I was even happy crammed inside a Lancaster bomber. But now that we're here this is where I want to be and to stay.'

'On Penmouth Pier?'

'On Penmouth Pier,' agreed Mr Livingstone. 'I feel as though I've come home.' He paused for a while. 'I hope that Schmidt woman isn't going to plunge a spanner into our garden of roses.'

'I wouldn't worry about it,' said Mr Hewitt, reassuringly. 'Mrs Caldicot will sort it all out.'

Mr Livingstone looked at him, smiled and nodded. 'She will, won't she?'

'She always does. Remarkable woman. She should be Prime Minister.'

The two old friends stood for a while, saying nothing, just looking around.

'You know,' said Mr Hewitt, 'when I was 20 I'd have settled for living to 70. It would have seemed like a decent lifespan at that point. But now it seems like no age at all. In my head I feel about 20. Maybe as much as 25 when I'm having a bad day. I'm a bit wobbly and I wouldn't go up a ladder. And if I kneel down it takes me a while to get up again. But I don't feel old, do you?'

‘Not at all. The list of foods I can’t eat goes up by the month. I wouldn’t eat a pickled gherkin if you paid me. And I’m glad Mrs Peterborough threw those pickled eggs at the bailiffs. If I had to run to catch a bus I’d wait for the next one. But inside I don’t feel more than about 18.’

‘Should we offer to help with painting the pier or shall we take a little ride on the train?’ asked Mr Livingstone.

‘Mr Merivale and Mr Roxdale seem to be getting on well with the painting. They both said they enjoyed it very much.’

‘So it would be a pity to interfere? It would spoil their fun?’

‘Definitely.’

‘We could help out in the shop for a while?’

‘Miss Nightingale and Mrs Peterborough seem to have that well in hand. I think we’d probably get in the way.’

‘It’s difficult to know where we’d be most useful. Maybe we ought to think about it before we go offering our services without a proper plan.’

‘Keep ourselves in reserve, as it were,’ agreed Mr Hewitt.

‘Ready for emergencies.’

‘Substitutes sitting on the bench, ready to leap into action whenever and wherever needed.’

‘Absolutely. Meanwhile shall I get a pair of train tickets?’

‘We don’t have to pay do we?’

‘Of course not. I’ll get us a stick of rock each, shall I?’

‘I’d rather have an ice cream.’

‘Two train tickets and two ice creams it is then,’ said Mr Livingstone heading for the shop.

‘Make sure they’re return tickets and bring two boxes of Turkish Delight for the journey back,’ called Mr Hewitt.

Chapter Twenty

While Mr Livingstone and Mr Hewitt had been entertaining Ms Schmidt, and her international band of colleagues from Penmouth Council's Department of Equality, Diversity and Sensitivity, Mrs Caldicot had been busy trying to work out how best to make use of the now apparently unwanted theatre on the accurately named Stone Rock at the end of the pier.

It was the theatre, she knew, which was one of the most notable parts of the pier and almost certain to be the most vital when it came to bringing in some money. Mrs Caldicot knew she had to find a way to make use of it if they were going to make the pier a commercial success.

And so Mrs Caldicot, together with Mrs Roberts and Ruth, the two permanent members of her ad hoc management committee, wandered down the pier to take a look at what was available in the theatre, and, as Mrs Caldicot put it, to 'brainstorm' in the hope that a suitable idea might appear.

The three of them had been in the theatre before. But they had only looked around in a vague sort of way; oohing and aahing as tourists 'doing 14 European countries in 11 days' might ooh and aah when visiting their fourth cathedral of the day. They hadn't really 'seen' anything.

But now that they had time to examine the theatre more carefully they found it enormously impressive.

'Wow!' said Ruth, who had never seen anything like it before. 'Does Mr Livingstone own all this? His very own theatre!'

'It would appear so,' said Mrs Caldicot. She too was terribly impressed by the beauty of the building and the way it had been decorated. The theatre had been built at a time when red velvet and gold paint were fashionable and when theatre designers had deemed it necessary to decorate every available square inch of space with masks of tragedy and comedy, with plaster cherubs and with bunches of grapes and other similar delights. The gold leaf had, admittedly, peeled off some of the plaster but the effect was still stunning. Mrs Caldicot and the other two members of the ad hoc committee were awestruck by the decorations in the auditorium.

Above them there were two levels of seating, the dress circle and the upper circle, and to the right and to the left there were several enormously impressive looking boxes wherein wealthier patrons could sit and stretch out a little while enjoying whatever show was on offer. The walls of the theatre were decorated with scores of photographs and posters in glass frames. There were pictures of singers, comedians and pop groups. There were posters for dramas, comedies and ballets. The Penmouth Pier theatre had, it seemed, played host to every conceivable form of entertainment.

'Crumbs!' said Ruth, examining the photographs. Most of the faces and names were unknown to her, since they had been famous before she was born, but occasionally she spotted a star she could identify.

'What on earth are we going to do with this place?' asked Mrs Caldicot, talking more to herself than to her two companions.

'It's marvellous!' murmured Mrs Roberts, gazing in astonishment at the decorations and rubbing her hand across the back of one of the velvet seats. The velvet was worn and a little faded but it felt wonderful. Mrs Roberts wondered how many people had sat there and been enthralled by what they'd seen on the stage. Attached to the seat in front there was a pair of opera glasses which could be released if you put sixpence into the slot. The mechanism which controlled the release of the glasses had never been changed to cope with decimal currency.

'It's a pity the local amateur dramatics group won't use the theatre,' said Mrs Caldicot. 'I wonder if they really know what they're missing.'

'They're damned silly!' said Mrs Roberts. 'If they're any good then I bet they could make far more money out of appearing here than they receive in grants. They could put on shows whenever they liked.'

'Maybe we could put on pop concerts,' suggested Ruth, who saw herself welcoming a string of famous singers and sitting with them while they sipped their lattes with cinnamon sprinkles.

'That's an idea,' agreed Mrs Caldicot, sounding wary. She didn't really think they were ready yet to become impresarios but she didn't want to dismiss Ruth's idea out of hand.

'I wonder if we would be able to cope with thousands of screaming girls?' asked Mrs Roberts.

'Do bands still have thousands of screaming fans?'

'Oh yes, I think so,' said Ruth.

'The carpet is wet here,' said Mrs Caldicot, who had wandered down one of the aisles and had found a damp patch. Mrs Roberts and Ruth joined her.

Mrs Roberts looked up. 'There's a hole in the ceiling,' she said.

'Oh dear,' said Mrs Caldicot looking up at a small piece of sky. The rest of the ceiling was covered in gold paint but there was definitely a blue patch of sky visible. Everywhere she looked there were things to do. And everything that needed doing meant more expenditure.

'It's only a small hole,' said Mrs Roberts, reassuringly.

The three of them walked down to the front of the auditorium and climbed up the wooden steps which led onto the stage. They then turned and looked back at the theatre; at the stalls, the dress circle, the upper circle and the boxes.

'I wonder how many people can fit in here,' said Mrs Caldicot.

'At least 1,500,' replied Mrs Roberts after looking around, counting the number of seats in a row, counting the number of rows and multiplying one by the other.

'We could organise lecture tours with famous people,' suggested Ruth.

'That's a very good idea!' agreed Mrs Caldicot, who liked that idea better than Ruth's suggestion that they arrange pop concerts.

'What sort of lecture tours?' asked Mrs Roberts. 'Do people pay to go to lectures these days?'

'I don't think people call them lectures anymore,' said Mrs Caldicot. 'But I've seen adverts for them. Politicians, writers and retired actors just sit on the stage and reminisce for an hour or so and then they answer questions from the audience. It's nothing new; Charles Dickens did a lot of it.'

'Oh,' said Mrs Roberts, who didn't seem terribly impressed with the idea.

Ruth wandered off to the left of the stage.

'We could organise our own variety shows,' suggested Mrs Roberts, who always liked variety shows especially when there was a good singer and a conjuring act.

'Oh, I don't think we could manage that,' said Mrs Caldicot. 'Not just yet. We'd have to do the bookings and arrange for all the artistes and the band. We might be able to do it one day. But not just yet.'

They stood for a few minutes, both wondering what on earth they could do with such a wonderful theatre when Mrs Caldicot looked up and spotted another small hole in the roof. There was another small, damp stain on the floorboards of the stage.

They were still thinking when Ruth came running back onto the stage. 'There's all sorts of exciting stuff back there,' she said excitedly. 'There are costumes and props and I found a huge chest filled with old posters.'

She led Mrs Caldicot and Mrs Roberts back stage and took them to a small props and costumes room that was absolutely crammed with bits and pieces left over from old theatrical performances. There were suits of armour, spears, swords and golden crowns. There were even a dozen tickling sticks which were, presumably, left over from a Ken Dodd performance.

'Look!' said Ruth, opening the lid of a huge, very solid looking cabin trunk.

Inside the trunk there were hundreds of old posters, all pristine and laid flat. They were all perfectly preserved. 'There are posters for performances by all sorts of famous people!' she said. 'People from before my time but people even I have heard of!' She lifted up corners of the posters and started reading off names: Judy Garland, Bill Haley, Eddie Cochran, Bob Dylan, Gene Vincent, Frankie Vaughan, Tommy Cooper, the Glen Miller Band, the Rolling Stones and all sorts of other people. Oh, look! There is even a pile of posters for the Beatles!'

'Did the Beatles perform here?' asked Mrs Roberts impressed.

'I don't think so,' said Mrs Caldicot. 'Mr Pickering said they had only nearly appeared on the pier. But they must have been booked here and so the promoter had some posters printed.'

'Even if they are posters for a concert that never took place they're probably quite valuable!' said Mrs Roberts. 'People collect anything to do with the Beatles.'

'There are scores of them!' said Ruth, rifling through the posters. 'Do you really think they're worth anything?'

'They might be worth a few pennies,' agreed Mrs Caldicot, sceptically. 'And we could probably sell some of this other stuff. We might be able to raise enough money to pay for the roof to be repaired.'

They closed the lid of the trunk, left the store room and wandered back onto the stage.

'That poster of Judy Garland reminded me of 'The Wizard of Oz!' said Mrs Roberts. 'I saw it years ago in the cinema.' She smiled as she remembered the film. 'I saw it in a cinema rather like this place. It was all red velvet and gold paint. They brought round ice creams and popcorn. I used to love going to the cinema.'

'I loved all those old Bogart films!' said Mrs Caldicot. ''Casablanca', 'African Queen' and 'The Big Sleep'.'

"The Maltese Falcon' and 'To Have and Have Not'!' continued Mrs Roberts.

'I haven't seen any of those!' said Ruth.

'Oh you must!' said Mrs Roberts. 'And you need to see them on the big screen – not just on a television.'

'That's it!' cried Mrs Caldicot.

'What's what?' asked Mrs Roberts, slightly confused.

'We'll open a cinema. We'll put up a screen and rent old films which we can show. We don't have to worry about looking after artistes or dealing with screaming fans. We just show classic old movies. We show films with Humphrey Bogart, Cary Grant and the Marx Brothers. We have a season of films by favourite stars or directors. We could have a Hitchcock season and show films like 'The Thirty Nine Steps'.'

'What about old musicals?' asked Mrs Roberts.

'Brilliant!' agreed Mrs Caldicot. 'We could show 'My Fair Lady' and 'The Sound of Music' as a double bill.'

'And horror movies?' said Ruth. 'I love those old Dracula movies with Christopher Lee and Peter Cushing.'

'That's a terrific idea!' agreed Mrs Roberts. 'And the Vincent Price films.'

'What about the leaks in the roof?' asked Ruth.

'I don't remember that one,' said Mrs Roberts, thinking Ruth was talking about a movie title.

Ruth explained.

'Oh we can soon deal with those,' said Mrs Caldicot, who was now in an optimistic mood. 'We can position buckets under the leaks.'

'And if the weather is bad we can give people umbrellas if it turns out they are being rained upon,' suggested Mrs Roberts. 'English customers won't mind a bit!'

'That's an excellent idea,' agreed Mrs Caldicot.

'We could show children's movies on Saturday mornings!' said Mrs Roberts. 'Cartoons and so on. Just like they used to do in the good old days. I bet we'll do a roaring trade when the weather is too bad for people to sit on the beach.'

'That's a good half of all the days in an English summer,' Ruth pointed out.

'Exactly!' said Mrs Caldicot. 'It shouldn't be difficult to arrange films for all ages and all tastes. This cinema thing is a wonderful idea. Who thought of it?'

'It was you,' said Ruth.

'Oh was it? Well I get a free cup of tea and a bun. And you two get free cups of tea and free buns for agreeing that it's a great idea.'

'Oh goody,' said Ruth. 'Dorothy said she was going to the bakery to buy some cakes. I hope she bought some éclairs.'

And so the three of them locked up the theatre and walked back down the pier towards the café.

As they went, Mrs Roberts and Mrs Caldicot looked at each other, smiled and skipped for a couple of paces.

Chapter Twenty One

While Mrs Caldicot, Mrs Roberts and Ruth had been examining the theatre, and trying to work out how best to use it, Ms Schmidt and her entourage had been wandering up and down the pier trying to find someone who was in charge or, failing that find someone who would tell them who was in charge or, failing even that, hoping to find someone whom they could impress and intimidate.

There is absolutely no point at all in working for the council, and having an important title and an entourage, if you can't find someone to impress and intimidate.

Unfortunately for Ms Schmidt, the members of Mrs Caldicot's gang had long ago decided that talking to people wearing suits was never a particularly good idea, and if the person wearing the suit looked or seemed full of their own self-importance, then it was invariably a very bad idea.

'What good has talking to someone snooty in a suit ever done anyone?' enquired Mr Merivale.

And answer came there none.

There was, instead, simply much pursing of lips and shaking of heads.

No one could think of an occasion which had been enlightened or enlivened by a conversation with someone (male or female) in a suit. And at the first sight of a cluster of be-suited figures, Mrs Caldicot's gang had pretty well disappeared from sight.

And the members of the pier staff who had not arrived with Mrs Caldicot (and who were, perhaps, not yet as allergic to people in suits) were all busy. Mr Rowbottham the silhouettist was in his booth, snipping away and providing happy holidaymakers with extraordinarily lifelike silhouettes of themselves, or their loved ones, on black cartridge paper. Mr Pickering, the train driver, was driving the train, and far too busy collecting tickets and avoiding holidaymakers to people who were patently not on the pier to have a Good Time. He had a little brass bell attached to the front of the train and occasionally he rang it to warn pedestrians that the train was coming. He liked ringing the bell.

Mr Pickering's granddaughter Dorothy and Miss Pettifer, the erstwhile Fat Lady and newly appointed waitress, were in the café where they were busy quenching thirsts and appetites with an apparently endless stream of cups of tea, buttered crumpets, toasted teacakes and home-made sandwiches and, of course, the inevitable packets of fish and chips.

If business slowed (which it did only rarely), Miss Pettifer would stand outside the café holding and nibbling from a bag of freshly made chips. The wonderful aroma would immediately inspire passers-by to rush into the café to order their own supplies.

It was only on their way back down the pier that Ms Schmidt and her multinational band of authorised marauders eventually spotted Mrs Caldicot, Mrs Roberts and Ruth who were heading back towards the café and their ice creams. Mrs Caldicot had stopped to pick up a newspaper which had been abandoned and was about to flutter into the sea.

'Are you something to do with the pier?' demanded Ms Schmidt.

'In a way I suppose I am,' answered Mrs Caldicot, warily and very reluctantly.

'I am looking for the owner,' snapped Ms Schmidt. She had never been a woman over-imbued with surplus quantities of natural charm, patience and good manners but she had found that these shortcomings had been a considerable help to her in her short but dramatic career. She was now reaching the end of a very short tether.

'I don't know where the owner is,' said Mrs Caldicot quite honestly.

The last time she had seen Mr Livingstone he had been sitting on the little train with Mr Hewitt. They had both been travelling up the pier and enjoying large ice creams; the fluffy sort of ice cream that has at least one bar of chocolate stuffed into it. That had been some while earlier, when she and her ad hoc committee had been heading up the pier to the theatre.

'Who are you?' demanded Ms Schmidt, who could not have asked the question more forcefully if she'd been working in a cellar with a floodlight shining into Mrs Caldicot's face.

'My name is Caldicot,' said Mrs Caldicot who was no longer the meek, mild and easily bullied woman she had been when Mr

Caldicot had been alive and moaning. 'And I am not accustomed to being addressed in such a manner. Who are you?'

Ms Schmidt took a deep breath and explained, once again, who she was and why she was there. It took her nearly two minutes.

'Well I'm the Pier Master,' said Mrs Caldicot, perhaps a trifle rashly.

'No, no, I need the person in charge,' insisted Ms Schmidt dismissively. 'I must speak to the owner.'

'Then you'd better find them,' said Mrs Caldicot. 'And good luck with that,' she muttered under her breath as the little train hummed past them, going back down the pier. Mr Livingstone and Mr Hewitt shouted greetings and held up cubes of Turkish Delight. The pair had found that neither of them could eat a whole box of Turkish Delight in one ride down the pier and so they'd stayed on the train. This was, they thought, probably their sixth or seventh journey along the pier.

'Well, I suppose you will have to do for now,' said Ms Schmidt with the rudeness of self-assured youth. 'What did you say your position is?'

'I'm the Pier Master,' replied Mrs Caldicot.

'What does that mean precisely? What qualifications do you have? Are you trained? You seem very old to be a Pier Master. And the term 'Master' is quite unacceptable to my Department.'

'I don't know. None. No. Don't be so rude,' said Mrs Caldicot, answering Ms Schmidt's barrage of questions.

'I must say it seems to me that you are far too old to take on responsibility for a structure of this magnitude,' said Ms Schmidt.

'I'm so sorry,' said Mrs Caldicot, feeling her blood begin to bubble. 'Is there a preferred age for pier management?' she asked. 'How old should I be? Would you like me to have cosmetic surgery to make myself look younger?'

She was furious. She had spent much of her life being bullied. She had been bullied and taken for granted by her first husband. She had been ignored by shopkeepers, Post Office staff, bank tellers and a wide variety of utility company employees. She had been treated with scant respect by more people than she could possibly remember.

'Why, does everyone think they can patronise older people?' demanded Mrs Caldicot. 'You remind me of those people in shops and offices and on the telephone who talk down to pensioners and treat them as though they're members of some sub-species, or aliens from another planet. If I have to ring the gas or the electricity people they always want to know my date of birth. I can't imagine why but they do. Maybe you're not allowed to have gas or electricity if you're too old. And then when I've told them how old I am they always say 'Well done!' as if I've just discovered a new way to split the atom or won a gold medal in the Olympics. All I've done is get my date of birth right but they congratulate me as if I've really astonished them with my brilliance. Why do people under 40 always assume that anyone over 60 must be senile, and then act all surprised and delighted when they turn out not to be?'

Ms Schmidt, startled by the fact that Mrs Caldicot had the temerity to stand up for herself, frowned but didn't say anything at all. Like all bullies she didn't like it when people stood up for themselves.

Mrs Caldicot hadn't finished. She looked sternly at Ms Schmidt, taking in her shapeless suit and her scalped hairstyle. 'Maybe I should get someone to trim my hair with a lawn mower. Would that make me look younger, do you think?'

'Do you have relevant life experiences?' demanded Ms Schmidt, trying to retake control of the conversation. She didn't understand the remark about the lawn mower. She was very proud of her hairstyle. Her hair was cut by a Syrian refugee who had received his hairdressing training while serving as a soldier in the Syrian army. He cut everyone's hair in the only way he knew how, but had won two trophies for hairstyling and was so busy cutting hair that he was booked up three months in advance. *The Guardian* newspaper had printed a long interview with him.

'I always used to go on the pier when I was little,' replied Mrs Caldicot. 'So my on-pier experience goes back well over half a century. What qualifications do you have?'

'I have a diploma in Asylum Studies from the University of Banbury and a certificate in Golf Course Management from the University of Bakewell,' said Ms Schmidt very proudly. 'I also have a post graduate diploma in Transcultural Gender Studies from the University of Eccles.'

'It's a pity you didn't get a diploma in something from Chelsea where the buns come from,' said Mrs Caldicot.

'I beg your pardon?'

'Don't mention it. I often feel that way if I've had a heavy lunch.'

Ms Schmidt, who felt that the conversation had passed her by on the other side of the road, and who was not enjoying what she had expected and believed would be an easy day of unopposed confrontation and flagrant bullying, looked around desperately as if hoping that someone would leap to her rescue.

Naturally, no one did. Actually, none of her entourage had managed to follow more than a quarter of the conversation.

'As a person of authority you are required to give me details of everyone working on the pier,' said Ms Schmidt. She held out her hand and one of her aides, spotting the gesture and knowing it well, placed a small computer in it. All of her aides were carrying nylon computer bags or plastic briefcases and between them they had enough computing power to put a satellite into space or, at a push, even adjust the wing mirrors on a BMW motor car.

'Oh my word,' said Mrs Caldicot.

She thought for a moment and then slowly rattled off a list of names. 'Pinhola, Nwanga, Kwindja, Nowak, Kowalczyk, Okereke, Azikiwe, we've got two of those, Tinibu, Nzeogwu, Iwu, Dokubo, Muller, Ursache, Dobrescu and Balescu. Oh and I nearly forgot Mr Manescu and Ms Popescu. How could I forget them? Silly me.'

'Is that everyone?' demanded Ms Schmidt, when she'd finished putting all the names into her keyboard.

'Oh yes, that's everyone.'

Ruth, who was standing open mouthed at the imaginary list of names which Mrs Caldicot had recited with such ease, felt herself being nudged. She looked. It was Mrs Roberts, who was opening and closing her mouth. Ruth closed her mouth.

'How many of these peoples are of ethnic origin?'

'Oh, all of us I would say. Yes, definitely all of us are ethnic.'

'Your English is very good.'

'Thank you. I practise it every day.'

'Good, good. But don't neglect your own language. You must retain your ethnicity.'

'Oh yes. Thank you. I make sure that I speak my native language on holidays and every Sunday.'

'And are you all members of population subgroups within dominant natural or cultural groups?'

'Definitely,' confirmed Mrs Caldicot. 'All of us. We often laugh about us all being members of population subgroups.' She laughed lightly to illustrate what she meant. 'Being members of subgroups within dominant natural or cultural groups is something that brings us all together.'

'By my reckoning there are 18 peoples working here,' said Ms Schmidt, studying her computer 'How many of these peoples are of Non English speaking Eastern European origins?'

'I don't know,' said Mrs Caldicot. 'I never like to enquire. But when Mrs Pinhola went to Gdansk she talked for months about how much she was looking forward to going home. Do you remember that, Mrs Nwanga?'

'Definitely,' replied the woman more customarily known as Mrs Roberts. 'She went back twice I think. While she was there she visited a tractor factory and brushed up on her plumbing.'

'Splendid. And how many asylum seekers do you have employed here?'

'Including the illegal ones?'

'Oh yes, we would be very happy to include them. We like to have the illegal ones included though we would not, of course, pass their details on to the authorities.'

'I would say maybe at least half could be considered worthy of inclusion in your list of people who would be suitable for an asylum,' said Mrs Caldicot. 'It may be more.'

'Splendid!' said Ms Schmidt, who seemed pleased by this. 'Thank you for sharing this with me.'

It clearly did not seem to Ms Schmidt to be in the slightest bit strange that everyone working on the pier should be so very foreign.

Mrs Caldicot thought the wretched woman probably felt that it was such a Good Thing that she didn't like to question it, or even to suspect for a moment that it might not be entirely true.

'And how many homosexuals and gender variants do you have?'

'Oh I haven't asked,' confessed Mrs Caldicot. 'I would say at least half but maybe more.' She turned to Mrs Roberts. 'What do you think Mrs Nwanga?'

'I would say at least half,' answered Mrs Roberts, with a nod. 'At least half – and we have a lot of variants here.'

'And how many of your peoples are disabled?'

'Oh I think everyone is suffering from one handicap or another,' said Mrs Caldicot. 'Mrs Kwindja has terrible trouble with her knees.'

'That's the mother of the lady who went to Gdansk,' said Mrs Roberts helpfully. 'The one who looked at the tractors and brushed up on her plumbing while she was there. She enjoyed herself so much that I think she went twice.'

'I see there is a small train running on the pier,' said Ms Schmidt. 'What facility do you have for peoples in wheelchairs to board the train?'

This rather stumped Mrs Caldicot. It had not even occurred to her that people who were in wheelchairs, and who already had wheels of their own, would want to board the train.

'We have a hook on the back of the train,' said Mrs Roberts helping out Mrs Caldicot at her time of need. 'And we have a piece of rope handy at all times. We just tie the wheelchair to the back of the train and pull it along.'

Ms Schmidt frowned. 'Is that safe?'

'Oh yes. There's never been an accident,' said Mrs Roberts. And since the experiment had never been tried she was being perfectly honest.

'Thank you, so much,' said Ms Schmidt, switching off her computer and handing it back to one of her assistants. 'I will report back my findings. I am quite delighted with what I've heard from you today.' She started to leave and then turned back. 'When we came onto the pier,' she said, 'I talked to two men who were standing there. Are they anything to do with the pier?'

'Would they be distinguished looking gentlemen of mature years?'

'Mature, yes,' said Ms Schmidt, a little cautiously.

'Was one of them wearing a sports jacket with patches on the elbows and the other wearing an old suit jacket with a maroon jumper underneath it?'

'Exactly! That is precisely them. You know these persons?'

'I've seen them around.'

'Are they employed by you?'

'Most definitely not!' said Mrs Caldicot emphatically. She shook her head. 'I have no employees.'

'I am so pleased,' said Ms Schmidt. 'They seemed very confused and not at all ethnically acceptable.' She lowered her voice. 'In fact,' she said, 'I strongly suspected that they might be English!'

And with that she hurried off, her entourage racing after her.

'Golly,' said Mrs Roberts, when she'd gone. 'Where did you get all those names from?'

Mrs Caldicot held up the newspaper she was holding. 'From the sports page,' she said. 'They're the names of footballers playing for clubs in the English league.'

She was silent for a moment.

'I feel bad about telling her porky pies but I was worried we'd all get into trouble for not being foreign enough.'

'You did the only thing you could,' said Mrs Roberts. 'She'd have probably closed us down if she'd known we were all British.'

'I liked the bit about the asylum!' said Ruth, giggling.

Mrs Caldicot looked at her and raised an eyebrow. 'Which bit was that?'

'The bit when you said that half of us would be suitable for an asylum.'

'Oh,' said Mrs Caldicot, rather pleased. 'I think my estimate was a little on the low side, don't you?'

'I definitely do,' agreed Mrs Roberts. 'We're definitely all suitable for an asylum. In fact, we should turn the entire pier into an asylum! We could probably get a grant for it.'

Giggling, they continued on their way back down the pier, towards the café and their cups of tea and buns (or, in Ruth's case, a cream filled éclair).

Ten minutes later, they were sitting down enjoying their very welcome comestibles.

'Oh, I'd love one of those,' murmured Mrs Caldicot appreciatively, as Ruth bit into her éclair and cream squeezed out at both sides.

'The girls have got two or three more!' said Ruth. 'Shall I fetch you one?'

'No thank you, dear. I'd love one but it wouldn't love me. I'd be poorly for a week. I'm happy with a nice iced bun.'

So Ruth enjoyed her éclair at first hand and Mrs Caldicot and Mrs Nwanga (nee Roberts) enjoyed it vicariously, at second hand. And, surprisingly perhaps, the two of them enjoyed it almost as much as

Ruth had; comfortable in the knowledge that the éclair would not have a chance to get its own back on them.

Chapter Twenty Two

They all met that evening in the ballroom, which had now become their living area. There was a small dining area at one end, a television set at the other and enough chairs and tables for them to sit down and relax. There was, suggested Mr Roxdale, even room for a table tennis table and a pool table.

It quickly became apparent that Mrs Caldicot's suggestion that the theatre be turned into a cinema was a popular one. The proposal was met with universal approval.

'It's a wonderful idea!' said Dorothy, who was excited at having a cinema within walking distance. 'There isn't a cinema in Penmouth. The nearest one is nearly thirty miles away.'

Mrs Caldicot had worried that young locals and visitors would be disappointed if they showed old films instead of the latest blockbusters but it seemed that her fears were unfounded. Dorothy, like everyone else, thought that the idea of showing old films was a terrific idea.

'Can we have lots of old cowboy movies?' asked Mr Roxdale. 'I like those John Wayne films. And I love films starring Clint Eastwood. Films like 'A Fistful of Dollars' and 'The Good, the Bad and the Ugly'.'

'That's a terrific idea,' agreed Mrs Caldicot. She made a note of this in her notebook.

'And a season of war films?' suggested Mr Livingstone. 'The Dam Busters?', 'The Battle of Britain' and 'Where Eagles Dare'? I like films where they kill a lot of Germans.'

'Can we get hold of all those old films?' asked Mrs Merivale. 'Are they still available?'

'Definitely!' said Mrs Caldicot. 'An hour ago I spoke to Jenkins, who is very well but missing us all very much, by the way, and he gave me the telephone number of a film distributor called Rufus Strutt in London. I then rang Mr Strutt and he was very helpful. He told me that hardly anyone shows old films anymore. We can show them for a fraction of the cost of showing new films.'

'What about a screen?' asked Mr Merivale. 'We can't just show films on an old sheet – even though it would probably be a cheap way to do it.'

'Mr Strutt was very helpful about that too,' said Mrs Caldicot. 'He gave me the name of an old cinema that's just closed down. He said he thought we ought to be able to buy their screen and projection equipment for next to nothing. Apparently their equipment is considered out-of-date but it would be perfect for showing old movies.'

It was generally agreed that all of this was excellent news.

'By the way,' said Mrs Caldicot, turning to Mr Livingstone. 'Did you talk to a woman called Schmidt today?'

'A German woman with a huge entourage?'

'That's the one.'

'Well we did and we didn't,' said Mr Livingstone. 'She wanted to speak to the owner.'

'So you didn't tell her that you're the owner?'

'It slipped my mind,' admitted Mr Livingstone. 'But we had a nice chat,' said Mr Livingstone. 'I told her all about my one and only visit to Hamburg.'

'You didn't tell her that you'd been in a Lancaster Bomber when you called?'

'He damned well did!' said Mr Hewitt with a chuckle.

'Oh dear me!' said Mrs Caldicot. She paused and thought for a while. 'Never mind I think I managed to convince her that we're following all their regulations.'

She looked at Mrs Nwanga (aka Roberts) and winked. Mrs Nwanga (aka Roberts) winked back.

'Jolly good,' said Mr Livingstone. He turned to Errol. 'I don't think you need worry too much about the council closing us down, young man! Mrs Caldicot will keep them under control.'

Errol, like everyone else, was relieved. Mrs Merivale had found him a small, empty bedroom and told him that he was welcome to stay there if he wanted to. No one was much surprised when he said he wanted to.

The truth is that they were all enjoying life on Penmouth Pier. They had settled into their rooms upstairs. And the massive ballroom had become their communal living room.

An hour or two later that evening there was particularly good news for Ruth.

The gates were locked and padlocked and Mr and Merivale had just decided to take a stroll along the deserted pier when they heard a familiar voice calling to them. They turned and saw Jean-Jacques, the young man whom Ruth had met when they had all gone to Paris for a few days. Jean-Jacques had an arm stuck through the gate and was waving to them. 'Can I come in?' he called.

'Won't be a minute!' called the Merivales.

And while Mr Merivale rushed to find Mr Livingstone, who had the key to the padlock, Mrs Merivale hurried off to find Ruth.

Not surprisingly, it was Ruth, whose legs were over half a century younger than Mr Livingstone's and who was so eager to get there that she would have given any Olympic champion a good run for their money, who got to the gates first.

'I didn't expect to see you for ages!' she cried, tears of delight running down her cheeks.

'I thought it would be a surprise!' said Jean-Jacques.

'When did you leave Paris?'

'I left Charles de Gaulle airport early this morning. But it has taken me three times as long to get to Penmouth from London as it took me to get to London from Paris! I had to get a train into London and then a train across London and then a train from London. Oh la la! So many trains.'

'Are you hungry?'

'I am starving. I tried to eat a sandwich I bought at the railway station but they made it out of cardboard by mistake.'

'Could you eat some fish and chips?'

At that point Mr Livingstone arrived with the key. And a moment later Ruth had her arms around Jean-Jacques's neck, and the Merivales and Mr Livingstone were looking away and discussing what they thought the weather was going to be like the next day.

'Did you ask me if I could eat some fish and chips?' said Jean-Jacques a few minutes later.

'I did.'

'I would love some of your famous fish and chips!'

'I'll ask Dorothy if she can make you some,' said Ruth. 'She makes the very best fish and chips in the world.'

'I'll pop off and find her,' offered Mrs Merivale. 'The fat will still be hot. Meanwhile I'll make a nice pot of tea.' Making a nice pot of tea was Mrs Merivale's first course of action whenever something out of the ordinary occurred. If there was good news then she made a nice pot of tea to celebrate. If there was bad news then she made a nice pot of tea to settle everyone's nerves.

'I cannot believe that you own a pier!' said Jean-Jacques, straining to look through the gloaming, down the seemingly endless length of the pier. 'It's huge and so magnificent.'

'It belongs to Mr Livingstone,' said Ruth. 'But we all live and work here now. Mrs Caldicot is going to open a cinema in the theatre at the end of the pier. And Mrs Torridge has become a Fortune Teller. I am so pleased that you brought your accordion. We have a really nice man who cuts pictures out of black paper. And there is a train that runs up and down the pier. How is your father? I am so sorry I should have asked sooner. Why didn't you tell me that you were coming? When did you decide to come?'

Jean-Jacques, who was laughing, looked at her. 'My father is very well. He sends everyone his love.'

'Can we do some busking?' asked Ruth. 'Just you and me?'

'I hope so very much!' said Jean-Jacques. 'I will play my accordion and you will sing.'

'I'll ask Mrs Caldicot if we can stand at the entrance to the pier,' suggested Ruth. 'It'll help draw attention to the pier and entertain people as they come in.'

Naturally, Mrs Caldicot, and indeed everyone else, thought that a little music was just what the pier needed and it was agreed that a pair of buskers at the gate would be a marvellous attraction.

Chapter Twenty Three

The man who had the cinema screen and the projection equipment for sale turned up with everything packed up in a large van. He was a long standing lover of old movies and he was delighted to know that his equipment was not to be recycled into a local landfill site. He was keen to install it in the theatre straight away.

'But we haven't agreed a price yet!' protested Mrs Caldicot.

'And we haven't got any money,' pointed out Mr Livingstone, practical for once.

'You can have it all for £1,000,' said Mr Strutt with a shrug. 'The stuff is too old for anyone else to use and not old enough to have any value for a collector.'

Mrs Caldicot and Mr Livingstone exchanged glances. 'I'm afraid we haven't even got £1,000,' said Mrs Caldicot apologetically.

Mr Strutt shrugged. 'Pay me when you've got going,' he said.

He and the assistant he had brought with him piled all the equipment onto the little train and walked beside it as it was driven along the pier to the theatre. Within a surprisingly short period of time, they had the screen installed and the projection equipment set up in the Dress Circle, where they had removed twelve seats to make room.

'I suggest you build a little, wooden wall around the projection area,' suggested Mr Strutt. 'Just to give the projectionist a little privacy. You don't want someone bumping into the projector and knocking it off line!'

Mrs Caldicot and Mrs Roberts, who had been watching in awe, said they thought this would be an excellent idea. The ad hoc committee had been temporarily reduced to two for Ruth was with Jean-Jacques, busking at the pier entrance.

'Who is going to be the projectionist?' asked Mr Strutt.

Mrs Caldicot and Mrs Roberts looked at each other. 'We hadn't thought about that!' admitted Mrs Caldicot.

'Well, why don't I teach you two ladies how to do it? And then you can show anyone else how it's done. The equipment is really very simple. You can't go wrong.'

And so Mrs Caldicot and Mrs Roberts learned how to become cinema projectionists.

'If you have any problems just give me a call,' said Mr Strutt.

'Before we take you and your assistant back to the café for a cup of tea and a meal, may I ask you if you know anything about cinema and theatre memorabilia?' asked Mrs Caldicot.

'I've just sold all the stuff from my cinema,' said Mr Strutt. 'So, I've got a rough idea of the sort of prices things fetch these days.'

They took him and his assistant down to the small room behind the stage where they had found all the old theatrical props.

'These are very nice!' agreed Mr Strutt. 'They'll fetch a very decent price at auction. Collectors love this sort of stuff. What about the posters and photos you've got on the walls? They're probably worth a few bob. People love old posters and old film star photos.'

'I think we'd like to leave the posters and the photographs on the walls,' said Mrs Caldicot. 'If we take them down we'll need to redecorate all the walls.'

'But there are the posters that Ruth found in that old trunk,' pointed out Mrs Roberts.

'Of course!' agreed Mrs Caldicot. She crossed the room and opened the lid of the trunk in which Ruth had found the old theatre posters. 'We've got heaps of old posters in here.'

Mr Strutt stared in astonishment as the lid went up.

'Are they worth anything?' asked Mrs Roberts.

Mr Strutt didn't reply for he was too busy flicking through the posters.

'Do you know how many there are in here?' he asked.

'No idea,' replied Mrs Caldicot.

There was a silence while Mr Strutt did some counting. 'You've got some posters here for the Beatles!'

'Yes.'

Mr Strutt carefully counted the Beatles' posters. 'There are 100 of these!'

'Yes, but I'm afraid that I don't think The Beatles ever appeared here. According to Mr Pickering, they were booked to appear but something happened and they didn't come.'

'Who is Mr Pickering?'

'He's the gentleman who drives our little train,' said Mrs Roberts. 'He's been working here for ever. He knows everything about the pier.'

Mr Strutt was so excited he could hardly speak. He looked at his assistant who was grinning and then he looked at Mrs Caldicot. 'Do you have any idea how much these are worth?'

'None whatsoever,' said Mrs Caldicot.

'If I offered you £200 for all these posters, would you take it?'

'I'd have to ask Mr Livingstone,' said Mrs Caldicot. 'He owns the pier and everything on it.'

'But he might accept £200 – for the lot?'

'I suppose he might,' agreed Mrs Caldicot.

'Well, it's a good job for you that I'm honest,' said Mr Strutt. 'Each one of these old theatre posters is worth between £150 and £200 and the Beatles' posters are easily worth £500 each.'

Mrs Caldicot and Mrs Roberts just stared at him in astonishment.

'But they're just old posters! And the Beatles never even appeared here.'

'People love these things,' insisted Mr Strutt. 'Interior decorators will kill one another to buy these. They put them into big aluminium frames and hang them in posh London apartments.'

'Even the Beatles' posters?'

'Oh, especially the Beatles' posters.'

'It doesn't matter that The Beatles didn't appear here?'

'No. In fact it probably adds to their value. These are the missing posters for the missing concert!' said Mr Strutt. He smiled at Mrs Caldicot and Mrs Roberts. 'I think you'll be able to pay for the screen and the projection equipment.'

'If Mr Livingstone agrees would you take them and sell them for us?' asked Mrs Caldicot. 'We would obviously pay you a commission.'

'Delighted!' said Mr Strutt immediately. 'I'd be delighted. Pay me 15% of the price you receive and I'll find you the best buyer. I'll try a few dealers here and in America and if they don't offer the right money we'll put everything into an auction. But if we go straight to a dealer we won't have to pay the auctioneer's commission and the dealer will save money too so we'll probably make more money that way.'

'How much do you think they're all worth?' asked Mrs Caldicot.

'You won't get the prices I quoted, of course,' said Mr Strutt. 'Those are the retail prices. But you should get half of those prices from a dealer.'

Mrs Caldicot and Mrs Roberts waited while Mr Strutt did some sums in his head.

'I think there are about 200 mixed posters here,' he said. 'And there are the 100 Beatles' posters. So, conservatively, I'd expect a dealer to pay at least £40,000 for the lot. If I break up the collection and sell them in separate lots I might be able to get more.' He paused, thinking. 'Then you'd have to take my 15% out of that. Oh, but you've got all that theatrical memorabilia as well. Those old suits of armour and the spears and whatnot should be worth another few thousand. I think I should be able to get you a cheque for something between £40,000 and £50,000, less the £1,000 for the projection equipment and my 15% commission.'

'I think we might be able to get the roof repaired,' whispered Mrs Caldicot to Mrs Roberts.

They hurried back down the pier to tell Mr Livingstone the good news. And to ask if he was happy to sell the collection of posters he didn't even know he had.

'I need to consult my adviser here,' said Mr Livingstone, turning to Mr Hewitt. 'What do you think we should do, Mr Hewitt? Do you think we should keep a pile of old posters in a trunk so that they can quietly go mouldy and rot away or should we flog them, put a big chunk of loot in the bank and then buy Mr Strutt's projector and repair the cinema roof?'

'It's a difficult one,' said Mr Hewitt, pretending to think about it.

'Very tricky,' agreed Mr Livingstone.

Mrs Caldicot and Mrs Roberts, who knew they were being teased, just smiled and waited. Mr Strutt, who didn't know Mr Livingstone at all, simply stared in astonishment.

'On balance I think maybe you should sell them,' said Mr Hewitt eventually.

'OK, we'll sell them!' agreed Mr Livingstone. He and a relieved Mr Strutt then shook hands.

And so, after they'd all had lunch and a nice cup of tea, Mr Strutt and his assistant loaded the trunk full of posters, and the theatrical memorabilia, onto the little train. Mr Pickering drove the train down the pier and Mr Strutt and his assistant loaded everything into their van.

Chapter Twenty Four

Naturally, things weren't allowed to go quite so swimmingly without there being a serious setback.

Mrs Caldicot really wasn't terribly surprised.

She had become accustomed to the fact that life was very much like a game of snakes and ladders. She just rather wished that the ladders were longer and the snakes a little shorter.

A small expeditionary force of men and women in suits returned to the pier two days later.

There were three of them and Ms Schmidt, the head of the Department of Equality, Diversity and Sensitivity was not among them. Nor were her acolytes to be seen.

'I think you rather pulled the wool over our Ms Schmidt's eyes,' said a man who introduced himself as Mr Chapman. He looked to be in his forties and was short and notably overweight. Actually, he was very short. He looked a little bit like Dudley Moore, except that he was about two feet shorter and not as good looking. And he was very fat. So fat, indeed, that Mrs Caldicot thought that God could have probably made two quite average sized executives out of him and still had enough material left over to make a Great Dane.

Mr Chapman was addressing Mrs Caldicot who had identified herself as the Pier Master. Most of the others were there too. Mr Pickering was driving the train, and Dorothy and her new waitress were working in the café. But everyone else was gathered around Mrs Caldicot. Even Ruth and Jean-Jacques, the French accordionist, had stopped playing music to pay attention to what was happening.

'May I ask who you are?' asked Mrs Caldicot, very politely.

'I'm the council's Deputy Chief Executive,' replied Mr Chapman. 'We haven't met though you did meet Ms Schmidt, the Directrice of our Department of Equality, Diversity and Sensitivity. Ms Schmidt is German and therefore humourless. I am from Dundee, and therefore not German, and for a Scot I have a terrific sense of humour.'

‘We rather thought we could rely on our Ms Schmidt to find a way to close you down,’ said a woman who introduced herself as Ms Trench and who said that she was the council’s Chief Planning Officer. ‘The equality, diversity and sensitivity legislation governing small businesses is very strict these days.’

Like Mr Chapman, the Chief Planning Officer looked to be in her forties. She had no discernible curves whatsoever and was what used to be called stout.

‘In the report which she submitted after her visit, Ms Schmidt said that you were fully compliant with all the legislative requirements,’ said Mr Chapman. ‘And we both know that’s rubbish don’t we?’

‘I bet you thought you were very clever,’ said Ms Trench. She looked around. ‘Which one of you is Ms Nwanga?’

Mrs Caldicot and Mrs Roberts both examined their shoes. They both felt like naughty schoolgirls. Naturally, the others did not know what Ms Trench was talking about.

‘You should be ashamed of yourselves,’ said Mr Chapman. ‘Fancy taking advantage of a naïve and inexperienced young woman like that.’

‘A foreign woman too,’ said Ms Trench.

‘We’ve sent Ms Schmidt and her team off on another training course,’ said Mr Chapman. ‘They’ve all been sent to Venezuela for three months.’ He laughed. It was a mocking, derisory sort of laugh. ‘All expenses paid by the council and they’ll come back clutching another batch of diplomas.’

‘And after that we’ll send her off somewhere else,’ said Ms Trench. ‘They do lots of nice training courses in Russia these days.’

‘And Iceland too, I believe,’ added Mr Chapman. ‘They seem to do lots of diversity training in cold places.’

‘So, the bottom line is that the grown-ups are taking over,’ said Ms Trench. She looked at Mrs Caldicot, as though contemplating making a bid for her. ‘You’re a little old to be running a pier, aren’t you?’

‘I beg your pardon?’ said Mrs Caldicot.

‘You’re a little old to be running a pier, aren’t you?’ shouted Ms Trench. She leant forwards a few inches and spoke very slowly, and in that patronising way that television interviewers often adopt when they are talking to the deaf or the elderly, especially when they want to appear kindly and sympathetic. This time Mrs Caldicot understood her. She looked across at Mrs Roberts but did not reply to Ms Trench.

'You should be in a residential home,' said Ms Trench. 'Maybe we could find you and your many wrinkles a place in one of those places where you can sit down in a nice, plastic armchair and play bingo. Maybe they'll let you make a raffia basket.'

'I tried one of those,' said Mrs Caldicot drily. She was tempted to point out that her aches and wrinkles were badges of honour; proof that instead of just sitting round waiting for life to totter past she had, in recent years at least, gone out and met it head on.

'Well, you'll be trying another one soon because you're not going to stay here!' said Ms Trench. 'We've got great plans for this piece of outdated Victorian memorabilia.'

'The thing is,' said Mr Chapman, 'that there are people working on this pier and your elusive Mr Livingstone is, therefore, an employer. 'As an employer we can tie him up in several miles of red tape. There are laws governing the hours people can work. There are laws governing an employer's pension liabilities. There are, as I am sure Ms Schmidt pointed out to you, laws governing equality, diversity and sensitivity among employees.'

'There are so many laws,' said Ms Trench with a sigh. 'Working with our colleagues in various Government Departments we can have the missing Mr Livingstone arrested and fined. He is an employer and so he's fair game. Governments don't like small employers and so we can make his life an absolute misery.'

'But that's not fair!' protested Mrs Caldicot, rather weakly. She could feel her voice beginning to crack but she was determined not to cry. 'We're just trying to revive this wonderful old pier. We want to restore the theatre. We've reopened the café and the shop. We're providing entertainment for people; for locals and for holidaymakers. We're not expecting the State to support us or to provide us with grants. We're trying to make Penmouth Pier a real attraction in the town.'

Mr Chapman laughed scornfully. 'Who cares about fair?' he demanded. 'You don't get it do you?'

'Get what?' asked Mrs Caldicot. She spoke now in a whisper. She wished Jenkins were here. Just to hold her. It was all so damned, cruel and unfair.

'This isn't about a pier, it isn't about Penmouth, it isn't about holidaymakers, it isn't about people at all!' said Mr Chapman, rubbing his hands together. 'Don't take it so personally. This isn't about you or the pier. It's just business. It's just about the money.'

'This is Ms Rothstein,' said Ms Trench, introducing the third member of the small deputation. Ms Rothstein was a reed thin, dour faced woman in her thirties. 'Miss Rothstein represents a large consortium of commercial developers. And she is going to make you an offer you can't refuse. She has very exciting plans for the pier.'

'Maybe this is the moment when you'd better think about producing the pier's owner,' said Mr Chapman. 'He's going to have to make himself known at some point soon.'

'What sort of plans do you have for the pier?' asked Mrs Caldicot, speaking so softly she wondered if anyone could hear her.

'We're going to turn the buildings at this end of the pier into offices,' said Ms Rothstein, waving a hand in the direction of the archway and including the shop, the café and the former hotel in her wave. 'And we're going to knock down the theatre on Stone Rock and build a luxury hotel and a 2,000 seater conference centre. Neither the pier nor the buildings on it are listed or protected in any way and so the only permission we require is from the council's planning department.'

'Which we have given,' said Ms Trench.

'What sort of offices?' asked Mrs Caldicot.

'We're going to put up modern offices which we have been commissioned to build for a major international company called Community Protection,' replied Ms Rothstein. 'It's a company which has won numerous Government awards.'

'What on earth do they do?' asked Mrs Caldicot, who had never heard of them.

'They're the world's largest manufacturers of community protection aids.'

'What on earth are 'community protection aids'?'

'Oh, things like tear gas, pepper spray, CS gas, water cannon and rubber bullets. The company supplies governments all around the world. They are going to build a large factory near here. It will be a tremendous boost to local employment figures. The Government has approved the factory. The Minister said it would provide a great boost to exports. And it will help release the region from over-dependence on the dying holiday trade.'

'You're not really going to help employment in the area if you kill off the holiday trade in order to help establish a factory making tear gas and rubber bullets!'

'We've already approved Ms Rothstein's planning application,' said Ms Trench. 'So now we just need to purchase the pier and the work can go ahead.'

'It would be good for us to start soon,' said Mr Chapman. 'The contractors really need to begin the construction work before the winter starts. We're going to use the rubble we obtain from knocking down that old theatre to help us build an extension to the landing stage on Stone Rock.' He grinned. 'Now, where is that Mr Livingstone hiding?'

'In our letter to your solicitor, Mr Canterbury, we offered to take the pier off your hands for £1,' said Ms Rothstein. 'Given the circumstances we thought that was a very generous offer. As you will have now discovered it costs a good deal of money to run a pier. For example, our surveyors told us that the roof of the theatre is in a terrible state and urgently needs repair work. We don't think you'll be able to find the money to do even emergency repairs. So you really don't have much choice but to sell to us, do you?'

'But surely they won't let you do those awful things!' said Mrs Roberts. 'They won't let you knock down an old theatre and build a beastly conference centre!'

'Who do you think 'they' are?' asked Ms Trench.

Mrs Roberts looked as puzzled as she felt. 'I'm not really sure,' she said, hesitantly. 'The authorities. The powers that be. The people who make all the decisions on behalf of the community.'

'We are the 'they' you expect to come riding to your assistance!' said Mr Chapman smugly. 'And I'm afraid we're not on your side.'

'The council takes advice from its staff,' said Ms Rothstein. 'And the council staff, in the persons of Mr Chapman and Ms Trench, has advised the council to recommend our planned development. So, just who do you think is going to stop us?'

'I don't know,' said Mrs Roberts, sadly. 'But there must be people who protect structures like this from people like you?'

'Do you mean people like the Seafront Heritage Authority?' asked Ms Trench.

'Yes!' said Mrs Caldicot, leaping on the suggestion. 'They look after seaside buildings all around the coast.'

'We have their endorsement,' said Ms Rothstein. 'We cleared their staff pension deficit and coincidentally they have approved our plans unreservedly.'

'That's awful!' cried Mrs Roberts. 'You bought them!'

'It doesn't matter what you think,' said Mr Chapman, wearily. 'Where is Mr Livingstone?'

No one spoke.

'Where is Mr Livingstone?' demanded Mr Chapman. 'He's the nephew of the late, lamented Mr Livingstone and he's the current owner. He's the one we need to talk to. So fetch him.'

Mr Livingstone, who had been standing nearby, had heard everything. He was no longer prepared to allow Mrs Caldicot to be bullied by these people. He stepped forward and cleared his throat. 'Mrs Caldicot doesn't need to fetch me,' he said. 'I'm here.'

'Aha!' said Mr Chapman. 'So you're the elusive owner! You're Mr Livingstone?'

'I am.'

'Well, the good news is that Ms Rothstein has got a cheque in her briefcase for £1,' said Mr Chapman. 'It's her original and final, final offer. If you accept it, which I am sure you will, we will tear up all the charges we've got prepared for you. If you refuse it then we'll hit you with so much paperwork that you'll wish you'd never been born. Do you have any idea how many forms you have to fill in if you're going to be an employer these days? Have you thought about providing pensions for your staff? Have you made arrangements for taxes and national insurance and sick pay and holidays? Do you know anything about the regulations concerning working conditions?'

Mr Livingstone was silent for a moment.

'You see,' said Mr Chapman, 'it's really all over, isn't it?'

'I tell you what,' said Ms Trench. 'The three of us will take a walk down the pier and give you a few minutes to think over what we've told you. Then, when we come back you can sign the sale documents and Ms Rothstein will give you that nice cheque for £1! We'll even pay all the legal costs for you. Getting rid of the pier won't cost you a penny.'

And with that the three of them strolled along the pier as though they were holidaymakers who were enjoying the sunshine and the sea air and who did not have a care in the world.

Chapter Twenty Five

'They will never own this pier,' said Mr Livingstone quietly, when Chapman, Trench and Rothstein were out of earshot.

The others looked at him. They had never heard him so angry.

'I will give the pier to charity before I let them buy it.'

'I suspect that they will simply buy it from whatever charity you give it to,' said Mrs Caldicot softly and very sadly. 'We can run the pier because we care about it and we're not desperate to make lots of money out of it. But the man from the council is right: they can use the employment legislation to force any owner to sell.'

'I will blow it up before I sell to them!' insisted Mr Livingstone.

'You can't do that,' said Mrs Roberts. 'At least they aren't threatening to knock down the pier itself.'

'They might as well knock it down,' said Mr Livingstone. 'And they're talking about knocking down the theatre.'

'If you blow it up then they'll sue you for millions,' said Mr Hewitt.

'How can they do that?'

'They'll sue you for the cost of cleaning up the debris!'

'Then I'll just go bankrupt!' said Mr Livingstone, full of defiance. 'My old age pension is just over £100 a week. That's my entire income. If I go bankrupt then in one year my bankruptcy will be over and they will still be left with all the rubble to clear away.' There were tears forming in his eyes as he spoke.

'Blowing up the pier isn't the answer,' said Mrs Caldicot. 'If we do that then everyone loses – including us.'

'But what can we do?' asked Mr Hewitt. 'They've got us in a corner.'

'I like it here,' said Miss Nightingale. She sounded as broken hearted as everyone felt. There were tears running down her cheeks. 'I like it here very much.'

'We all do, dear,' said Mrs Peterborough, putting her arm around her friend's shoulders. 'We've only been here a couple of days but I already feel as if I've lived here all my life.'

They stood in silence for a few moments; all trying to think of an answer.

'There is one thing we could try,' said Mrs Caldicot.

They all looked at her. Suddenly, there was hope in everyone's eyes. Not a lot. But a little.

'We could telephone Mr Canterbury,' she said. 'He was very helpful when Mr Livingstone and I went to see him and he did tell us that we could ring him if we had any problems we thought he might be able to help us with.'

'That's a brilliant idea!' said Mr Livingstone. 'He seemed a damned good egg. Maybe he will be able to think of a solution.'

'We'll do it now, before those awful people come back down the pier,' said Mrs Caldicot. And she hurried into the building behind the café, followed by everyone else.

'You speak to him,' said Mr Livingstone to Mrs Caldicot. 'You're much better at this sort of thing than I am.'

Chapter Twenty Six

'I don't know whether you remember me,' said Mrs Caldicot when she had got through to Mr Canterbury and had introduced herself. 'I came to see you with Mr Livingstone who had inherited Penmouth Pier.'

'Mrs Caldicot! What a delight to hear from you,' said Mr Canterbury. 'Of course, we remember. How could we forget? You are Mrs Caldicot and you are also Mrs Jenkins but you are not Mrs Livingstone. We certainly remember you. We've never handled a pier inheritance before. How are we doing? We hope your call does not indicate that we have problems.'

'I'm afraid there are some difficulties,' said Mrs Caldicot. 'Do you remember telling us that a company of some sort had made an offer for the pier?'

'Indeed we do. A derisory offer of £1 was made for the freehold, as we remember.'

'That's right. Well, we've got a representative of that company here on the pier today. She tells us that the council has approved their plans to knock down the pier entrance and the theatre and to build some offices and a conference centre.'

'Send them away with a flea in their ear or simply toss them overboard,' suggested Mr Canterbury, in a most un-lawyerly way.

'Unfortunately, two members of the council have come with them,' said Mrs Caldicot. 'They say that if Mr Livingstone doesn't sell them the pier they will make our lives very miserable. Apparently there is a lot of employment legislation they can use to cause us trouble.'

'Ah,' said Mr Canterbury. 'Pares cum paribus facillime congregantur. Birds of a feather flock together. We fear that your unwelcome visitors may have exaggerated their powers somewhat. Much of the employment legislation relates to Departments of Central Government and so is, strictly speaking, outside the remit of the council. But there is no doubt that a local council official with a bee in his bonnet, so to speak, and a link with financially ambitious corsairs, could cause a considerable amount of trouble for a business operator with little experience of these matters. Would we be correct in assuming that you and Mr Livingstone have little experience of these matters?'

'You would, indeed,' said Mrs Caldicot.

'Then we think you need help!'

'We do! That's why I rang you. Both Mr Livingstone and I hoped that you might be able to give us some advice. You seemed very sympathetic and supportive.'

'We are delighted to hear that. And we'll be delighted to help. Our first advice is that neither of you should speak to anyone. Don't agree to anything. And above all don't let Mr Livingstone sign anything – whatever it is.'

'OK,' agreed Mrs Caldicot. 'Don't do anything. I think we can manage that.'

'We need to talk in person,' said Mr Canterbury.

'Of course,' agreed Mrs Caldicot. 'I'll check out the train times and ring you back. We'll come and see you as soon as we can.'

'No, no! This needs to be sorted out in situ. We'll come there, down to Penmouth. We have high hopes of a satisfactory outcome and a case of Nolle prosequi!'

'A case of what?' asked Mrs Caldicot, assuming that Mr Canterbury was talking of something bottled and alcoholic.

'Nolle prosequi,' said Mr Canterbury. 'The abandonment and withdrawal of the case by the plaintiffs.'

'Really? That would be marvellous. Thank you very much! But, er...'

'Your fear, perhaps, is that you don't have any money and you are concerned about our fees?'

'Yes, to be honest, I am.'

'Then worry not. It will be a delight to help. Yours is by far the most interesting case we have had for some considerable time.' There was a pause and Mrs Caldicot could hear Mr Canterbury rifling through some papers on his desk. 'We can't get down there until tomorrow morning. Just tell your friends from the council that you cannot speak to them until your legal advisor arrives.'

'Oh that's wonderful. Thank you so much,' said Mrs Caldicot. 'You're our knight in armour!'

'It would have to be a very large suit of armour and a very strong horse,' said Mr Canterbury, with a self-deprecating chuckle. 'Just make sure that Mr Livingstone does not agree to anything, does not say anything and…'

'…does not sign anything!'

'Absolutely. We will see you tomorrow and then we will see what can be done about frustrating these piratical endeavours. Meanwhile remember: absente reo! In the absence of the defendant there can be no unpleasant consequences.'

And so, as a result of this conversation, when the duo from the council and Ms Rothstein from the developers returned from their stroll along the pier there was no sign of Mr Livingstone.

'You go and hide somewhere,' Mrs Caldicot had told him when she'd given everyone the good news about the imminent arrival of their legal advisor. 'Mr Canterbury says you mustn't sign anything or even say anything. So it's probably best if you go and have a nice, quiet cup of tea.'

And so Mr Livingstone, together with Mr Hewitt, had gone into the café to have the prescribed 'nice cup of tea'. They also had a Chelsea bun each.

Mr Chapman, Ms Trench and Ms Rothstein were not well pleased when Mrs Caldicot told them Mr Livingstone was not available.

'I'm afraid Mr Livingstone has disappeared. Perhaps you'd like to come back tomorrow afternoon,' suggested Mrs Caldicot. 'The fact is that we do need a little more time to discuss what to do. We can see you tomorrow afternoon and discuss everything then.'

'Tomorrow afternoon then,' said Mr Chapman, wagging a podgy finger at Mrs Caldicot. 'You've got 24 hours and not a minute longer.'

'You really don't have much choice, do you?' said Ms Trench.

Mr Chapman, Ms Trench and Ms Rothstein then marched off the pier and climbed into a very large, chauffeur-driven Mercedes that had been parked on double lines waiting for their return.

Chapter Twenty Seven

Mr Canterbury arrived just before lunch the following day. He had travelled down to Penmouth in a black taxi cab – one of the rather cubic cabs that are so commonly seen in London. He looked just the same as when Mr Livingstone and Mrs Caldicot had met him in his office. He was still on the large side of substantial. And, as before, he wore pince nez with a gold frame, a dark-grey pinstripe suit with a broad chalk stripe, a celluloid wing collar and a black bow tie. Over the pinstripe suit he wore a Victorian Ulster, a day coat in herringbone tweed which had the traditional cape attached at the shoulder. On his head he wore a black fedora which gave him a distinctly theatrical air.

He looked extremely imposing, and both Mr Livingstone and Mrs Caldicot remembered that when they first met him they thought he looked as though he had climbed out of the pages of a novel by Charles Dickens. He could only have been a lawyer.

Both Mrs Caldicot and Mr Livingstone felt much better when he arrived. He was a man whose very presence was comforting.

'We hate motor cars,' he explained when he had successfully decanted himself and told the taxi driver to park nearby and wait for him. He had with him a very old and battered briefcase which appeared to be bulging with paperwork. 'Motor cars are all so tiny,' he added, with a shudder of distaste. He explained that only in the back of a London style taxi cab could he have room to sit comfortably.

Mrs Caldicot and Mr Livingstone formally welcomed him to Penmouth Pier and introduced him to everyone around. To their astonishment, Mr Canterbury seemed able to remember everyone's name after a single introduction.

'Would you like something to eat?' asked Mrs Roberts. They had temporarily closed the café so that they could entertain the solicitor in some privacy.

'What do you have?' asked Mr Canterbury, brightening up noticeably.

'We can offer you fish and chips, hot, buttered crumpets, cheese on toast, hot, buttered teacakes and a variety of sandwiches,' offered Mrs Roberts.

'Splendid,' said Mr Canterbury. He thought for a moment. 'Those sound very satisfactory.' He stood for a moment gazing up the length of the pier. A broad smile appeared on his face as he did so. He seemed transfixed with delight as he looked at the pier, the stalls and, most of all, the little, red and yellow train.

'Which would you like?' asked Mrs Roberts, rather diffidently.

Mr Canterbury looked confused and rather disappointed. 'Do we have to make a choice?'

'No, no, not at all,' said Mrs Caldicot quickly. 'Would you like some of everything?'

'Oh, I think so, yes. I haven't eaten since breakfast.'

'We have also managed to buy you a loaf of nice, crusty bread and a pound of cheddar cheese,' said Mrs Caldicot.

'Splendid!' said Mr Canterbury, smiling. 'That will do very nicely for later.'

'And I managed to find you a nice bottle of port,' said Mr Livingstone. 'The man at the off licence said it was the best they had.'

'Even better!'

They led Mr Canterbury into the café where a table for one had been prepared for him. The bottle of port which Mr Livingstone had purchased was sitting on the table, together with a rather good lead crystal wine glass which Mr Livingstone had discovered in a cupboard upstairs.

'We can talk while we eat,' he said, when he'd removed his ulster and fedora and had settled down, putting his briefcase on the chair beside him.

A moment later Miss Pettifer put a large plate of buttered crumpets on the table in front of him. 'What sort of fish would you like?' she asked. She seemed flustered at having to wait on such an important guest.

'What sort of fish do you have, Miss Pettifer?'

'I'll go and ask Dorothy,' said Miss Pettifer, blushing.

She returned a moment later. The blush was now a little more noticeable.

'Cod,' she said.

'Then cod would be very satisfactory,' said Mr Canterbury, with a smile. He watched her go back across the café and then picked up a buttered crumpet and took a tentative nibble. After a moment he nodded, as though approvingly, and then took a much larger bite.

'I think it would perhaps be easier if you and Mr Livingstone were to sit with me,' said Mr Canterbury to Mrs Caldicot. 'The three of us can then discuss the possibilities which must be considered, before summarising the situation to the remainder of your party. Does that sound acceptable?'

'Very,' agreed Mrs Caldicot.

'Absolutely,' said Mr Livingstone.

'Now, the current situation is, as we understand it, that you, Mr Livingstone, are still the sole owner of the Penmouth Pier. Are we correct?'

Mr Livingstone agreed that this was correct.

'And all these other people whom we have met are employed by you to help run the pier? All have different roles and responsibilities? Dorothy Pickering and Miss Pettifer run the café, Miss Nightingale and Mrs Peterborough operate the shop and so on.' Mr Canterbury finished off the crumpet and started on a teacake. He ate slowly but methodically.

'That's about it,' agreed Mr Livingstone. 'Everyone does what they feel best suits them.'

'And they are all employed by you?'

'No, not really,' said Mr Livingstone. 'I've never had any employees.'

'How can that be? How can they not be employed by you?'

'Well, we haven't really thought about it in those terms,' said Mr Livingstone. 'They're all friends rather than employees.'

'Are all these people residents of the former nursing home where you met?'

'Oh no,' said Mrs Caldicot. 'There's Dorothy and Miss Pettifer who run the café, as you know, and there's Dorothy's father, Mr Pickering. He drives the little train. Miss Pettifer used to be the Fat Lady but she lost a lot of weight.'

'Good heavens!' said Mr Canterbury, he looked across at Miss Pettifer and then returned his attention to his teacake. 'How large was she?' he asked. 'She's very slender now.'

'I'm not really sure,' admitted Mrs Caldicot, who would not have described Miss Pettifer as slender and would, indeed, have thought the word 'plump' more accurate.

'Good heavens!' said Mr Canterbury again. When he'd taken another decent sized bite of the teacake he opened the bottle of port and filled the glass in front of him. He then took a healthy sip from the glass and nodded his approval. 'Excellent!'

'And there's Errol,' said Mr Livingstone. 'He's a friend of Dorothy's, but he lives and works here now. And Mr Rowbottham.'

'What does Mr Rowbottham do?'

'He makes silhouettes of people.'

'Using scissors and black card?'

'Well, it's sort of thick paper really.'

'Good heavens! We didn't know anyone was still doing that. We must take a look afterwards.' He took another large bite from the teacake and looked up as Miss Pettifer brought him a large plateful of cod and chips. He smiled and thanked her.

'I'm sure Mr Rowbottham will be delighted to make your silhouette!' said Mrs Caldicot.

'He'll need a large piece of paper!' laughed Mr Canterbury. Several chins wobbled when he laughed. 'And Errol? What does he do?'

'He helps Mr Williams.'

'And what does Mr Williams do?'

'He's our pier photographer. And there's Jean-Jacques,' added Mrs Caldicot. 'I'm not sure how long he'll stay. He's the nice, young French boy who was playing the accordion in the archway when you arrived.'

'Very well, too,' said Mr Canterbury. 'And the young lady who was singing?' He poured vinegar over his cod and chips and then added salt in plentiful quantities.

'Oh, that's Ruth,' said Mrs Caldicot. 'She came with us. She's the assistant housekeeper.'

'So she's an employee?'

'Well sort of I suppose.'

'Do you pay her?'

'We provide her with accommodation and food and give her £30 a week pocket money,' said Mrs Caldicot.

'Is she happy with that?'

'Oh yes, I think so.'

'How many hours a week does she work?'

'I'm not really sure.'

'Have you heard of the minimum wage for employees?'

'Yes,' murmured Mrs Caldicot. She thought for a moment. 'Oh dear,' she said.

'Oh dear, indeed,' said Mr Canterbury. 'And how many other employees do you have?'

'Well, there's Mrs Roberts,' said Mrs Caldicot. 'I suppose you could call her an employee. She's our housekeeper.'

'And how much do you pay Mrs Roberts?'

'She gets her accommodation and food and expenses and so on and she has £60 a week for her personal spending.'

'Does she have duties every day?'

'Oh yes.'

Mr Canterbury looked at Mrs Caldicot and waved his fork in her general direction as though about to say something. He then shook his head, abandoned whatever it was he was going to say, and then picked up two chips with the fork and popped them into his mouth.

'We do keep accounts,' said Mrs Caldicot. 'Mr Twist used to work for the Inland Revenue when it was called the Inland Revenue and before it became Her Majesty's Customs and Revenue. He looks after the accounts for us. He makes sure that all the bills are paid.'

'Well, that's something!' said Mr Canterbury, who seemed to be coming to terms with the rather unusual way that Mrs Caldicot and her companions managed their financial affairs. He finished chewing the two sample chips and swallowed them. 'Splendid!' he said. 'These are excellent chips!'

'Good,' said Mrs Caldicot. 'I'm pleased.'

'A good chip is a joy to behold,' said Mr Canterbury with a poignant sigh. 'As the years go by so the body's betrayals accumulate. We know well that one day we will find ourselves no longer able to enjoy a full range of gustatory joys and so we take our pleasures while we can; while the body may protest but does not yet forbid.'

‘I’m so glad you’re satisfied,’ said Mrs Caldicot. ‘The girls will be pleased.’

‘We can see that your unusual financial circumstances were possibly acceptable when you just lived together in your former nursing home,’ said Mr Canterbury. ‘You were not running a business and we assume that your income came largely in the form of pensions and so on.’

‘Mostly, yes,’ said Mrs Caldicot. ‘Mr Williams has an income from his photographs but he has an agent who looks after his accounts for him and makes sure that his taxes are paid on time. Mr Twist checked everything and said it was all perfectly proper.’

Mr Canterbury frowned. ‘That wouldn’t by any chance be Mr Henry Williams, would it?’

‘Yes, that’s him!’

‘The photographer who is famous for his pictures of Paris?’

‘Yes, that’s right.’

‘He lives with you, here?’

‘Oh yes. He’s now our pier photographer. He has a Polaroid camera and he wanders up and down the pier taking pictures of holidaymakers.’

Mr Canterbury stopped with a forkful of cod half way to his mouth. ‘Mr Henry Williams takes photographs of holidaymakers on Penmouth Pier with a Polaroid camera?’

Mrs Caldicot nodded.

‘We have three of Mr Williams’s photographs on our dining room wall,’ he said. ‘We paid several hundred pounds for them many years ago.’ Mr Canterbury completed the journey with the fork and the cod disappeared.

‘I’ll introduce you later,’ said Mrs Caldicot. ‘You’ll like him. He’s a really nice fellow.’

‘Good heavens!’ said Mr Canterbury. ‘Good heavens!’ He shook his head as though finding everything he was hearing rather difficult to accept. For a few minutes there was silence as he finished off his plateful of cod and chips. When the plate was empty he sat back and wiped his lips with the napkin with which he had been provided.

‘Now, we need to look at our options,’ he said. He drank some more of his port and then picked up a crumpet and took a large bite. Mr Livingstone and Mrs Caldicot just sat and waited.

'Would you like your Welsh rarebit now?' asked Miss Pettifer, who had hurried over to collect Mr Canterbury's empty plate. She seemed to blush every time she spoke to the solicitor.

'That would be excellent,' said Mr Canterbury, who was both a gourmet and a gourmand. 'Thank you, my dear. Did you cook the chips and the fish with your own fair hands?'

'No, Dorothy did the cooking,' said Miss Pettifer with clear regret. 'I'm just the waitress.' She was very taken with Mr Canterbury. She had always been attracted to large men and she had never met a larger man than Mr Canterbury.

'Not just the waitress!' said Mr Canterbury, putting the emphasis on the word 'just'. 'Good heavens, you are not just the waitress, my dear. To convey food with such delicacy requires an honest and willing spirit. But please convey my thanks and congratulations to Dorothy for an excellent plate of cod and chips; thoroughly delectable; most welcome; exquisitely enjoyable.'

'I'll bring over your Welsh rarebit as soon as it's ready,' said Miss Pettifer, now blushing even more. 'Would you like some more crumpets and teacakes?'

Mr Canterbury looked at the plates which had contained the buttered crumpets and teacakes. Both were empty. He thought for a moment. 'Not just now,' he said. 'After the cheese on toast I'll have the fresh bread and the block of cheddar. Just for nibbling.'

'Wonderful!' said Miss Pettifer, who loved to see a man with a healthy appetite and who, it has to be admitted, had never seen a man with a healthier affection for his food. She was still blushing as she hurried away with the empty plates.

'What a lovely, young lady!' said Mr Canterbury, who seemed quite taken with his waitress. 'You say she used to appear on the pier as the Fat Lady?'

'That's right,' said Mrs Caldicot.

'On this very pier?'

'Yes.'

'It's very difficult to imagine,' said Mr Canterbury.

Since there now wasn't anything on the table for him to eat he poured himself another glass of port. 'Difficult to imagine,' he repeated to himself. He closed his eyes as though trying to do just that.

Miss Pettifer then came back with Mr Canterbury's cheese on toast. On a second plate she had put a French baguette and a large chunk of cheddar cheese. She put this down on the table but to one side.

'Thank you, my dear,' said Mr Canterbury.

'My pleasure, sir,' said Miss Pettifer. She was blushing again.

'Roland,' said Mr Canterbury. 'You must call me Roland.'

'Roland,' said Miss Pettifer. She paused, smiling. 'I'm Emerald,' she said at last, suddenly realising that she was expected to tell Mr Canterbury her Christian name. The blush deepened still further.

'Emerald!' said Mr Canterbury. 'Emerald.' He pronounced the word twice, as though entranced by it. Although he was a professional whose life depended upon utterances, observations and pronouncements, he was a man whose private affection for words usually extended only to nouns such as 'cheese', 'port' and 'crumpet'. Now, suddenly and unexpectedly, he had a new favourite word. He murmured the word to himself a third time. 'Emerald.' He thought that it had an exceptional ring to it.

'Please call me if there's anything else you need,' said Miss Pettifer.

'We will,' said Mr Canterbury.

'Would you like any sauce for your Welsh rarebit?'

'Do you have brown sauce?'

'Of course! Would you prefer HP sauce or Daddy's sauce?'

Mr Canterbury did not hesitate. 'Oh, HP sauce, of course.'

'I'll fetch it.'

A moment later Miss Pettifer returned and carefully placed the bottle of HP sauce on the table. Mr Canterbury removed the top from the bottle and sprinkled liberal amounts of sauce on top of his melted cheese.

'Call me if you need anything else,' said Miss Pettifer.

'We will, Emerald,' said Mr Canterbury. 'Thank you.'

'It's a pleasure, said Miss Pettifer. 'Roland,' she added. 'It's my pleasure, Roland.'

When Miss Pettifer had gone, Mr Canterbury cut himself a large slice of his Welsh rarebit and popped it into his mouth. He couldn't remember the last time anyone had called him Roland. He thought it might perhaps have been his mother but she had died over 20 years ago. He was the sort of man who always managed to remain on formal terms with everyone he met. On the one occasion when he'd had to go into hospital even the nurses had, to their own surprise, found themselves calling him 'Mr Canterbury' – even when he wasn't present. They customarily addressed all the other patients by their Christian names but none of them quite felt able to refer to Mr Canterbury as 'Roland'. He was, they realised instinctively, a man who was naturally blessed with more than his fair share of dignity and presence. He was, one nurse had said to another reflectively, 'an old-fashioned gentleman'.

Mr Livingstone and Mrs Caldicot looked on amazed and impressed. They'd never seen anyone eat so much. It was not difficult to see why Mr Canterbury was the size he was.

'There are several possible solutions to your immediate problem,' said Mr Canterbury. 'On our journey down here it did occur to me that one possible answer to your problems might be to turn your pier into a church.'

'A church!' said Mr Livingstone and Mrs Caldicot together.

'It is remarkably easy to form a new religion,' said Mr Canterbury. 'If our pier were a church then we would be exempt from a good deal of legislation. If, for example, you became the Church of St Piers or the Church of Divine Intervention or some such thing then we would be able to argue that the council's representatives were targeting us because of our religion. That would be religious intolerance and would, of course, be a very serious crime against your various persons.'

'That sounds a good idea!' said Mr Livingstone. 'I like the idea of being a church!'

'It would, without doubt, be pleasantly mischievous,' said Mr Canterbury, cutting another large slice from his Welsh rarebit. He popped the slice into his mouth and chewed silently for a couple of minutes. Mr Canterbury was not one of those eaters who gobbled their food. He genuinely seemed to enjoy every mouthful. Miss Pettifer, Emerald, remained constantly in attendance, occasionally checking to make sure that Mr Canterbury did not need more sauce or additional supplies of condiments.

'We could have our own patron saint,' suggested Mr Livingstone. 'St Piers of Penmouth! Being on the pier is his way of walking on the water.'

'But,' Mr Canterbury continued a few moments later, 'turning ourselves into a religion would not deal with our fundamental problem. Even as a church we would be obliged to obey employment legislation. We would be exposed to a considerable amount of potential legal trouble. We would still be liable to obey the requirements related to minimum wages, working conditions, pension contributions, sexual discrimination and so on and on.'

'So the church isn't a good idea?' said Mr Livingstone sadly.

'It is now clear that it is not our best option,' said Mr Canterbury who, having finished his Welsh Rarebit had now taken out his penknife and was using it to slice pieces from the block of cheese before him. 'In a way, it's a pity because it is a neat and rather attractive solution.'

'So what can we do?' asked Mrs Caldicot. 'Is there any other solution?'

'Oh yes,' said Mr Canterbury. 'In our experience, there is always another solution. When questions are asked, answers are usually forthcoming.' He turned to Mr Livingstone. 'Mr Livingstone, you said that you are still the sole owner of the Penmouth Pier, did you not?'

'Yes. Nothing has changed since we came to your office and I signed those papers you gave me.'

'So everyone else working on the pier must, ipso facto, be an employee of ours. And we, as their employer must be responsible for ensuring that the laws of the land which relates to employment are adhered to in every respect.'

'Yes, I see that,' said Mr Livingstone, with a nod. 'Owning the pier is a good thing but it is also a bad thing.'

Deep down, he was beginning to wonder whether inheriting the pier had been such a piece of good fortune after all.

'However, there is one simple solution which we could adopt and which would, at a stroke, render us immune to these administrative imprecations and, thereby, render our opponents impotent,' said Mr Canterbury.

Mrs Caldicot and Mr Canterbury looked at him and waited.

'What we have in mind is a solution which we would not even consider offering to 99 clients out of 100,' he warned them.

'Oh dear,' said Mrs Caldicot. 'It sounds a bit frightening.'

‘Not frightening, my dear,’ said Mr Canterbury. ‘But it is an unusual answer to our problems. And it is a solution which requires a sacrifice on behalf of the proprietor.’ He cut himself another piece of cheese and slipped it into his mouth.

‘Ah,’ said Mrs Caldicot, looking at Mr Livingstone who, in turn, looked rather alarmed.

‘The advantage of it is that the council would be quite unable to take action against us in any of the ways they have threatened. We would, at a stroke, become inviolable. They would, we suspect, take their trials and tribulations to some other victim.’

‘Well, I think I’m probably all for it!’ said Mr Livingstone. ‘What’s the sacrifice? Do you want to take an arm, a leg or something more personal?’

‘No, no, no,’ said Mr Canterbury, holding up a hand. ‘There will be no need for that sort of sacrifice. Our solution is, we are pleased to say, quite bloodless.’ He tore a small piece of bread from the supply in front of him, considered it for a moment and then popped it into his mouth. There was then a short delay for Mr Canterbury was far too polite to talk while chewing.

Eventually, after swallowing, the solicitor continued. ‘At the moment, our problems arise from the fact that we are the employer and our colleagues working on the pier are our employees. We have legal responsibilities towards them all. It is this relationship which affords your tormentors the opportunity to threaten us with the many annoying facets of the nation’s complex employment legislation.’

‘I understand,’ said Mr Livingstone with a nod. He had to concentrate hard when Mr Canterbury was talking.

‘So our best solution is to find some way to rupture that relationship.’

‘I understand,’ repeated Mr Livingstone. He looked at Mrs Caldicot, who nodded that she too understood the problem. Neither of them, however, could see any sign of any solution.

‘The answer,’ said Mr Canterbury, tearing off a piece of bread, ‘is for everyone to become an owner.’ He chewed the bread and swallowed. He took a sip of port. ‘If everyone is an owner then there are no employees. Everyone is, by the very fact of their ownership, an employer. Ipso facto we have our solution! You cannot be both an employer and an employee.’

Mrs Caldicot and Mr Livingstone just stared at him. 'How could we do that?' asked Mr Livingstone at last.

'We would have to share the ownership of the pier with all our colleagues.'

'Is that all?'

'That is all.'

'That would get rid of all my problems?'

'In an instant.'

'Then let's do it!' cried Mr Livingstone.

Mr Canterbury put down his penknife and looked at Mr Livingstone very carefully. 'Are we sure we understand? It would mean that we would no longer be the sole owner of the pier. The ownership would be shared between us and all your colleagues.'

'It's brilliant!' said Mr Livingstone. 'I didn't like being the owner. It felt uncomfortable. I'll feel much better if we all own a bit of the pier. And if it helps keep those buggers at arm's length then it's clearly the thing to do. How do we do it? Do we have to divide up the pier into bits? Do we put up signs saying which bit belongs to which one of us?'

'Not at all,' said Mr Canterbury, with the hint of a smile. 'We form a limited company, distribute some shares and then everyone becomes a part- owner.'

'With equal shares?'

'The shares do not have to be equal,' said Mr Canterbury. 'But they could be. That is for us to decide. We could, in theory, divide the pier into 100,000 parts and then keep 99,000 of the parts for ourselves, distributing the remaining 1,000 parts among the other owners.'

'Like holding company shares?' said Mrs Caldicot, whose first husband, Mr Caldicot, had once bought 100 shares in a company called British Gas and who had, ever-after, regarded himself as a red-blooded capitalist.

'Exactly,' said Mr Canterbury with a nod. 'Precisely! Rem acu tetigisti. The only important thing is that everyone working on the pier becomes an owner and not an employee. The extent of their personal ownership is of no relevance. When no one is an employee and there is no employer then the employment legislation becomes irrelevant.'

'What's that rem acu whatever you said?' asked Mrs Caldicot. 'Is that Latin again?'

'Rem acu tetigisti,' said Mr Canterbury. 'It means 'you've hit the nail on the head'.'

'I should write down all these Latin phrases,' said Mrs Caldicot. 'I could use them when Jenkins gets back from America. He'll be terribly impressed!'

'Jenkins is your husband?' asked Mr Canterbury.

'That's right.'

Mr Canterbury nodded.

'If we all own a bit of the pier, how do people get paid?' asked Mr Livingstone.

'The owners must receive their remuneration in the form of dividends,' explained Mr Canterbury. 'If they are paid salaries or wages then there is, once again, an employee-employer relationship and our endeavours will have been without purpose and we will have made no progress in thwarting and confounding our tormentors.'

'May I ask Mr Twist to come over?' Mrs Caldicot asked Mr Canterbury. 'He'll be the one who will have to arrange things financially.'

'Of course you may.'

'This is brilliant!' murmured Mr Twist, the accountant and former tax inspector, when he had been invited by Mrs Caldicot and Mr Livingstone to listen to Mr Canterbury's solution. 'The easiest thing to do is to set up a limited company which owns the pier. There is no practical obstacle to making that arrangement. I can then do the accounts and share out the income to all the shareholders. And we all get paid dividends rather than wages.' Mr Twist, who was clearly delighted at the simplicity and effectiveness of the scheme, beamed broadly. 'Since the pier has already been valued at £1 there will be no capital gains liabilities in transferring shares in the business.'

Mr Livingstone stood up and, much to Mr Canterbury's astonishment and, it has to be said, a certain amount of embarrassment, insisted on shaking the solicitor by the hand. And Mrs Caldicot then insisted on kissing him on the cheek.

'Everyone who works on the pier gets an equal share,' said Mr Livingstone firmly. 'That's the fairest way to do it.'

'Would you like some Turkish Delight to celebrate?' Mrs Caldicot asked the solicitor.

Mr Canterbury's eyes widened. 'You have Turkish Delight? Here on the pier?'

'Oh yes!'

'We love Turkish Delight,' said a delighted Mr Canterbury. 'It is the only sweetmeat we enjoy.'

Mrs Caldicot popped across to the shop and fetched a box of Turkish Delight. She put the box down in front of Mr Canterbury. He opened it, took a piece and then pushed the box back across the table towards Mrs Caldicot.

'Thank you, that was splendid!' he said, a few moments later, savouring the taste and texture of the sweetmeat.

'The box is for you,' said Mrs Caldicot, pushing the box back towards Mr Canterbury.

'The whole box is for us?'

'Oh yes.'

If Mr Canterbury had been a cat he would have purred. He was, he thought, as close to heaven as a lawyer can ever be.

'When we look around,' he said softly to Mrs Caldicot and Mr Livingstone, 'we realise that we have discovered that life is something to be enjoyed. As an Englishman, and as a lawyer to boot, this is not something to which we are accustomed. It is, to be perfectly frank, a concept which has always rather unsettled us.' He paused, contemplating the open box of Turkish Delight. 'But it is a notion to which we are becoming increasingly well adjusted.' He took another piece of Turkish Delight and popped it into his mouth. 'We really should have had more fun in life,' he murmured to himself. 'We haven't had nearly enough.'

'It's not too late!' said Mrs Caldicot, who still remembered her own dull, grey years; years when life had been an endurance event rather than offering much in the way of hope or delight. She now looked back on those waste land years as though they had been lived by someone else. 'It's not too late at all.'

'Potius sero quam nunquam,' said Mr Canterbury. 'Better late than never'. We are beginning to realise that we haven't take enough risks in our life. We really don't want to find ourselves wearing Velcro fastened trousers and having nothing to remember but a bunch of regrets about the things we could have done but didn't.'

'I would like you to be one of the shareholders,' said Mr Livingstone to the lawyer. 'Would you accept?'

Mr Canterbury, clearly startled, looked at him and raised two bushy eyebrows.

'I'd be honoured if you would,' said Mr Livingstone.

'Well, we are not sure...,' protested Mr Canterbury.

'It would be a very small way for us to reward you for your work,' said Mrs Caldicot. 'When we pay out the dividends it would enable us to pay you a little for your work.'

'And if there's anything else we can do for you...' said Mr Livingstone.

Mr Canterbury took a large, freshly laundered white handkerchief from a trouser pocket and dabbed at his eyes. 'The sea air must be affecting our eyes,' he said apologetically.

When he had wiped his eyes he blew his nose. 'We would be delighted to accept a small shareholding in the pier,' he said, when he had eventually put away the handkerchief. 'We would be absolutely delighted.'

Miss Pettifer, who was standing beside the lawyer in case he needed more crumpets or teacakes, was so affected by Mr Canterbury's happiness that she added to it by kissing him on the cheek.

It occurred to Mr Canterbury, with Miss Pettifer's kiss still fresh on his cheek and a box of Turkish Delight before him, that if he were to die at that moment he would not feel inclined to consider himself ill done by.

'There is one small thing which has been on our mind,' said Mr Canterbury. He spoke softly, rather hesitantly. 'It concerns the little train which runs up and down the pier.'

'Do you like it?' asked Mr Livingstone. 'Or is there a problem with it? Does it have to go?'

'Oh no, it doesn't have to go,' said Mr Canterbury quickly. 'There is no problem. It's just that when we were a boy our parents took us to Weston-super-Mare on our holidays. There was a little train which ran up and down the pier and ever since those days we have always wanted to drive something similar.' He spoke very quietly.

'Would you like to drive our train?'

Mr Canterbury was so overcome that he found it difficult to respond.

'That's no problem at all!' said Mr Livingstone.

'Do you know if there is a bell? Is there a bell which the driver has to ring to warn pedestrians that the train is coming?'

'Oh yes,' said Mr Livingstone. 'There's definitely a bell. One of those big brass bells, like an old school bell. It's fixed to the cab, just where the driver sits, and you ring it by waggling a bit of rope from side to side.'

'And we could…?'

'Definitely!' said Mrs Caldicot. 'You can drive the train and ring the bell to your heart's content.'

'It's quite easy once you've got the hang of it,' added Mr Livingstone. 'And although Mr Pickering doesn't usually bother to wear it there is a special driver's cap with a shiny peak that you can wear. It says 'Driver' in gold letters across the front.'

'You have driven the train?' asked Mr Canterbury, as though Mr Livingstone had just confessed that he had walked on the moon.

'Oh yes!' said Mr Livingstone. 'Mr Pickering was a little cautious at first, but he gave Mr Hewitt and myself a few driving lessons and now he lets us drive it whenever we like. I think he likes having a couple of assistant drivers. It means he can stand on the pier and do a little fishing occasionally.

'You are officially an assistant driver?'

'Yes,' said Mr Livingstone with a big grin. 'Pretty good, eh?'

'Do you have a badge?'

'You mean a badge that says 'Driver'?'

'Precisely so.'

'No, I don't. But I suppose we could have some made. Actually, we ought to have some made.'

'And you have definitely rung the bell?'

'Oh yes.'

'While wearing the driver's cap?'

'Oh yes.'

'And driving the train up and down the pier?'

'Many times.'

'Mr Pickering would be happy to teach us how to drive the little train?'

'Definitely. I'm sure he would.'

'And allow us to wear the driver's cap?'

'Oh yes. Until we have some badges made it would be a good idea for you to wear the cap,' agreed Mr Livingstone.

Mr Canterbury, who was now almost certain that life could not get any better than this, closed his eyes and took several deep breaths. Miss Pettifer, who could tell that he was affected emotionally, put her arm around his shoulders and gave him a squeeze. Mr Canterbury now knew, with total certainty, that life could not get any better.

And then, without any more ado, Mrs Caldicot and Mr Livingstone rounded up every one of their friends, old and new, and they held a meeting upstairs in the ball room, where there was much more room than in the café. And there, in the ballroom, Mr Canterbury, who stood clutching his box of Turkish Delight in one hand and a glass of port in the other, explained that unless there were any objections he intended to draw up the papers making everyone an equal owner of the Penmouth Pier. The shares would, he said, be distributed on condition that no one could sell their part ownership of the pier to an outsider.

The news was greeted with universal acclaim.

Well, who wouldn't want to be a part owner of Penmouth's seaside pleasure pier?

Chapter Twenty Eight

It was just after three o'clock that afternoon when the deputation from the local council arrived.

By then Mr Canterbury had drawn up the necessary papers and the Penmouth Pier belonged to everyone.

All of those present, (together with Jenkins, who was in America but never forgotten) had become owners of the Penmouth Pier.

And, at Mr Livingstone's insistence, all of them, including Mr Canterbury, had become equal owners.

Moreover, Mr Pickering had happily agreed to train Mr Canterbury to drive the train. ('The most important thing to remember,' he said, 'is to keep ringing the bell.') And Mrs Caldicot had agreed that they should order some impressive looking badges which had the words 'Train Driver' printed on them in gold letters, and had also agreed that they should order another driver's hat in a slightly larger size, especially for Mr Canterbury. It had also been agreed that Mr Canterbury would stay the night on the pier, in one of the spare bedrooms, so that he could complete his driving course before he had to go back to his office and his other, more tedious responsibilities.

'That room will always be yours,' Mrs Merivale told him. 'I shall keep it for you and for you alone. Only you and I will ever be allowed to go in. And I will only go in to make your bed, change your bed linen and do a little dusting from time to time. I'll be very happy to do your laundry for you.'

The room was small and did not have much of a view (although you could just see the sea if you opened the window) but Mr Canterbury could not have been happier or prouder if he had been told that a suite at the Ritz hotel was being reserved exclusively for his personal use at any time.

'Shall we handle this business?' Mr Canterbury asked Mr Livingstone and Mrs Caldicot, as the official deputation approached.

Mr Chapman was in the lead, his short and stubby legs striding forcefully ever onwards and his rather high-heeled shoes clomping on the wooden pier. Ms Trench, the Chief Planning Office, followed him, scurrying along obediently a pace or two behind. And Ms Rothstein, representing the developers, strode alongside her, carrying a bulging briefcase in her right hand and clutching a document case across her chest with the other.

'Oh, I think so,' said Mrs Caldicot.

'Definitely!' agreed Mr Livingstone, who would, in all honesty, have happily been somewhere else – riding up and down the pier on the little red and yellow train, for example.

'So, have you made up your mind?' demanded Mr Chapman, as soon as he was within interrogating distance of Mr Livingstone.

'My name is Canterbury and we are handling everything for Mr Livingstone,' said Mr Canterbury, stepping forward.

Mr Livingstone felt a huge sense of relief.

Miss Pettifer could not help thinking how imposing Mr Canterbury looked. She was reminded of those wonderful, tales of mediaeval armoured knights riding into battle, ready to perform deeds of derring-do; rescuing distressed damsels by the armful as a delightful side-line. Though she rather hoped that in the case of Mr Canterbury just one damsel would be enough, and one not in any particular distress.

'Who are you?' demanded Mr Chapman, rather rudely.

'Canterbury, we are an Officer of the Court and we are the legal representative of the owners of the Penmouth Pier.'

Mr Chapman, rather startled, looked first at Mr Canterbury and then at Mr Livingstone and then, finally, at Mrs Caldicot. 'You're a lawyer?' he said at last. 'A solicitor?'

'Indeed so, sir,' agreed Mr Canterbury.

'And these people have hired you?'

'In a manner of speaking, that is quite so.'

'Well, it doesn't make much difference,' said Mr Chapman. 'Has Mr Livingstone explained the situation to you?'

'He has,' confirmed Mr Canterbury. 'Or, rather, I am cognisant of the situation as it was. I think you may find that circumstances have changed somewhat since your last visit.'

Mr Chapman, slightly puzzled, looked first at Ms Trench and then at Ms Rothstein.

'In what significant way have things changed?' Asked Ms Rothstein. 'As I am sure Mr Livingstone has explained to you, he is, as the owner of Penmouth Pier, legally responsible for meeting the various obligations which lay upon his shoulders with regard to his employees.'

'Mr Livingstone does not have any employees,' said Mr Canterbury.

Mr Chapman, Ms Trench and Ms Rothstein looked at him, looked at one another and then looked back at Mr Canterbury.

'I don't understand,' said Mr Chapman. 'Has he fired everyone? Is he going to try to run the pier all by himself? Or is he going to try to persuade us that everyone here is a volunteer?'

'Mr Livingstone has fired no one,' said Mr Canterbury. 'There are no employees because everyone you see here who is associated with the pier in any way is an owner.'

Mr Chapman, Ms Trench and Ms Rothstein stared at him disbelievingly. They simply did not understand that anyone would willingly give away chunks of his property without there being some trickery involved.

'What are you trying to pull here?' demanded Mr Chapman, who'd seen too many bad movies and was now trying to snarl and look threatening. Sadly, he wasn't tall enough or big enough to look threatening. He looked what he was: a small, stocky rather disappointed and indignant man in an ill-fitting off the peg suit.

'We are not, as you so clumsily put it, 'trying to pull anything',' replied Mr Canterbury. 'Your suggestion is a scandalum magnatum. A notable and malicious slur. Mr Livingstone, who was the former sole owner of the pier, has now shared ownership of the pier, including the former hotel and the theatre, with his former employees. There are now no employees working on the pier. And the owners of the pier have asked me to make it clear to you that they are not prepared to accept your derisory offer for the freehold of the pier. Indeed, they are not prepared to accept any offers for the pier. And since there are no employees working on the pier there is, of course, no need for any further mention of employment legislation. So, unless you have anything else to say, I wish you all good day. You are, of course, quite at liberty to remain on the pier to enjoy the facilities at your own expense.'

Mr Chapman, Ms Trench and Ms Rothstein stared at him, open mouthed.

And with that, Mr Canterbury turned and headed back to the café: a defiant and victorious knight returning to the castle keep to sustain his body with a fresh supply of essential victuals. It had, after all, been nearly half an hour since he had eaten.

He was followed closely by Mr Livingstone, Mrs Caldicot, Mr Hewitt, Miss Nightingale, Mrs Peterborough, Mr Roxdale, Mr and Mrs Merivale, Mrs Torridge, Mr Williams, Mr Twist, Mrs Roberts, Mr Pickering, Dorothy, Miss Pettifer, Mr Rowbottham, Errol and last, but certainly not least, Ruth and Jean-Jacques (who had temporarily suspended their busking).

The deputation from the council, deflated, defeated and temporarily demoralised, slunk away to the chauffeur driven Mercedes motor car which was, as before, waiting for them and parked on double lines. They were none of them well pleased but, as they all agreed as they drove away from the pier, there was absolutely nothing any of them could do.

'What about the old Imperial Hotel?' asked Ms Rothstein, taking a folder from her briefcase. 'It wasn't our first choice but if we can't have the pier then the old hotel will have to do. It's been empty for months.'

'We can definitely help you with the old hotel,' said Ms Trench. 'We can fix up planning permission for you in a jiffy. And in some ways, and I think Mr Chapman will agree with me on this, you might find the former Imperial Hotel preferable, in many ways, to the pier.'

'Oh most definitely,' said Mr Chapman, agreeing with her. 'The logistics make it a far superior choice.' He was bloodied and numbed but far too greedy to be unbowed.

Both Mr Chapman and Ms Trench had personal interests in the success of this operation. Decent sums paid into a couple of offshore bank accounts.

Naturally, Mrs Caldicot and Mr Livingstone, Mr Canterbury and the rest, knew nothing about this conversation for they were busy sitting down and preparing to enjoy a traditional, Devon cream tea: scones, jam and lashings of clotted cream.

Hastily written 'Closed for Tea' signs hung on the handle of the shop door, Mrs Torridge's Fortune Teller booth, Mr Rowbottham's booth, the little train and the handle of the café door.

Mr Canterbury's forgotten taxi driver was there with them, too. Errol had been sent to find him and to bring back to the pier for the sustenance he would require before making the journey home, without his passenger.

'I've always been a little confused about this,' said Mr Canterbury to Miss Pettifer as the latter put a large plateful of scones in front of him, and then add two decent sized pots of cream and strawberry jam. 'Should one put the cream on the scone first, with the jam on top of the cream, or should one put the jam on before the cream?'

'In Cornwall they split the scone in two and put the strawberry jam on first. They then put the clotted cream on top of the jam,' explained Miss Pettifer. 'But in Devon we split the scone in two and put the clotted cream straight onto the scone, as if the scone were being buttered. We then put the strawberry jam onto the top of the cream.'

'Ah, good,' said Mr Canterbury. 'And since we're in Devon…'

'…the cream goes on first!'

They both agreed that it was crucial to get the important things right in life.

'Emerald, would you be kind enough to come and join me as soon as you've finished serving the others?' Mr Canterbury asked Miss Pettifer.

'Thank you, Roland,' said Miss Pettifer. 'I would be delighted.'

Chapter Twenty Nine

Jenkins arrived in Penmouth a week later.

He had, of course, never even seen the pier because he had left for his speaking engagement in America some hours before Mrs Caldicot and the rest of the gang had set off on their journey to Devon.

'Golly!' he said, when he saw the pier. He was, he admitted later, terribly impressed.

It was early evening and everyone was very busy.

Ruth and Jean-Jacques were busking at the entrance to the pier.

Miss Nightingale and Mrs Peterborough were in the shop, serving up ice creams, postcards and tickets for the little train, which was on this occasion being driven by Mr Canterbury.

Mr Canterbury, who was having more fun than he could ever remember having before, had not been back to his office since he had arrived in Penmouth, and he showed absolutely no signs of going back to a life of mortgage deeds and wills. He had telephoned his secretary and receptionist and told them that he would not be back for a few months – at least. He had, however, assured them that he would continue to pay their salaries. It seemed easier than dealing with the paperwork required to close the business and to make arrangements for the two loyal employees to receive their pensions. There was, he knew, enough money in his bank account to pay their salaries indefinitely.

Mr Canterbury proudly wore a train driver's hat and had a newly made enamelled badge bearing the words 'Train Driver' pinned to his jacket. He was, it was generally believed, the only man in history to drive a train on a pier while wearing a stiff collar and a neatly knotted, black bow tie. 'A man is entitled to be a damned fool at my time of life,' he said to Mr Hewitt. On the seat beside him there lay a box of cheese and tomato sandwiches which Emerald, his fiancée, and still the café waitress, had prepared for him so that he would not go hungry as he travelled up and down the pier between meals.

Mr Roxdale and Mr Merivale were painting the railings at the side of the pier, Mr Twist was doing the accounts (he said it was much better to do them on a daily basis, rather than to wait until the end of the month, the quarter or, heaven forbid, the year) and Mr Williams was wandering up and down the pier taking snaps. Errol his assistant was hard at work in the darkroom. Mr Rowbottham was snipping profiles out of sheets of black cartridge paper and Mrs Torridge was telling people what their future held. Mrs Merivale was doing practical things upstairs in the old hotel, which was now their home, and Mr Pickering was showing visitors from Bristol how to fish for mackerel from the jetty at the end of the pier. Mr Pickering had never actually caught any mackerel but he had never really wanted to catch anything, so that was fine.

And Mr Livingstone and Mr Hewitt were sitting on a bench, in the sunshine, eating ice creams and watching seagulls swooping over the sea. The seagulls too were fishing and proving far more successful than Mr Pickering had ever been, or was ever likely to be.

'Do you believe in that Buddhist stuff?' asked Mr Livingstone. 'About us all being reincarnated according to how we behaved the last time we were here on earth?'

'You mean that Karma Sutra stuff?'

'I think the Karma Sutra stuff is something else. I meant the plain, vanilla karma stuff. Do you believe in it?'

'Believe in it?'

'Yes.'

'I suppose so. Possibly.'

'Because if it's true, if what we get in this life is a reflection of how well we behaved in our last life, then we must have been bloody good people in our last lives. If we were snails then we must have been pretty damned good snails.'

Mr Hewitt licked his ice cream, and nibbled a bit off the chocolate flake that was stuck into the top of it. 'You could be right about that,' he said at last. He thought for a while. 'I don't remember being a snail,' he added.

'I thought I might stroll down and get a newspaper from the shop when I've finished my ice cream,' said Mr Livingstone.

'Or we could catch the next train down,' suggested Mr Hewitt.

'Good idea,' said Mr Livingstone. He paused, and watched a cormorant dive into the sea. 'A bit later on, though.'

'I say! Look! Here comes Mrs Caldicot's other half!' said Mr Hewitt, using his ice cream to point to Jenkins, who had left his bags with Ruth and who was now strolling up the pier.

Ruth had promised to take the bags up to what had been Mrs Caldicot's room and what would now be Mr and Mrs Jenkins's room.

'You all seem well settled,' said Jenkins. 'There were no problems with the move?'

'No problems at all,' said Mr Hewitt. 'Everyone went as smooth as silk.'

'Nothing your wife couldn't handle!' said Mr Livingstone.

'Have you seen her?' asked Jenkins. 'Ruth said she thought I'd find her down this end of the pier.'

'She'll probably be in the theatre with Mrs Roberts,' said Mr Livingstone.

'They'll be getting ready for tonight's performance,' added Mr Hewitt.

Jenkins looked puzzled, as well he might have done. He was not aware that his wife had theatrical ambitions of any kind, although he was well aware that a film had been made about her early adventures. But he knew her well enough not to be surprised. And he would not have been unduly surprised if he'd been told that she and Mrs Roberts were rehearsing a tap dancing act.

'Just keep walking along the pier,' said Mr Livingstone. 'You can't miss it. The theatre is right at the end. If there wasn't a big rock there anyway the theatre would stop you falling into the sea.'

'It's a big building with the word 'THEATRE' on it,' said Mr Hewitt, helpfully. 'I think you'll find that Mrs Caldicot will be inside.'

'Thanks,' said Jenkins, smiling to himself and continuing along the pier. As he did so he heard a bell ringing. He turned and saw a red and yellow train approaching. He stepped aside and saw to his surprise that the train was being driven by a very large man whom he had never seen before and who was wearing a driver's cap and a stiff collar with a bow tie.

As promised, Jenkins found Mrs Caldicot in the theatre.

She put down the box of Turkish Delight she was holding and threw her arms around her husband's neck. They kissed and hugged for a while. Mrs Roberts hurried off, muttering something about needing to do something with some posters that needed pinning up in the foyer.

'I've missed you terribly,' said Mrs Caldicot.

'And I've missed you.'

'How did things go in America?'

'I think things went well, thank you.'

'And was your flight OK?'

'The people at Yale paid for an expensive seat so I stretched out and slept most of the way.'

'So you're not too tired?'

'No, not at all, surprisingly.'

'Good. Because you're on in…' Mrs Caldicot looked at her watch '…forty seven minutes.'

'What do you mean 'I'm on'? asked Jenkins, rather startled.

'Well, we bought a projector and a screen from a man who sold some old posters for us and everything works quite well except for the sound thingy. I rang up the man we bought them from and he said it happens sometimes. Apparently we need a new carburettor or a battery or a speaker or something and so he's going to come down and fit one but he can't do it for weeks and we are showing a film this evening and we've sold quite a few tickets.'

'And so the show must go on?'

'Exactly! I knew you'd understand!'

'I don't really. You're showing a film tonight?'

'Yes, that's right. We've converted the theatre into a cinema and we're showing old black and white films. Lots of Gary Cooper, Clark Cable and Jimmy Cagney.'

'And what are you showing tonight?'

'Casablanca. With Humphrey Bogart.'

'Together with Ingrid Bergman, Peter Lorre, Sydney Greenstreet, Claude Rains and Paul somebody.'

'That's the one. It's Paul Henreid who plays the hero in the story. It's funny. I always forget his name. I only know it now because we've got posters with his name on. It's like that chap in the Magnificent Seven.'

'The one no one can remember?'

'That's right. Can you remember his name?'

'Brad Dexter,' said Jenkins. 'He was a chum of Frank Sinatra's. Saved him from drowning and got a medal for it. Did you say we had forty seven minutes?'

'Forty four now.'

'What am I doing? If you've got no sound and you're hoping that I'll play the piano then I'll have to disappoint you. I can't play the piano.'

'No, no, we need you because we're going to dub the voices. Isn't that what they call it? Dubbing?'

Jenkins, puzzled, looked at his wife. 'I don't understand.'

'We've got hold of two copies of the script,' explained Mrs Caldicot. 'And we have a loudspeaker system in the theatre, it's there really for making public announcements, but it's quite good and so we can use that.'

Jenkins, still puzzled, looked at his wife.

'Mrs Roberts is playing the Ingrid Bergman part, Mr Canterbury does Sydney Greenstreet ever so well and Mr Twist does a marvellous Peter Lorre.'

'You mean, you've got people reading out the script while the film is shown on the screen?'

'Yes. We've been doing it for several days now. It's gone down ever so well.'

'Who is Mr Canterbury?'

'Oh, of course, you haven't met him, have you? Do you remember that Mr Livingstone and I went to see a solicitor when he heard that he'd inherited a pier?'

'Yes I do.'

'Well, the solicitor was a really nice fellow called Mr Canterbury. He helped us a good deal and then we had a little problem the other day and he came down to help us sort it out.'

'You didn't say anything about having problems when we talked on the phone! Once you'd got rid of the bailiffs you said everything went smoothly.'

'No, well, I didn't want to bother you. Anyway, Mr Canterbury sorted things out and now we all own a bit of the pier. You're an owner too.'

'I own a bit of the pier?' said Jenkins, startled. 'I own a bit of this pier?'

'Yes. Mr Livingstone signed some papers and now we're all joint owners. It made tremendous sense. It was all very clever, really. Mr Canterbury has some papers for you to sign when you've both got a minute. He's a really lovely man. He's marvellous in the Sydney Greenstreet part. And he's engaged to Miss Pettifer.'

'Miss Pettifer?'

'She used to be the Fat Lady but now she's a waitress in the café, she helps Dorothy.'

'Dorothy?'

'Dorothy Pickering. She's Mr Pickering's daughter. She's going out with Errol who helps Mr Williams develop his photographs.'

'I don't suppose that was Mr Canterbury whom I saw driving the little red and yellow train?' said Jenkins, who was beginning to wonder how long he'd been away. 'He had on a train driver's cap and a stiff collar. He looked like a lawyer out of a novel by Dickens.'

'Yes, he does, doesn't he?' said Mrs Caldicot. 'That would be Mr Canterbury. He loves driving the train. Mr Pickering used to drive it but he seems quite happy to spend his days showing people how to fish off the side of the pier. No one ever catches anything but they all seem to have a good time. Mr Pickering drives the train during cinema performances and while Mr Canterbury has his breakfast, his elevenses, his lunch, his afternoon tea and his dinner.'

'You said you needed me to do something to help with the film in forty seven minutes time.'

Mrs Caldicot looked at her watch. 'Thirty nine minutes now.'

'What am I doing in thirty nine minutes time?'

'We need you to be Humphrey Bogart. To play Rick – the bar owner. You don't have to do any acting. You just read out Rick's lines when he's supposed to be speaking. Mr Williams was going to play the Bogart part but he's got a very strong Welsh accent and he doesn't think it's quite suitable for the part. We're going to show 'How Green is My Valley?' next week and he's playing several parts in that. You must hear Mr Roxdale do the Claude Rains part. He's marvellous though he's a little deaf and when it's his turn to speak we have to nudge him a little bit to get him going.'

'And what about the piano playing? How do you manage that?'

'Well, we've got a piano and Mr Livingstone plays it. He's very good.'

'And the singing of the Marseillaise?'

'We all sing that together. The audience love it. They laughed ever such a lot last night and everyone joined in singing it with us. People who came out of the theatre had such a good time that they were crying. And we're getting massive numbers of people booking seats. Mrs Roberts says she thinks that we shouldn't bother with fixing the sound when we get the new carburettor or battery or whatever it is but that we should carry on reading all the lines ourselves.'

Jenkins looked at his wife. She never failed to amaze him. He really did love her so very much. He decided that he really didn't ever want to go away from her again.

'We're going to show 'Gone with the Wind' in a couple of weeks' time. I know it's in colour and we usually only do black and white but I think it will be very popular. We want you to read Rhett Butler's part. Mrs Roberts says she thinks you'll make a marvellous Cary Grant.'

'Clark Gable.'

'Clark Gable?'

'It was Clark Gable in 'Gone with the Wind', not Cary Grant.'

'Well, she says you'll make a marvellous Clark Gable. And I think so too. Although, you'll definitely sound much sexier than he did.' Mrs Caldicot looked at her watch. 'We're on in twenty nine minutes. And then after the performance you can have one of Dorothy's fish suppers. Mr Canterbury says she makes the best chips he's ever tasted.'

'He looks as if he should know!'

'Oh yes. He's got a marvellous appetite. I think that's why Miss Pettifer fell for him. She used to be the Fat Lady on the pier. Did I mention that?'

'I think so but I'm not entirely sure.'

'And Mr Roxdale and Mr Hewitt are planning to build a rockery on Stone Rock.'

'Isn't that the lump of rock on which the theatre is built?'

'That's it.'

'But it's enormous! How big a rockery are they planning to build?'

'I have a suspicion it will probably end up in the Guinness Book of Records,' said Mrs Caldicot. 'Oh, and we have a lot of Turkish Delight. Tons of it!'

'Tons?'

'No, not really tons. But there were 868 one pound boxes in a cupboard at the back of the shop. The man who used to run the pier seemed to like ordering stuff. I think perhaps he was getting a kick back from the wholesaler.'

Jenkins thought for a moment. 'That's nearly half a ton. That's a lot of Turkish Delight.'

'I know,' smiled Mrs Caldicot.

'I saw some in the airport shop,' said Jenkins. 'I very nearly bought you a boxful!'

'That would be a case of 'Alcinoo pom dare; crocum in Cilician ferre; noctuas Athenas ferre'!' said Mrs Caldicot.

Jenkins stared at her.

'It's Latin!' said Mrs Caldicot.

'I know it is,' said Jenkins. 'But what the devil does it mean?'

'To give apples to Alcinous, to take saffron to Cicilianus and to carry owls to Athens!'

'To carry coals to Newcastle?'

'That's right. Mr Canterbury uses a lot of Latin phrases. He taught me that one.'

'Mr Canterbury being the driver of the little red and yellow train?'

'That's him!'

Jenkins swallowed hard. It was clear that a good deal had happened while he'd been away. 'Did the pier shop just have vast quantities of Turkish Delight? No seaside rock?'

'Oh yes, absolutely tons of pink seaside rock too – all peppermint flavoured. But the lettering inside was all misprinted. People don't seem to mind a bit. In fact, Mrs Peterborough says that they sell a lot of it and that when we have some more made we should make sure that it's misprinted again. We used to have a lot of coconut mushrooms. But Mrs Peterborough and Miss Nightingale used them as ammunition.'

Jenkins put his arm around his wife and pulled her close to him. 'I missed you,' he said. 'Life with you is never dull, is it?'

Mrs Caldicot hugged him back. 'It's really none of it my fault,' she said. 'Things just sort of happen.'

'If we ever have a quiet moment,' said Jenkins. 'Will you tell me everything that happened when I was away?'

'Oh, it was all really very boring,' said Mrs Caldicot dismissively. 'There's nothing much else to tell you. Let's get you into the cinema so that you can take a look at the script for 'Casablanca'.'

'Here's looking at you, kid,' said Mr Jenkins, doing his best Humphrey Bogart impression.

This is the fourth of Vernon Coleman's books about Mrs Caldicot. The other three are *Mrs Caldicot's Cabbage War*, *Mrs Caldicot's Knickerbocker Glory* and *Mrs Caldicot's Oyster Parade*. There is a full list of Vernon Coleman's other books on his Amazon author page and on www.vernoncoleman.com

Note from Vernon Coleman:
If you have enjoyed this book, I would be enormously grateful if you give the book a good rating on Amazon. A good review (however short) really does make a huge difference to my life and my books.

Appendix

A Very Short History of the British Pleasure Pier

Before I started to write *Mrs Caldicot's Turkish Delight*, I did a great deal of research and explored the history of Britain's seaside pleasure piers. I found it a fascinating story.

Piers, of course, have been with us for a long time – probably almost as long as there have been ships and boats – but back in the late 1700s, piers were nothing more than simple jetties, built so that large boats which needed deep water moorings could land people and goods without having to unload their cargo into smaller craft. The jetties had to be long so that they were useful whether the tide was in or out. Two hundred odd years ago, before railways and the lorry had been invented, manufacturers still preferred to send their heavier goods by sea rather than over land. Roads were so bad, rutted and ruled by highwaymen, that business folk didn't have much choice.

And for travellers, whether on business, making a Grand Tour or simply going on holiday, a journey by sea was the safest, fastest and most comfortable way to reach the resort of their choice.

If there was no jetty available then travellers would have to climb down into a smaller boat and either wade through the surf or head to shore while hanging onto the back of a porter. Once on the sand they would have a walk of anything up to half a mile across wet sand. Numerous porters and servants would be needed to carry the luggage since no wheeled conveyance could be pushed or pulled across the sands. It was a slow and tedious way to arrive; and there wasn't much dignity in it.

Meanwhile, despite these drawbacks, seaside towns had become popular because breathing the sea air and taking a refreshing dip in the sea were considered healthy activities – especially for those who lived in towns and cities and spent their lives breathing in foul air.

So, for example, in 1754, the town of Brighton on the English south coast became extremely fashionable after a certain Dr Russell pronounced seawater to be a cure for all imaginable ills. You could bathe in it, splash about in it or drink the stuff. Naturally, Dr Russell recommended that the sea should be taken under the direction of a knowledgeable physician. And, unsurprisingly, his preferred choice of knowledgeable physician was himself.

The result of Dr Russell's widely publicised recommendation was that the sick raced down to Brighton to be cured while the healthy rushed there even more speedily so that they could stay healthy.

Huge, complicated bathing machines were built and rented out to all and sundry so that men and women could take a dip in the sea without exposing themselves to the eyes of curious onlookers. Even so, for the sake of common decency, and to avoid the danger of arousing the enthusiasms of onlookers beyond self-control, bathing costumes were voluminous, covered all and left absolutely everything to the imagination.

And so, gradually, the idea of travelling to an English seaside resort for a holiday became increasingly fashionable.

And that enthusiasm accelerated in the latter part of the 18th century when the Napoleonic Wars made foreign travel distinctly unhealthy and quite inadvisable. Wars have always had a tendency to interfere with continental travel and the once popular Grand Tours of Europe quickly became quite impractical. From the year of 1793, it was actually illegal to cross to France. As a result, even those continental travellers who had previously travelled across the English Channel with retinues of servants and scores of trunks, and who had returned a year or two later laden with artwork, antiquities and carpets (some bought and some liberated from natives who didn't realise the value of what they had) had to give up their travels. Instead of touring France, Germany, Italy, Switzerland and Greece they took their holidays at British seaside resorts such as Brighton, Blackpool and Penmouth.

So business in the seaside towns was booming.

There was, however, one big problem.

When they arrived at their destination, and their boat docked, these wealthy travellers had to walk or be pushed or carried along the jetty to the shore. The jetties were an improvement on the alternative but they were bare, dull, dirty and boring. And the shoreward ends of the jetties were invariably in uninspiring parts of the resorts. After all, the jetty had almost certainly been built to carry raw materials or manufactured goods, rather than ladies in fashionable dresses and gentlemen wearing top hats and carrying ebony canes.

The time was ripe for the first pleasure piers to be built.

The first pleasure pier was built at Ryde on the Isle of Wight at the start of the 19th century. The foundation stone was laid at the end of June in 1813 and when the pier was opened, just over a year later, it was a little under a third of a mile long. It was built entirely of timber; the piles were made of wood and the promenade was built with wooden planks.

Within a couple of decades piers were springing up all around the coast and every town which wanted to cater for holidaymakers simply had to have at least one.

The new piers enabled visiting ships to drop off both goods and passengers and the longer the pier, and the further out into the sea it stretched, the bigger the ship that could visit the town.

Moreover, local boat owners quickly realised that they could use their nearest pier as a point from which to take holidaymakers on boat trips to nearby attractions, or for a simple 'trip around the bay'. Fishermen started offering fishing trips so that travellers could catch their own mackerel. And businessmen vied to build new hotels as near as possible to the pier for the convenience of holidaymakers coming to the town by sea.

Railway lines were laid along the piers so that passengers and goods could, for an appropriate fee, be transported from the head of the pier to the landward end. The railway on the pier also made it possible for holidaymakers to take a trip to the pier head during their stay in the town. More energetic holidaymakers could simply walk along the pier – which became a sort of promenade.

And gradually, the piers' owners realised that they could put entertainments on the immensely long structures which they'd built over the sea – bringing in more revenue. A range of other entertainments were quickly added. Many newly built piers had extensions built at the seaward end so that theatres could be built. Older piers were extended so that new buildings could be added and additional jetties, at various heights, were built on to accommodate the requirements of vessels large and small. Booths were erected to provide accommodation for fortune tellers, weighing machines, silhouette cutters and a whole range of other entertainments.

By the second half of the 19th century, piers were opening at the rate of one a year. Some of the new structures were immensely long. The pier at Southend, which was built in 1890, was one and a third miles long. On this part of the Essex coast the tide goes out a long way and steamers bringing visitors needed to be able to land their passengers at any time of the day and any state of the tide. By 1925, when paddle steamers were operating shuttle services between Southend and Tower Bridge in the heart of London, the pier was bringing 1.5 million people a year to the resort.

The stars were aligned for the success of all these new piers.

The new-fangled notion of giving workers annual holidays and the introduction of official bank holidays at various times of the year made seaside resorts even more popular with people looking for somewhere to spend their few days of freedom. And just when it didn't look as if things could possibly get any better for English seaside towns, along came the new railway network.

Within a very short space of time, it became possible for people to travel around the country without having to bounce around on top of a rickety stage coach. Leading citizens in every seaside resort in the country wanted their own railway station and, if necessary, demanded that a branch line be built. As far as the seaside resorts were concerned, the icing on the cake was an Act of Parliament, passed in 1844, which forced the railway companies to provide cheap travel for everyone. If you were a successful hotelier in a seaside town and your resort didn't have a pier, you would either build a pier yourself or you would do your best to make sure that someone else did. During the later years of the reign of Queen Victoria, pier building turned into a frenzy.

By the end of the 19th century, the popular resort of Blackpool in Lancashire had three full length piers. The North Pier provided classical music concerts and catered for the gentry while the Central and South pleasure piers were built to provide more down-to-earth attractions for workers coming from the Lancashire cotton mills. End of the pier shows provided employment for comedians, singers and dancers and the same entertainers who worked in pantomime during the winter season moved en masse to the end of the pier theatres for the summer shows. More than anything else, it was the existence of those three piers which helped to make Blackpool the most popular seaside resort in the United Kingdom. The philosophy was simple: if one pier was good and two were great then three piers must be marvellous.

Of course, what goes up must, generally speaking, come down and the rise and rise of the British seaside pleasure pier, having continued on its upward trajectory for well over a century, was slow, steady and painful.

The low point for piers came during World War II when some piers were deliberately breached to prevent the Germans using them as landing points. And while essential repair work had to be abandoned, the sea and wind continued to damage the piers which remained. In the years following the Second World War, a good many piers, weakened by the lack of maintenance, were lost to storms and fires. The availability of cheap flights to Spanish, French and Italian resorts with guaranteed all year round sunshine meant that seaside resorts, and their piers, hit hard times.

And that pretty well brings up to date – and to the day when Mr David Livingstone inherited Penmouth Pier from his Uncle Bertram Livingstone.

Note from Vernon Coleman:
If you have enjoyed this book, I would be enormously grateful if you give the book a good rating on Amazon. A good review (however short) really does make a huge difference. God willing, Mrs Caldicot will be back.

This is the fourth novel about Mrs Caldicot. The first three are *Mrs Caldicot's Cabbage War*, *Mrs Caldicot's Knickerbocker Glory* and *Mrs Caldicot's Oyster Parade*. For a full list of the books by Vernon Coleman which are currently available please see his author page on Amazon or visit www.vernoncoleman.com.

Printed in Great Britain
by Amazon

23604966R00131